# Sea Dust

# Sea Dust

Margaret Muir

ROBERT HALE · LONDON

ISBN 0 7090 7989 3

Robert Hale Limited
Clerkenwell House
Clerkenwell Green
London EC1R 0HT

2  4  6  8  10  9  7  5  3  1

Typeset in 11/13pt Garamond
by Derek Doyle & Associates, Shaw Heath.
Printed in Great Britain by St Edmundsbury Press
Bury St Edmunds, Suffolk.
Bound by Woolnough Bookbinding Ltd.

*For my son Bill*
*For me your light will always shine*

luminescent particles
stirred by the ship
dark sea's illusive diamonds

# Acknowledgements

To my agent, Bob Tanner, and publisher, Robert Hale Limited, thank you for taking me on board. Also to Richard Rossiter, Glyn Parry and Chris McLeod for their constructive criticism in the early stages of the novel.

For information about old Whitby, I thank Geoff Vasey, and for a hand on to the first rung of the publishing ladder, my thanks to novelist, Anna Jacobs.

Finally, to my dear friend Peter Ryan, thank you, PJ.

# Chapter 1

## Whitby, North Yorkshire,
## February 1856

Emma shivered. The cold spell had been cruel, very cruel. Yet the picture, framed by the window, had a stark beauty about it.

The fishing port nestled in the valley was shrouded in white. Snow covered the docks and wharfs, the sand flat, Belle Island, and the hills and open moors beyond. Only the treacherous face of the crumbling East Cliff had escaped the winter mantle.

From the attic, Emma gazed down on the rooftops to the chimney stacks poking up from the snow like bare stumps awaiting spring, to the icicles hanging from the clay tiles like a line of glass organ pipes, and to the street below. Vestal white. Untouched.

To the north, the sea was strangely still. There were no white caps on the water. No waves breaking along The Scaur. The grey sky and sea melded in a haze of mauve. There was no horizon.

Near the old lighthouse, half hidden by the pier wall, Emma could see the masts of a ship. It was moving slowly towards the fishing harbour, but it carried no sail.

A bird fluttered moth-like against the window and distracted her. It landed on the sill settling its claws into the mat of tangled snowflakes. She watched as it hopped to the end of the ledge and started pecking at the crack in the corner of the glass. She listened to it, tap-tapping on the window as if wanting to be invited in. Then she remembered the other sounds she had listened to in that room: the cough, the wheeze, the crackled breath. Now those sounds were gone and the room was silent save for the bird's beak tapping on the pane.

It regarded her, or appeared to, cocking its head from side to side. She wondered if it could see her. She thought not. Her dress was dark. Her shawl, spun from the fleece of a black Corriedale, even darker. And there was no lamp.

How long was it since the sun had warmed the town?

The bird fluffed out its rust-red chest feathers and stretched one of its wings.

She heard stockinged feet padding up the stairs and waited for the distinctive creak of the three steps outside the attic door. The latch clicked as it was lifted. The bird cocked its head and, when the door rasped on its hinges, it flew away.

She knew it was Joshua.

He moved close beside her and waited for a few moments before he spoke. 'Are you all right, Mama?'

She nodded.

'What are you looking at?'

'A ship,' she said quietly.

Joshua pressed his forehead against the glass and scanned the harbour. He could see the masts of the tall ships moored at the wharfs. He counted several others anchored in the deeper water, their sails hanging lankly in the still air. To the right, three flat-bottomed Whitby cats sat almost upright on the snowy sand waiting for the tide to refloat them. He knew there would be other ships hidden by the houses but he could see no movement on the harbour.

'Where, Mama?'

'By the West Pier. See, the three masts moving very slowly.'

Joshua looked to the left. 'I see it. A barque, I think. Or a ketch, maybe. Hard to tell from this distance.' He slipped his hand into his mother's. 'You are cold, Mama,' he said. 'You must come downstairs. The kitchen is warm.'

'Seems strange to see a ship moving without sails,' Emma murmured.

Joshua looked at his mother. 'The men are warping her in.'

'Yes,' she whispered.

'Please, Mama, come down. Father is getting angry.' He rubbed her hand. 'Your fingers are frozen.'

'Look,' she said. 'Do you see it? On the roof near the chimney stack. A robin.'

Joshua glanced across as the bird fluttered from one sooty stack to another.

'I see him.'

They watched for a moment.

'Mama,' he said softly, 'there is nothing more you can do here.'

'I know.' Emma turned to her son and smiled. Something of her own pain was reflected in his hazel eyes. 'I will come in a moment. It will be dark soon. I must light a candle.'

'Let me do it.'

She watched as he lit the stump of tallow. Watched his movements, his easy gait, the movement of his wrist and hand. His profile. How well he stood, she thought. How tall he had grown. Almost thirteen years old, and grown almost to a man.

He handed the holder to her.

The voice which bellowed up the stairwell startled them. 'Get down here, woman!'

'Mama, you must go down.'

'One last moment,' she said. Lifting her skirt she held the candle towards the cradle nestled in the recess beside the fireplace. The flickering light wavered across the wooden headboard. The gossamer wings of the hand-painted fairies glimmered in the yellow light.

In the cot the child lay swaddled in fresh linen. A bonnet trimmed with white lace framed the infant's ashen cheeks. Two bright new pennies rested on the tiny eyelids.

Leaning down, Emma loosened the bow under the baby's chin, then retied it neatly. She touched the lips. They were cold. Alabaster cold.

'Bessie! My lovely Bess!'

'Come down at once!' the voice demanded. 'Don't make me come up there to get you!'

Emma stiffened.

'I hate him!' Joshua cried.

'You must not speak like that.'

His eyes were level with hers. 'But I hate him for what he does to you. It isn't right. He isn't fair.'

'Enough, Josh! Now is not the time.'

'But he doesn't care for you!'

Emma turned towards the empty hearth and folded her arms across her chest. 'This house is cold, isn't it?'

'Please, Mama, go down. Please do what he says.'

Emma sighed. 'You go. I promise I will follow.'

The boy turned.

The top stairs groaned as Joshua stepped down slowly. Emma listened. Heard him stop for a while on the first-floor landing. Then heard his feet thumping down the last flight of stairs and the stairwell door close behind him.

Hot wax trickled over her fingers. The wick was almost spent. Carefully, she placed the holder on the mantelshelf. The flame spluttered.

At the door, Emma stopped and looked back. Across the room the mouth of the fireplace gaped open, black and cold. Pockmarked grey cinders littered the grate and particles of white ash dotted the rug like flakes of newly fallen snow.

Emma knew it was time to leave: to leave the cradle shrouded in the shadow; to leave the child she had failed to raise; to leave behind another splintered fragment of her life. So short. So precious.

She lifted her skirt and stepped down into the gloom. Within the stair-well the musty smell of lingering mould exuded from the faded roses peeling from the walls. Soon it would be mingled with the scent of death.

Sweet. Sour. Unforgettable.

'What have you been doing up there? Wasting time again, no doubt!'

Emma closed the door quietly.

'Now the child's dead you have no reason to go up there. You're like a rat in a barn, up and down the steps. I am sick and tired of it.'

Slipping the shawl from her shoulders, Emma folded it over the back of the chair and took an apron from the dresser drawer. The crease running down the bib and skirt was quite sharp. She must have folded it when it was still hot from the iron. As she smoothed the line with the palm of her hand she could feel his eyes on her.

'I am waiting for my tea! I am going out!'

She knew his routine well enough where he went every day at this time.

'The snow is getting quite deep,' she said, not needing to look at his face to gauge his expression. 'There is a pot of broth on the stove. Sit at the table and I will get some for you.'

George shuffled from the fire where he had been toasting his back. He mumbled to himself as Emma lifted the vase of catkins from the table and slid the velvet cloth from under his elbows.

'Joshua! Put your book away and come to the table.'

From the pot, Emma ladled the broth into a china bowl. A few drops spilled and sizzled on the coals.

'Mutton,' she said, placing it on the table.

He sniffed, splayed his knees to accommodate his paunch and rested his forearms on the table.

'At least I will not need to waste any more money on medicines,' he announced, flicking the linen napkin and tucking it inside his collar. 'Dr Throstle will get nothing more from my pocket.'

' 'Twas only once I called the doctor.'

'Then why does he keep sending his bills?' He tore a chunk of bread from the cob and dipped it in the fluid.

'Perhaps if you would pay him . . .' she whispered.

George Quinlan glared as Emma tipped the contents of her bowl back into the pot. Her appetite was gone.

'You should eat something, Mama,' Joshua said.

'Later, perhaps.'

As she lifted the kettle, she could sense her husband watching her, waiting for her to turn and look at him. But she kept her gaze to the fireplace, hiding her face, her frustrations, pain and resentment. After placing it on the hob and moving the soup pot away from the fire, Emma added another lump of coal.

'Didn't I tell you, that child would never thrive?' he said. 'Weakling from the start. I knew it all along.'

She knew he was goading her.

Joshua looked up at his mother. 'Are you all right, Mama?'

She nodded as she poked the fire.

'A waste of good money!' he announced.

Emma knew better than to be drawn into an argument. She dare not chance upsetting him. She could speak with Joshua when he had gone. She wanted to reassure her son, tell him she was all right. She knew he was concerned.

George mopped his dish with the remaining bread. Broke the cheese into two large chunks and swilled them down with a pot of ale. After polishing the grease from his whiskers with the back of his hand, he dusted his chest, turned his chair from the table, stretched out his legs and belched loudly.

Joshua turned his face away. His cheeks were sallow. Thinner than she had ever seen them. His eyes red. The spark of youth was no longer there.

Emma fetched her husband's boots from the hall, knelt down on the mat beside the hearth and forced them over his swollen ankles. His face spoke of pain.

With the boots laced, George raised himself and stomped his feet on the floor.

Without a word, Emma fetched his coat and helped him into it, though her fingers struggled to squeeze the buttons through their matching holes.

'Have you sponged this again?'

'Only to wipe away some stains.'

'Haven't I told you before? Do not touch it! Don't you ever listen to me, woman? Can't you see you've shrunk it?'

Emma wound the knitted muffler firmly round his neck and tucked the ends under his coat lapels. She watched as he considered his figure in the hallstand mirror and slapped his hands on to his belly, signifying, as he did every morning, that he was satisfied with his reflection.

Emma opened the door and waited on the doorstep. The air was icy cold. In one hand she held his hat and gloves, in the other his walking cane.

'Do you think it wise to go out in this weather?' she asked quietly.

He looked at her scornfully but did not answer.

Snowflakes floating over the threshold melted into spots of wetness on the floor. Across the street, the gas lamp, lit earlier than usual, glowed through a halo of misty air. Seal Street's surface of grey cobbles had been replaced by a carpet of white almost six inches deep.

From the parlour, the clock chimed the half-hour.

'And I hope you don't expect me to pay for an expensive funeral,' Quinlan added, as he stepped down the stone steps on to the street. 'Paid enough for the child while it was alive; I'm not paying any more now that it's dead.'

Joshua's chair scraped noisily on the kitchen floor.

'Be careful not to slip,' Emma called, not expecting a reply. She got none.

As he walked awkwardly down the street, snowflakes settled on his hat and shoulders. A hungry dog sniffing at his boots received a stinging stroke of the cane for its trouble. It ran off, yelping.

Emma closed the door on the cold.

'I hate him,' Joshua said.

# Chapter 2

The rain fell straight and constant. Drenching rain which bounced down to the cobblestones and oozed up from the hillside at the same time.

The wooden wheels of the handcart splattered through the puddles as it rumbled up Church Street. A stream of clear water raced along the gutter in the opposite direction. When he reached the stone steps, Reginald Beckwith eased his cart into the verge. The newly painted sign hanging from the cart read: MASTER CRAFTSMAN – CARPENTER – WOOD-TURNER and beneath that in fine copperplate scroll, the name, *Reginald G. Beckwith*. While his cart was a familiar sight on the Whitby streets, carrying wood, or fish, or turnips as the demand required, to the townsfolk of Whitby, Mr R.G. Beckwith was best known as the grave-digger.

Straightening his back, he glanced up the hillside towards St Mary's, but the old stone church together with most of the East Cliff had been swallowed in misty cloud. Pulling the cape of felted wool close around his neck, he lifted the wooden box from the cart, leaned it against his stubbled cheek and settled it on to the wet wadding on his shoulder. When he was satisfied the box was seated properly, he signalled to the parson with a nod of the head.

The few mourners, standing in a silent huddle, did not see his gesture. Their faces were hidden beneath umbrellas.

'Ready, ladies?' Parson Wakeley said, one foot poised on the first step, ready to go.

His wife, close behind him, sighed loudly as they began the long climb up to the top of the cliff. 'Dreadful weather,' she said.

'Yes,' Emma replied without thinking.

Joshua held the umbrella over her as she gathered several folds of skirt

17

into one hand. In the other hand she carried a bunch of snowdrops which she had picked early that morning.

It must have been raining when she went out. It hadn't stopped since the previous day. But she couldn't remember. Her mind was occupied with thoughts of other things; her little Bess, her family, her home – not the tall house in Seal Street, nor her life in Whitby, but the place where she had grown up, her parents and her sister.

'Dreadful weather,' the portly lady muttered again, flicking at the rain as it soaked the front of her black satin skirt.

Dreadful weather, Emma repeated in her head. No, she thought, on the contrary, there was something comforting about the rain. Since it had started, the biting cold had gone. Almost all of the snow and ice had disappeared, washed to the sea. The streets and yards had been sluiced clean. Grass growing in the ditches looked green and fresh, and the water running down the hill was clear as glass. She envied the water's flow. It ran so freely and always knew which way to go. No, she thought, she didn't mind the rain.

Mrs Wakeley continued grumbling. 'Why on earth they built the church at the top of a cliff, I will never know.' Her cheeks resembled two ripe pomegranates both in colour and in size. Emma wasn't sure if the deepening hue was the result of her frustration, or if the lady was just running out of puff.

'Would you care to rest for a while?' she asked.

'No, must keep going!'

Ahead, the slab steps, 199 in all, curved around the hillside, disappearing halfway up into the cloud which showed no signs of shifting. Emma considered the parson's wife would have made it easier for herself had she saved her breath and conversation until they reached the top.

But the remonstrations continued, one following the other and all quite unrelated: the number of new taverns in the town; the children who had not attended Sunday School; the cost of tea; the pain from her bunion. She stopped at every resting place. The mourners waited patiently, the water seeping through their boot seams and saturating the ladies' already sopping hemlines.

When she had regained her composure the party moved on and Parson Wakeley strode ahead, stamping his feet on each step as if in an attempt to halt the stream. But his efforts were in vain and succeeded only in jetting water at his portly wife, his practice providing her with yet another reason to complain.

Whether he chose to ignore her protestations or simply didn't hear them, Emma wasn't sure, but when the next resting place was reached, he strode on, seemingly unaware that he was leaving his wife and the rest of the party behind.

It was a small group. The parson and his wife, Emma, her son, Joshua, and two matronly ladies who walked arm in arm about a dozen steps behind.

Mr Beckwith followed at a respectable distance, occasionally tutting at the slow progress. But he neither tried to pass on the steps nor take the donkey track beside it; instead, he mumbled to himself and waited. It was a routine he was familiar with. Sliding the box across his back, he balanced it on to his other shoulder. It was becoming increasingly heavy.

George Quinlan was not amongst the mourners.


The furthest corner of the graveyard was swathed in the canopy of cloud and though the land leaned into the valley, nothing could be seen of the harbour below. Around the grave, the freshly dug earth which clogged their boots was soft and slippery. Emma slipped her hand into her son's for support.

Familiar with the burial service, the parson did not need to use his spectacles. He recited the text quickly but respectfully. Emma was not conscious of the words he spoke, only of the dreadful emptiness she felt inside. She gazed ahead as raindrops trickled down her face, in place of tears.

Mr Beckwith lowered the remains of Elizabeth May Quinlan with care. But the rainwater which had collected in the grave was trapped in its clay. For a few moments the wooden box floated like a small wooden craft on a becalmed sea. As water seeped in, it settled to the bottom of the hole.

When the formalities were over, Parson Wakeley excused himself to speak with Mr Beckwith. Emma turned to the two ladies standing behind her. She had been surprised at their presence, not expecting anyone to attend the burial besides herself and Joshua. She recognized their faces but knew them only vaguely.

'Thank you for coming,' she said.

Mrs Cooper and Mrs Bradshaw had been her neighbours since the Quinlans moved to Whitby more than four years ago. Mrs Bradshaw, the older of the two, lived directly across Seal Street. Mrs Cooper lived further up the hill, though Emma was not sure which house she lived in. She felt abashed that in the past she had spoken with both women very little. A brief 'Good day', or 'It looks like rain', was the extent of their previous conversations. George had always discouraged any dealings with the 'riff raff over the way', and had forbidden Joshua from associating with the local children.

But a funeral was different. The ladies had come to pay their respects and Emma welcomed their support.

'Would you care to join my son and me for some refreshments at the house?' she asked.

The response was unashamedly enthusiastic. It was the first time either lady had been invited to step over the Quinlans' threshold. It was an opportunity they would not miss.

'That would be very nice,' Mrs Cooper said. 'You can't beat a bite to eat and a nice chat after a funeral, that's what I always say. Don't you agree, Mrs Bradshaw?'

'Couldn't 'ave put it better myself. Be pleased to come and join you and your boy.'

Emma had earlier extended the invitation to the parson and his wife, but Mrs Wakeley had offered her apologies, explaining that her husband had urgent work to attend to. Emma considered that as a result of the freezing conditions of the past week, both the parson and Mr Beckwith would have plenty of work to do, and Mrs Wakeley would have more than her fill of funeral teas. She felt sorry for the lady. Such a depressing pursuit. It was no wonder the poor woman suffered from frustration.

'You'll excuse us if we get along now, Mrs Quinlan,' the parson said. 'Another bereavement to attend to, I'm afraid.'

Emma thanked him for conducting the service and his kind words.

'You mind you look after your mother, young man,' he said, patting Joshua on the back.

'Yes, sir.'

'Goodbye, my dear,' Mrs Wakeley said, hesitating for a moment as if she had more to say. Then she smiled sympathetically at Emma and took her husband's arm for the long walk back down to the town.

The heavy clay clung to Mr Beckwith's spade as he struggled to shovel it back into the hole. Emma and Joshua stood in silence as the oak coffin disappeared beneath the dirt and a plain wooden cross was hammered into the ground at the head of the mound. It sank in easily. Emma laid the posy of snowdrops beneath it. She could think of little, save for the fact the funeral was over.

The two ladies waited by the church wall.

Through the lifting cloud, the outline of the old abbey appeared dark and hazy in the distance. On a clear day its stark features dominated the cliff top. From the still shrouded harbour the clang of the Whitby bell rang out its warning to shipping. A sea fret had moved in from the North Sea. It was a familiar sound for the folks in the fishing port.

The group of four walked down the hill together. Down Church Street and through the older part of town. Along Bridge Street to the draw-bridge which joined the east and west sides of Whitby and separated the harbour in two. The bridge provided the only way to cross the River Esk. They crossed and made their way past Flowergate to Spencer's Ghaut which led them up to Seal Street. The Quinlans lived at number twenty-nine.

'Please come in,' Emma said, as she opened the door.

The mud which had caked their boots in the churchyard had washed away but the ladies' skirts and petticoats were sopping. Despite their efforts to shake off the excess water, it was impossible to prevent the trail of drops which followed them into the house. Both ladies apologized. Emma assured them that they should not concern themselves. A wet floor would soon dry.

With heavy velvet drawn across the windows, not a chink of light spilled in. The kitchen was dark save for the glow from the coals. But the fire had kept the room warm. The company would add to that.

'Please light a lamp, Joshua.' Emma said.

Mrs Bradshaw surveyed the living-room, good furniture all polished, brass shining and linen crisp. It was clean and fresh though somewhat austere. Her attention was attracted to a picture on the wall. A pen and ink drawing. She stood in front of it. 'Your parents?' she asked.

Emma didn't need to look to know which picture she was referring to. 'Yes,' she said quietly, before inviting the ladies to sit down.

Mrs Cooper gave an involuntary shudder. 'Nice and cosy in 'ere,' she said. 'If you don't mind, luv, I'll hang me cloak near the fire. It's a mite wet I'm afraid.'

'Of course,' said Emma, 'Let me help you.' She drew a chair closer to the fireplace. Mrs Cooper draped her cloak over it. Mrs Bradshaw removed hers and did the same.

Emma was aware of Joshua hovering near the stairs.

'May I go upstairs, Mama?'

She nodded. 'Leave your wet jacket. Change into some dry clothes then come down to talk with the ladies.'

'Let the boy go,' Mrs Cooper said. 'He don't want to be talking with us old fuddy-duddies.'

Joshua looked across to his mother.

She smiled. The woman was quite right.

Relieved, Joshua took off his boots, rested them against the fender and ran upstairs.

'A good lad, you've got there,' Mrs Bradshaw said.

'Thank you,' Emma said, as she slid the smoke-blackened kettle over the flames. The lid was soon rattling. From the glass-fronted cabinet she took a china teapot, with matching cups, saucers and plates. She arranged them neatly on the red velvet cloth. After warming the pot she made the tea.

'My, this is pretty,' Mrs Cooper said, lifting an empty cup and turning it in her hand.

Her friend gave a disapproving look.

'The china was my mother's.' Emma said.

'That's nice.'

'Thank you. I don't have much occasion to use it.' As she spoke, she realized it was the first time she had used it since they had moved to Whitby four years ago. It was also the second time that day she had thought about her mother and her life before she came to the fishing village.

Emma removed the doilies covering the plates on the table. 'A biscuit, Mrs Cooper, or a scone?'

'Thank you. Don't mind if I do,' Mrs Bradshaw said. 'Nice words, the parson spoke, don't you think?'

The other woman agreed. 'Indeed they were. You know, I always enjoy a good funeral. I ain't much for church and Sunday service, but I do like a nice funeral,' she said. 'Likes to show me respect, you know what I mean?'

'I thank you both for coming today.'

'Shame the father couldn't be here. Mr Quinlan away on business, is he?'

Emma felt embarrassed.

Mrs Bradshaw didn't wait for a reply. 'Seems to me, it always comes down to us women. We bring 'em into the world and we have to see 'em out of it.'

'Sugar, Mrs Cooper?'

'Thank you, my dear.' The woman stirred her tea and helped herself to a biscuit.

'Bad business that funeral last week,' she continued.

Mrs Cooper nodded.

Emma wasn't particularly interested in tittle-tattle. Sometimes she overheard snippets of local gossip when she went shopping, but because of Bessie's death, she felt she would rather not hear about someone else's misfortune. But the ladies meant no harm, and as she did not want to appear rude, she felt obliged to ask the question. Besides, she could see that Mrs Bradshaw was intent on relating the story anyway.

'I didn't hear about it,' Emma said.

'Bad business,' Mrs Bradshaw repeated. 'Ruth Nichols, young lass, lived down bottom of Spencer's Ghaut. Pretty girl. Not more that twenty-two years old.' She sipped her tea. 'They say she fell down the stairs, poor girl, but I got it on good authority her husband pushed her. Bad business, I tell you.'

'Bad business,' the other woman echoed.

'They say she lay there all night and most of the following day. Couldn't move. They say they might have saved her if her man had called the doctor. But he wouldn't call for help. Too tight with his money he was.'

'You can bet he always had money for his drink!' Mrs Cooper added.

Emma turned away, picked up a lump of coal and added it to the fire.

'Died there where she fell, they say. At the bottom of the steps.'

'Shame! Shame!'

'Two bairns, orphans now. He won't look after 'em.'

No one spoke. The three ladies reached for their cups and drank. After a moment's thought Mrs Bradshaw continued, 'It strikes me, in a situation like that, a woman's got two choices.'

Emma listened knowing there was no way of changing the course of the conversation, and besides, Mrs Bradshaw was intent on providing the solution.

'She can poison him, or run away! Two choices, that's how I sees it.' She nodded to reinforce her statement. 'A good dose of rat poison, that'd be my choice. That would fix a man like that.'

'Well, I have to agree,' said Mrs Cooper. 'But how's a woman going to support herself? Unless she's got means.' She dusted the crumbs from her lap into her hand and returned them to her plate. 'Or a fancy-man?'

'Mrs Cooper!' Emma said.

'Well, I ask you, what chance has a woman these days, running off on her own, especially in a sea port like Whitby? No chance at all. Too many of them foreign sailors around. Drunken louts every one of 'em. Just waiting, they are, for the opportunity to take advantage of a poor woman. I ask you, what can she do? Where can she go? Big towns is even worse.' She paused. 'I'd have to agree with you, Sadie Bradshaw – a good dose of rat poison would do the trick just fine.'

'More tea, Mrs Cooper?' Emma was finding the conversation quite entertaining.

'No thank you, my dear, I enjoyed that. But tell me, what about that lad of yours? Joshua. Is he all right?' She inclined her head toward the stairwell. 'Bottle it all up inside the boys do when someone dies. Don't like no one to see 'em bawling.'

Mrs Bradshaw agreed. 'That's right. My eldest he were the same. Never cried when the twins died of the pox. Not for six months that is, then one day some little thing happened— I'm dashed if I can think what it was.' She stopped and scratched at her bonnet. 'I remember,' she said. 'He tripped over and slopped a jug of milk on me.'

Emma covered her lips with her fingers.

'It were just an accident. Splashed the milk all down my apron and I got mad with him. You know how you do? It weren't now't much really, but he just cried and cried and cried. Six months' worth of tears there were came flooding out.'

'Is that so?' Mrs Cooper said. 'Well, I'll be!'

'All right he was after that. It had all been bottled up inside. Them tears had to come out sometime and spilling that jug of milk, that was what done it.'

'Joshua will be fine,' said Emma, 'but I thank you for your advice and I will mind how he is. Mrs Bradshaw, another cup?'

'Don't mind if I do, lass.'

As Emma drained the last of the tea from the china pot, the older woman squinted inquisitively at the expression on her face.

'Well, I must say! Do I detect a smile, my dear?'

Emma's cheeks flushed. 'I am sorry,' she said. 'I didn't mean to appear rude, but it was what you were saying about the spilled milk, it reminded me of something that happened when I was a girl. It was the memory of it which made me smile.'

'Come on then, lass – spit it out – don't keep it to yourself.'

Emma protested, 'No, I couldn't. It wouldn't be fitting – not in the circumstances – the funeral, I mean.'

'Now, we'll be the judge of that, won't we, Sadie? Darn it all, lass, you've done all you can for the bairn. You've given her a proper Christian burial.'

'And very nice it was too,' Mrs Bradshaw added. 'Very nice.'

'But I'll be betting that it's a long time since that pretty face of yours had anything much to smile about.'

The two women exchanged knowing glances.

'Come on, dear, we'd love to hear about it.'

'Aye, come on, luv, tell us about when you were a lass. A good yarn'll warm us up inside.'

Emma put her cup down. The two ladies were kind. Good-hearted. It was strange but she was enjoying their company. Mrs Bradshaw reminded her of the old housekeeper who had been so caring towards her mama when things had become difficult. Even her broad accent sounded similar. Something about their openness made her feel comfortable. She welcomed the opportunity to talk.

' 'Twas just a childish memory, but I sometimes think back to those days. Foolish really. But they were happy times. When I was a girl,' she sighed, 'a long time ago.'

'Not that long ago, I don't think,' Mrs Cooper said, her chin resting on her plump washerwoman hands. Emma could feel the woman's eyes examining her intently. 'I have to say, my dear, it's hard to believe that you have a lad the age of your Joshua. But I'm sorry, I was interrupting. Go on tell us your yarn.'

Emma returned her cup and saucer to the table. Her shoulders dropped forward slightly and she relaxed back into the chair.

'I was only nine,' she said. 'My sister, Anna, was thirteen. Papa was commissioned to work in London and Mama was invited to go with him. They were away for almost six months and the house was closed up.' Emma gazed into the fire and didn't see the raised eyebrows exchanged between the two women.

'I remember at the time, Anna and I were terribly upset. We had to be sent away to the country to stay with Mother's sister, Aunt Daisy. We did not know what a wonderful time we would have.' She explained, 'You see, until then, we had always lived in the city.'

The two women listened intently.

'My Uncle Jack had a small farm. In Lincolnshire. With some milking cows. I remember them well. The cows. They were big and brown and bony.' A grin spread across her face. 'One in particular, her name was Molly.'

'Molly,' Mrs Cooper echoed.

Emma nodded. 'I remember Anna and I running down to the cowshed early in the morning when it was still dark and cold. Uncle would follow carrying a lantern. "Don't run, girls", he would shout, and "watch where you are treading".'

The women smiled.

'Funny the things you remember, isn't it?' she said, as she watched the steam rising from the ladies' cloaks drying by the fire. 'I can remember the smell of that barn. It was strong and rank, and in the mornings steam would rise from the thick piles of old hay heaped at the back of the shed.' She breathed deeply through her nose. 'Uncle Jack taught us how to milk the cows.'

Mrs Bradshaw leaned forward resting her elbows on the table.

Emma corrected herself. 'No, I should say he taught Anna, my sister. She was good. Her hands were bigger than mine and she managed the job easily. I was envious when I heard the milk squirting into her pail. It just didn't matter how much I tried, I couldn't do it properly. Uncle Jack was very patient and would say "Try Molly, Em. You mark my words, you'll have no trouble this morning". But Anna would always have her pail full before I had a trickle in the bottom of mine.'

Emma looked across to the two faces framed in black bonnets wondering if she should continue.

'Don't stop,' Mrs Bradshaw said leaning back in the chair. 'I have to admit, that's something I've never done – milked a cow. Not much call for it on the harbour.'

Mrs Cooper laughed. 'You're right. The only milk we've ever had came out of a churn. Go on, luv. Don't stop.'

Emma continued, 'I would squeeze and squeeze but nothing would happen. And I would tell Uncle that I couldn't do it. Then he would whisper a few words in Molly's ear, and the milk would flow like water from a pump.

'But as soon as Uncle went off to milk one of the other cows, Molly would start moving, backwards and forwards and side to side. I would have my head pressed on her belly and I would call out, "Molly! Keep still!" but she would keep on swaying, and then I would feel the back leg of the stool sinking into the ground and I knew that if I let go, I would topple over and take the pail of milk with me. I would beg Uncle, "Please tell Molly to keep still", and he would stroke her on the nose and again whisper something in her ear and she would stand as still as any statue.'

'So tell me,' Mrs Bradshaw asked, 'did you ever fill your pail?'

'No. Never. Uncle always finished the milking for me.' She paused and smiled. 'And when Anna and I weren't looking, Uncle would squirt milk at us. And we would laugh and squeal and he said we sounded like a pair of piglets. And by the time we went back to the farmhouse we would have milk in our hair and milk down our aprons and Aunty would scold us.'

'Just like I scolded my boy when he spilled milk down my apron.'

'That is what reminded me,' Emma said. 'But I don't think she was really angry. She would tell us to be more careful next time. But then she would scoop the cream off the top of the milk and give us both a mugfull. It was so rich and thick. It lined our mouths and warmed our empty stomachs. I can almost taste it now.' Emma paused and took a big breath. 'There,' she said, 'it was just a childish memory.'

'It was a right fine little tale and I enjoyed hearing it. How about you, Sadie?'

'Good to see a smile on your face, my dear,' Mrs Bradshaw said, then with a serious tone to her voice, added, 'Strange where we end up, isn't it? Sometimes I think it's just as well we ain't all gypsies, as can gaze into a crystal ball and see what the future has in store.'

'Such talk, Sadie Bradshaw! If you'll excuse us, Mrs Quinlan, I think it's time we were off home. Our menfolk will be none too happy if there's no tea cooking.'

'Aye, I suppose you're right,' the older woman said. 'Though I don't feel much like shifting. Got right comfortable I have and I enjoyed listening to your story.' She gathered up her cloak and draped it round her shoulders. 'Now you mind and come and pay us a call sometimes.'

Emma promised that she would.

As she was leaving, Mrs Bradshaw touched Emma's arm. 'Now don't you forget, if there is ever anything you want – and I mean at any time – don't you be too proud to ask.'

'And that goes for me too,' added Mrs Cooper. 'I'm only a couple of doors up the street. Your lad knows where to find me.'

'Thank you,' Emma said. 'I will remember that.'

Outside the street was bathed in its customary shadow.

An assortment of urchins was crowded on to Mrs Bradshaw's doorstep, their gazes fixed like the faces often framed on a mantelshelf. The moment she appeared, the two smallest ones ran across the street to meet her, pulling at her skirt and wailing for her attention. But no sooner had the ladies left the Quinlans' house, than they became engrossed in conversation and seemed oblivious to the demanding cries.

Emma closed the door, thankful for their visit. They had lightened the burden of Bessie's death. The house felt warmer and her spirits had been lifted by their company. But most of all she felt satisfied that everything had been taken care of properly. Now she was sure her little girl could rest in peace.

She could relax.

George had hired a rig and pair to drive down to Robin Hood's Bay. It was a journey he made every three or four weeks sometimes not returning until the following day. She often wondered what business he had in the tiny fishing village, but she knew better than to ask. For the moment, she indulged herself in the knowledge that he would not be back until late that evening.

She looked around the room to the pictures hanging on the wall, to the one which had attracted Mrs Bradshaw's attention. The pen and ink.

How many times had she gazed at it? Been called by it. She knew it intimately. Every line, every stroke. Every detail replicated as perfectly as if captured on a photographic plate. For the picture revealed more to her than the subjects' images. Far more. The artist's pen breathed life on to the paper. More life and character than any flash of magnesium could duplicate. And in unwritten words a discourse spoke from it. Words of truth, humility and love.

Her fingers stroked the moulded frame.

From within the confines of the dark oak, the man and woman appeared at ease. This was no stiff, self-conscious tableau, powdered and posed for a portrait session; here the subjects were relaxed. The man seated in his horsehair chair. A gentle man with kindly face, clean-shaven save for a goatee beard gone white. His flowing hair, streaked with varying shades of grey, fell softly about his shoulders. And skilfully etched into his features, lines of joy, frustration, happiness delicately tinged with an air of grief.

But his eyes concealed the deepest mystery. Pale misty eyes that had a strange opacity. As if, when capturing his soul, the artist's pen had dried.

Instead of pools of black, the pupils were empty voids, not looking anywhere but seeing all. And yet, reflected from the face, here was a man accepting all life dealt with mellowness. A smile just past.

Perhaps it was his dress which had caught the onlooker's attention.

With neither coat nor waistcoat, his attire was quite unbecoming for a formal sitting. His silken shirt was open at the neck, its sleeves billowing down to hide slim arms which rested on the chair's wearied upholstery. His fingers, soft and slender, resembled those of a musician.

The fingers touching the frame were similar.

A walking cane leaned against his leg. Its tarnished handle was moulded to the shape of a mallard's beak.

Standing close beside him, the woman gazed down, her left hand resting over his protectively, as if a mother's hand upon her child's. An old woman, perhaps fifty years of age or more, her dress in keeping with her years: the neckline, high beneath the chin; the dress's yoke and sleeves edged with exotic lace, the fine threads fraying at the wrist. The satin cloth, shaded the colour of a winter's sky, reflected a subtle sheen and fell in gentle folds of which no crease escaped the artist's eye.

Her hair, combed loosely to a bun, showed not a trace of grey. The ringlets curling from her temples hid her ears. But, like the creases in her skirt, it seemed that every hair had been accounted for. Her skin was clear, save for the lines of life around her lips and eyes. Smiling, sad eyes, drawn to her man, her husband, lover, companion and friend.

And in her right hand, she held a rose, its stem still wet as if just lifted from a vase. A wild dog rose, whose petals were about to shed. One petal floating gently to the ground. A graceful movement captured in the stillness of the frame.

There was a knock on the door.


'Mrs Quinlan. I came to offer my condolences.'

Mr Albert Hepplethwaite was almost as round as he was tall. His frame filled the doorway. Doffing his hat, he lifted it only slightly from his head before settling it down again. He was breathing heavily.

The smile on Emma's face faded.

'Heard about your sad loss, my dear, and thought as I was just passing, I would call in to pay my respects.'

Something in his words rankled. If indeed Mr Hepplethwaite was *just passing*, then where was he going? Seal Street led up the western side of the valley. At the top of the street there was nothing but wind and heather.

The fact that his ruddy cheeks looked about to burst and he was quite out of breath, confirmed what Emma already knew, that he was not in the habit of taking walks up the Whitby hillsides. Furthermore, she had heard it said that Mr Albert Hepplethwaite was as much a fixture leaning across his shop counter, as the sign was which swung on the street outside his establishment.

The proprietor of The Harbour Pie Shop was highly regarded in the town, but in Emma's estimation, he was too familiar. The words, 'my dear', had an ingratiating ring. She did not like the man and he was the last person she would have expected to see standing on her doorstep.

'Condolences,' he repeated. 'Just paying my respects.'

'Thank you,' Emma said flatly.

'I was speaking with your good husband last week. Discussing the future of your boy, Joshua.'

She watched the rain stream from the brim of his hat, conscious that she did not want to invite him in.

He coughed into his podgy fist. 'He told me that the lad's had enough of schooling. Said it was time he had a job. An apprenticeship was what we were discussing.'

A scowl puckered Emma's forehead.

'Excuse my candour, Mr Hepplethwaite, but I do not think anyone can have enough schooling. However,' she said, 'Mr Quinlan has not spoken to me about the matter.'

She lied. She was neither prepared to discuss the issue with this unwelcome visitor, nor admit that she was keenly aware of her husband's intentions. George had made it very clear to her that Joshua should bring a wage into the house. He was not interested in what the boy wanted to do, stating that the boy was more than old enough to go out to work and that was the end of the matter.

But the idea of her son working for Mr Hepplethwaite was unacceptable to Emma. She had seen Mr Hepplethwaite's boys, their backs bent double, struggling with handcarts laden with sacks of flour. She had seen others running along the wharfside as if the hounds of Hell were after them. If this was the job which Mr Hepplethwaite was broaching, it was not Emma's idea of an apprenticeship.

Emma believed her son at least deserved the education she had had. If not more. He was intelligent, and if he continued with his studies he could gain a worthwhile career. She felt she owed him that. But she also knew George and if he said the boy must earn his keep then nothing would sway that decision.

'Mr Quinlan home?' Hepplethwaite asked, dabbing a silk handkerchief across his brow.

'No. He had business which took him out of town,' Emma said curtly. 'He was unable to attend the funeral.'

'Dear me, that is a pity.' There was no scrap of surprise in the shop-keeper's tone. Was he aware that George Quinlan had not attended the funeral? Did he know that her husband was not at home? How could he know unless someone had told him?

'Is the lad in?'

'Yes,' she said cautiously. 'If you care to wait a moment, I'll call him.'

'Kind of you, my dear,' he said. 'But no need to trouble the boy. If you don't mind the liberty, I'll just step inside out of the wet.'

Without waiting for an invitation Albert Hepplethwaite shook the rain from his hat, stepped across the threshold, and closed the door.

Emma's agitation quickened. Was her intuition wrong? He said he was just paying his respects. She wondered why she should doubt that. Had she been ungracious to leave him standing on the street? She was confused.

'It's no trouble,' she said politely. 'I am sure Joshua will be pleased to speak with you. Excuse me, I will only be a moment.'

The proprietor of The Harbour Pie Shop puffed out his chest and placed his top hat on the stand. The wiry red whiskers, which flared from the sides of his face, belied the fact that the top of his head was completely bald. He was uncomfortably fat and only marginally taller than Emma.

'No need to hurry yourself,' he called, as she disappeared up the stairs.

He waited for a moment, listening to the sound of the creaking timbers as Emma hurried to the top of the house. He looked around, tilting his head toward the stairwell to catch the drift of muffled voices floating down from the attic. Sidling between the furniture, he crossed over to the writing-desk and ran his hand across the polished timber. The lid lifted out towards him. He opened it sufficiently to peer inside. Small bundles of letters, tied with ribbon, were housed in individual compartments. A bottle of ink rested on a well-used blotting pad. A black quill lay beside it.

At the sound of descending footsteps he closed the desk lid and shuffled back leaving behind a trail of damp footprints.

'So here you are, lad,' he announced. 'I trust you have been looking after your dear mother?'

'Yes, sir,' Joshua replied, buttoning his shirt at the neck.

Emma realized that the remains of the afternoon tea were still on the table. She wished that she had cleared them away.

'Your father had words with you, boy?'

'About what, sir?' Joshua looked across to his mother.

'Very likely I have a job for you, lad. Your father and I have spoken about it. Good strong boy like you will be very useful to me. An apprenticeship with the Pie Shop.' He waited for a response. 'What say you, boy?'

'I go to school,' Joshua said hesitantly.

'Don't you worry about school, lad. You'll learn more working with me than sitting behind a desk. I'll see to that.' Reaching into his waistcoat pocket he withdrew a fob watch and flipped it open.

'I need another pair of hands this afternoon. Stores to deliver to one of the ships,' he announced. 'Your father said I should come and get you whenever I needed you.'

So this was the purpose of his call.

'Which ship is it?' Joshua asked, hiding the hint of excitement in his voice.

'Barque. Name of the *Lady Cristobel*. She's due to sail in the morning.'

Joshua looked to his mother and then back to Mr Hepplethwaite.

Emma picked up his boots from the fireplace and handed them to him. They were still wet. But she was relieved that Mr Hepplethwaite would leave at last.

'Go along, Joshua, and do whatever Mr Hepplethwaite tells you.'

'Good. That's settled then,' the shopkeeper announced. 'Will Mr Quinlan be away for long?'

'I expect him home quite soon.'

'Well, it is time I took my leave.' He turned to the boy who was sitting on the doormat lacing his boots. 'Now you be a good lad and run along. You'll be much quicker than me. Down at the shop, Mrs Hepplethwaite will tell you what to do. The sooner you are off, the sooner you'll be finished.' He opened the door. 'On your way, boy!'

Joshua grabbed his cap, glanced back at his mother and dashed off down the street.

'And I will bid you good day, Mr Hepplethwaite,' Emma said, endeavouring to usher him out of the door.

But Hepplethwaite made no effort to move.

'A good boy,' he said, combing his fingers through his knotted whiskers. 'Now if your boy is going to work for me, perhaps we could be a little less formal. You must call me Bert.' The smile on his face was false. 'The missus and I treat all the lads we take on like family, especially when they're fresh away from their mothers. The wife, she's soft with 'em. Likes to give 'em a treat if they work hard. Piece of pie or a jam tart.' He sneered. 'Likes to spoil 'em a bit. Too soft, she is, in my estimation.'

Emma was hardly listening. She was considering the foolish expression on the man's face, likening it to that of a boy with nothing but holes in his pockets, looking through a shop window with mischief in his eyes.

'Of course,' he said, 'I've no time for lazy louts. No time at all. A boy's to pull his weight if he's working for me.'

'I assure you, Mr Hepplethwaite, you will have no problems with my boy.'

'Good. Then that is all settled,' he said again. 'Now let me once again offer you my condolences.'

Before Emma had time to step back, the man reached forward and grasped her hand. He placed his other hand on top of it, holding it like a waffle in an iron.

Emma tried to draw away but she was firmly secured.

'You must call into my shop one afternoon,' he said. 'I am sure I have something that will take your fancy. My special treat,' he smirked. 'You understand. Perhaps I can help you to get over this unfortunate business.' Unable to bend from the waist, the shopkeeper inclined his head towards the hand he had caught.

At that moment the door opened. George Quinlan had returned early.

'So! What do we have here?'

Albert Hepplethwaite dropped Emma's hand. 'Ah! Quinlan. Good day. Yes. I was just leaving. Just paying my respects on this sad occasion.'

Quinlan's eyes by-passed the baker. His fiery gaze set on his wife. Bert Hepplethwaite retrieved his hat from the hallstand and shuffled out sideways on to the street. The door banged behind him.

'He came to pay his respects. He came to fetch Joshua,' Emma cried. 'I didn't invite him in. I wanted him to go.'

Quinlan wasn't listening. He leaned back against the door unbuttoning his coat, his eyes still fixed on his wife. He let his coat fall on the floor. The wet wool smelled of tavern smoke. The buckle of his belt cut tight into his belly. He tugged it free and slid the leather strip from round his waist.

Emma backed towards the stairwell. Afraid. He followed her, eyes glaring. Before she reached the door, his arm shot forward. He slammed it shut behind her.

'It was the rain,' she begged. 'He came in out of the rain.'

His ruddy face pulsed.

Crossing her arms over her chest, Emma dropped her chin into them. She thought of Joshua and prayed he would not come home till late.

'You slut! You common whore!' George Quinlan yelled. 'So this is what you do when I'm away!' Firelight glinted on the buckle. 'I'll show you what you get for entertaining men under my roof! This time I'll teach you a lesson you will not forget!'

# Chapter 3

There was little movement on the headland, save for the solitary figure.

From a recess in the abbey wall, the seaman watched, his interest stirred by the sight of a woman walking alone. He had noticed her when she had first appeared from the direction of the church. Watched her wandering aimlessly, stumbling at times, the sprigs of heather tugging at her skirt.

He wondered why she was there. Why she had not taken the path, hard-padded over the centuries by the silent feet of monks and foxes. Why, instead, she had chosen to trek across the damp untrodden ground towards the cliff edge.

High above, a lone seagull hovered. It observed the intruder approaching its colony. It cried, one long wailing cry, and gave itself up to the wind, peeled back from the land and dived.

Two hundred feet below, the North Sea gnawed at the clay cliffs, spewing its foam on the bedrock beach in a rumble of distant thunder.

The seaman poked a stained finger into the bowl of his pipe, tapped the ash on to his leathered palm and watched as the particles danced off. For a while, he toyed with the narrow shaft. Sucked on it. Then returned the pipe to his pocket. He leaned back against the weathered wall and rubbed the itch from his shoulders.

She was wearing neither gloves nor bonnet. Surely she was cold.

The March wind combed the spiked grass in sweeping waves. The woman's hair floated across her face like the tentacles of a jellyfish. She was oblivious to it.

He could not see her features. He watched her slow. Then stop. Not wanting to be seen, he dropped down to his haunches. But she had no interest in the land. Her gaze was directed firmly to the sea.

He picked a blade of grass and chewed its sappy fibre. Following her every step, her gait stirred in his groin the tingling urge which life at sea deprived a seaman.

Between her legs her skirt flapped like a poorly set sail.

He spat the grass from his mouth, stood up and scanned the horizon.

To the east the leaden sea supported nothing but a billow of dark clouds. There were no ships. No sails. Nothing on the seascape save the mewing gulls, their cries muted by the offshore wind.

What was she looking for?

Was she waiting for a ship? The return of a husband, father, brother? Was she come here to mourn a vessel already lost. Dashed to flotsam on some uncharted reef?

He pulled a pouch from his pocket, pinched at the dried leaves and stuffed them into his pipe. The skeleton of the abbey towered above, its voided windows, once decked in shards of coloured glass, now framed a cold chameleon sky. The wind soughed through the empty nave. The ruin's transept long silenced to the peel of bells, a sanctuary to bats and passing birds.

The seaman watched. She lifted her skirt. Walked forward. Her movements slow but deliberate.

Perhaps now she would turn and retrace her steps. Or find the path. Return to the town. He would follow at a distance, taking care not to be seen. He would find where she went. Where she lived. He coveted this strange intimacy.

But she bore neither right nor left. She was heading for the cliff edge.

His uneasiness quickened. Surely she did not intend to give herself to the wind as the white bird had?

His buckled shoes caught on the tussocks as he lumbered awkwardly over ground unfamiliar to his sea legs. But he covered the distance quickly and slowed only when he was close behind her. A few yards ahead, the land ended, the remnant vegetation dangling from the edge by woody tendrils.

He touched her arm.

'*Pardonnez mois, mademoiselle*. Are you all right?'

'*Mais oui.*'

'*Vous êtes Française?*'

'*Non,*' she sighed.

'Please, *mademoiselle*, I fear something is wrong. Let me help you.'

As he reached out to touch her, her knees buckled, her body crumpling like a falling sail.

He supported her, cupped her chin in his hand and lifted her face towards him. The hair layered across her face streamed back on the wind.

'*Mon Dieu!*' The colour of old blood trapped beneath skin was not what he had expected. 'What has happened to you? Your face.'

Her fingers traced the swollen contours of her cheek. She looked into the swarthy face appealing for an answer. None came.

'I don't remember,' she said. 'A fall I think.' Her head rolled against his leg. Her eyes closed.

*Mon Dieu!* At sea, men fell from the yards. He had seen their broken faces. He had seen them when they crawled back to the ship after brawling in the taverns. He knew the difference. He knew the damage one man's fist inflicted on another's face. He knew the mark a knuckle could imprint upon a cheek. What man had done this? What coward? If he were here now he swore he would kill him.

Lifting the woman, he carried her to the shelter of the abbey. On a patch of soft green, between hewn stones, he laid her on the earth, swung the coat from his back and draped it over her.

'Can I bring someone to you, miss?' he asked, sliding his fingers under a ringlet which lay across her brow. Her skin was smooth. Warm. She smelled good.

Emma stirred. She remembered the gesture. The soft touch of a hand across her forehead. The scent of the spring flowers around her. The warmth of the sun. And the sound of a fountain pattering softly on to a lake. She closed her eyes and drifted back into the dream.

'*Mademoiselle?*'

'Thank you,' she said, forgetting what he had asked.

'Let me take you home, or bring help to you.'

'Let me just rest a while. I will be fine presently.'

For three hours Emma slept, slept as the wind whipped the clouds out to sea. As the pockets of sunshine drew clouds in their wake, grey shadows slithered over her body like drifting veils. She slept on the dank ground unaware her every breath was being watched. Slept, unaware of the seaman, squatting against the wall, waiting for her to wake. She slept beneath his coat tainted with the smell of salt and tar, soothed by the rhythmic sound of a knife blade drawn against a sharpening stone.

But there was no dream in her sleep though at times her mind fought to capture some memory. Like a drowning soul struggling in the ocean, she needed something to cling on to. She thought nothing of past or future, but a single image fluttered behind her lids. A mound of earth. A bunch of withered snowdrops. A wooden cross.

When she opened her eyes, the sky above was blue. She could hear a skylark singing. It was the first she had heard this year. She moved her head and recognized the contours of the abbey. Why was she lying on the ground? What had brought her to this long abandoned place?

The seaman returned the knife to its scabbard and stood up. 'At last the princess awakes!'

Emma was confused but not afraid. The Frenchman's tone was gentle. 'What am I doing here? What has happened?'

'I thought you would be able to tell me.' he said.

'I cannot remember.'

He leaned over and offered her his tar-stained palms.

'Perhaps you can sit up?' he said. 'Let me help you.'

As she placed her hands on his and allowed him to draw her up, the coat slid from her knees.

'Yours?' she said. 'You must be cold.'

'It is much colder on the sea.'

She looked up at him.

'Sometimes it is so cold, the fingers, they almost freeze. The ropes, they cut across my feet like knives. No,' he said, 'this is not so cold.'

'Please take it anyway. I am better now.' She gathered up the coat and held it out to him.

He thanked her. 'I am pleased. I was concerned.' He donned the coat and took a step back. 'Perhaps, I should introduce myself.'

Standing almost six feet tall, the sailor bowed. 'My name is François le Fevre. At your service, *mademoiselle.*'

Emma smiled. Held out her hand. 'I am pleased to make your acquaintance, Monsieur le Fevre. I am Emma Quinlan. Mrs Emma Quinlan.'

'Ah, *madame.* I beg your pardon. But you look so young.'

She could feel the blood flush in her bruised cheeks. 'I think I should not be here.'

'And, I think I am glad that I visited this place, otherwise I would not have met the Mrs Emma Quinlan.' He inclined his head graciously then turned his face into the wind, flicked back his hair and retied the strip of rag which held it.

How becoming he was. This seaman. This miscreant. The very type of man she had been warned to be wary of. Yet this sailor provoked no fear in her. Quite to the contrary: she felt safe with him.

What was it about him? His touch? The deep walnut of his eyes? His weathered face? Or was it the lilt of his French accent? Soft. Haunting. Lyrical.

As if reading her thoughts, he said, 'I am inquisitive, *madame*. You speak French?'

'A little. Why do you ask?'

He laughed. 'Because you spoke to me in French.'

'I do not remember.'

The seaman shook his head. 'This is very strange,' he mused. 'Here I am, alone on the top of a cliff, in the ruins of a great church, with a beautiful woman who I do not know. A beautiful woman who speaks to me in French but says she cannot remember. *Mais oui!* I think this is very strange.'

'Please, *monsieur*, do not make fun of me. I think I have been a little crazy in the head. But now I am well.'

'My dear *madame*, forgive me. I am not making fun, as you say.' He kneeled down beside her. 'I would not do that.'

'I must go home.'

'Then let me help you.' He eased her to her feet.

Emma looked about, swaying unsteadily. A sudden sickness churned inside her belly. They were alone. Alone on the cliff top. Had anyone seen them there? Seen her with the sailor? How long had she been there? What had happened there? Now she was afraid.

'Perhaps, *monsieur*, if you would help me as far as the church stairs, I will manage on my own from there.'

François understood.

She leaned heavily on his arm as they walked slowly back towards the churchyard and the steps which led down the valley side.

'Will you be all right?'

She nodded.

He stood for a moment considering his farewell.

'*Au revoir, madame.*'

'*Au revoir, monsieur.*'

'My ship will be in port for a few days.'

She smiled. 'Goodbye, *monsieur.*'

He hesitated for a moment, then turned and sped off.

The potato soup bubbled with the smell of sweet onions. A jet of blue spurted from a piece of coal. Emma drew the curtains against the growing dusk and considered what she had achieved in the past few hours. She had scraped and polished. The brass fender gleamed. The room looked fresh. Even the household items, lined up neatly, appeared to have adopted a different appearance. Why? She did not know. Did not know what had awakened her enthusiasm and granted her renewed energy.

On returning from the abbey she had first relit the fire, then peeled the potatoes and boiled several pots of water. Stripping off her clothes she had stood naked by the hearth and sponged herself. The tepid water, scented with a dash of salts, had felt good as it trickled down her legs. As she dried herself she had watched the tiny beads of water run from her feet and settle between the knots of the rag rug. She had dipped her hair into the china bowl and washed her head. After rinsing the soap from her eyes, she had admired the porcelain decorated with swirls of damask roses intertwined with curling ribbons. It was a long time since she had examined the delicate artwork.

From her wardrobe she picked the blue merino. It was soft and warm. And an apron edged with a frill of French lace. She wound the wisps of hair which fell around her face, in strips of cloth, then sat by the fire to hasten it drying.

The smell from the pot reminded her she had an appetite. It was getting late.

From the doorway of the brick terrace, she could see as far as the corner where Seal Street turned down towards Flowergate and the harbour. George was standing in the middle of the narrow street no more than twenty yards away. He was going neither forward nor back. Just standing. Legs apart. Hands on hips. Swaying. As she watched, he leaned forward and projected a concoction of dark-coloured fluid on to the cobbles. The best port from the Faith and Compass, several pots of rum and more than a little ale. It splattered back at his legs.

He straightened. Leaned back and waited but he had no encore. Saliva dribbled from his bottom lip. He wiped his sleeve across his mouth, spat, and continued his perambulation to the house. Two dogs snapped at each other while lapping up the liquid treat.

Emma returned to the fire and waited. The soup bubbled. The clock in the parlour ticked loudly. But George did not arrive.

Beneath the lamp pole, across the street, he had settled himself in the gutter.

The lamplighter leaned over him. 'You 'right, squire?'

'Fine! Absolutely fine, my man!' he drawled, a cock-eyed grin contorting his face.

Working with his pole above the drunken man, the lighter opened the glass and ignited the mantle. The flame burned blue for a moment then burst into a cool white haze. Doffing his cap, the workman continued on his rounds. The sound of his pole tapped its way up the hill.

The smell of burning brought Emma back to the stove. The soup! As she pushed the pot from the heat, the lid slid towards her. She tried to catch it in her lap but it went clattering noisily to the tiles.

'You are useless, woman. I always said you were useless.'

George Quinlan was propped against the door. He turned the key in the lock. Suddenly the room seemed quite dark. Emma had grown accustomed to the firelight and had forgotten to light a lamp. She hoped he would not notice.

She retrieved the lid, wiped it and returned it to the pot.

George stumbled against the chair and grunted. He was peering at her, eyes half closed, his head poised at a strange angle. The corner of his mouth twitched foolishly.

'Sit down,' she said.

He followed her instructions, sat in his armchair and stared, gazing for a while at the fire. Then the kettle. The poker. The box of kindling. The coal-scuttle. He studied each one in turn, inclining his head as if questioning its function. When his eyes returned to the fire, the lids were almost shut.

Emma wondered, as she had so many times, what had become of the upstanding man she had met twelve years earlier? What had reduced him to this pathetic figure? Reeking of alcohol. Fat. Unkempt. Old, though not yet fifty. She remembered him when she was first introduced: his proud though somewhat pompous bearing; how he had seemed kind at first. And generous. How could she forget his visits to her parents' house? How the idea of a union between them had at first been distasteful, no, appalling to her, but how she had considered her situation against that of her family. After all, he had provided Joshua with the father he never had. Given her a home. But most importantly had shouldered the burden which she and Joshua had become to her dear Mama and Papa. She was grateful to him for that. And she remembered how she had endeavoured to love him albeit in a respectful way.

The George she had married had at least been amiable, quick-witted, astute. A sound businessman. He had promised to provide for her and her son. The prospects had been good. But over the years, George had changed and Emma's situation was far from that which she, or her parents, had envisaged.

'Mama! Mama!' Joshua tapped on the door. The brass handle rattled but the man snoring in the chair did not stir. 'It's me, Mama. Please open the door!'

Emma unlocked it.

'From Mr Hepplethwaite,' he said, thrusting a brown paperbag into her hands. 'And Mrs Cooper wants to know if you have a spare candle. She says she's down to her last one.'

George's lips puffed out on every breath.

'Mama?'

'I heard you, Joshua. Wait a moment.'

From the dresser drawer she sorted through the stubs of tallow.

'Take these. Tell Mrs Cooper it's all I can spare. Then hurry back.'

George Quinlan stretched out his legs, kicked at his boots and groaned. 'I'll fetch some water. You can soak them,' she said.

As Emma eased his feet from the stained boots, he grumbled. She loosened his belt. He squinted at her from one eye as she performed the ritual. She was used to it. It was a nightly chore. She always strove to make him comfortable. She wanted him to remain in his chair. Wanted him to fall asleep so she could go to bed alone, so she could fall asleep out of reach of his grappling hands.

Joshua returned quietly and placed his boots in the hearth. In the fire-light, his hair was the colour of polished teak.

'Mrs Cooper said, thank you.'

He pointed to the paperbag on the table. 'Some jam tarts! Mr Hepplethwaite said to say that you deserved a treat. And that you must call into his shop one day.'

'Hush,' said Emma, glancing at her husband. 'Please ask Mr Hepplethwaite not to send anything more,' she whispered.

'But, Mama, they're fresh.'

'I don't doubt they are!'

Emma lifted her skirts as she stepped over George's outstretched legs. Asleep, he was just another piece of kitchen furniture.

From the cooking pot she ladled a large bowl of thick white soup for her son and a smaller serving for herself.

'Tell me about your day.'

'I went to the wharf. And a sailor, from one of the sailing ships, told me about the whales. He said that they are as big as a ship. And that they rise out of the water to the height of a ship's mast. And they can stand upright on their tails and stare at a ship from their evil eyes before falling back. And he said the sound is like the waves crashing against the West Pier. Whoosh! Splash!'

'Tall tales!'

'But it's true, Mama. And he told me that there are flat fish the shape of a serving plate, as big as this room, that glide below the surface. And snakes in the sea, bright orange and thick as a man's leg that kill a man if he tries to grab it.'

'Goodness, son! You mustn't spend all your day gossiping. Don't let Mr Hepplethwaite catch you or you'll be for it. You must forget about ships and sailing. You are supposed to be working. You have a job now.'

'But, Mama, I was working. I took eight cartloads of flour to the jetty. And the sailor let me carry them on to the ship. Right down into the hold. And Mr. Hepplethwaite gave me a macaroon when I got back. And he asked me if I wanted to go to sea.'

'Who did? Mr Hepplethwaite.'

'No, Mama! The seaman!'

'And what did you say, pray tell?'

'I said that I wanted that more than anything in the world.' His smile faded. 'But I told him that I had a job with The Pie Shop. And besides, I know Father wouldn't let me.'

'I should think so, too. Now eat your tea.'

'But he said if I go back tomorrow, and if the captain is not on board, he will let me climb the rigging.'

'Enough now, Joshua! Eat your tea.'

'But it's a real sailing ship. Not like the Whitby ships. And he said they needed boys like me. And maybe one day I could be a captain and have my own ship. Oh! Mama. You know it's what I want.'

'Enough of that talk, Joshua. Finish your meal.'

'But, Mama. . . .'

'Enough!'

Emma lay awake listening to her husband stumbling around the kitchen. When finally he mounted the stairs, she counted each footfall. She knew the distinctive sound of each creaking stair. Anticipated the moment the door handle would turn.

She moved closer to the edge, closed her eyes and feigned sleep.

The bed sagged as he dropped on to it rolling her body back to his. His coal-shovel hand flopped on to her belly. She didn't move. From beneath the bedding, his sickly odour drifted into her nose.

As was her custom, she lay still, hardly daring to breathe, praying he would fall asleep, grateful that he was usually incapable of making love to her properly any more. But his lack of manhood made him angry. She knew he blamed her for his inadequacy, reminding her that she did not tend to his needs as a good wife should, lashing out at her in the darkness with his knee or foot or elbow.

But this night, unlike any other, Emma did not close herself off to his penetrating hands. This night, she relaxed. She allowed her chest to rise and fall rhythmically. Her mind was awash with thoughts of the seaman. She could see him leaning over her. She quivered to the thoughts of his touch. Breathed deeply on the memory of his briny smell.

She revisited their conversation on the cliff top, pondering on every word, wishing there were more. She recalled his gestures. The flick of his hair as he tied it. The colour of his hands as he held them out to her. She considered every minor detail, over and over again.

She wanted it to be him lying next to her. Wanted his hands on her. Touching her. Feeling her. Such thoughts! Yet she could not make them pass. Nor wanted to. How could she feel this way for such a man? A common seaman.

George turned over dragging the bedclothes with him.

Carefully, so as not to disturb him, Emma pulled the nightdress around her shoulders and fastened the buttons under her chin. Her breasts were cold. She folded her arms across them. Her thoughts were not of sleep. But of one thing. Of being with the sailor. Of what might have happened in the ruins of the abbey. But didn't. Of his concern for her and of his parting words which echoed through her head – *My ship will be in port for a few days.*

She knew she must see him again.

# Chapter 4

It was the first time Emma had ventured along the old waterfront. A compulsion to see the Frenchman had been nagging at her for several days and despite her conscience telling her to forget the seaman, the desire to meet him had welled to overflowing. She had to see him and speak with him, though she had no thoughts about what she would say.

Beside the wharf, ketches, sloops and barques lolled on the shallow water. Further out an old collier drifted on its anchor chain, its seasoned sails hanging out to dry, limp and lifeless.

On the dockside, an engine clattered, slapping at the air with its leather belts and shooting out spurts of pressured steam. Barrels, near the height of a man, rumbled over cobblestones, along swaying planks and across decks while up above them, wooden tackle blocks swung wildly from braced yard-arms. Crates and boxes caught in webs of hemp netting disappeared into the seemingly insatiable ships' holds. A mule bellowed and kicked as it was hoisted from the ground. Ducks clacked through slats in wooden boxes. A cooper's hammer thrummed. Grubby sailors gawked. It was an uninviting place. No place for a lady.

Emma pulled the plaid tightly around her shoulders and hurried on scanning the bow of each ship for its name, searching for the one the Frenchman had mentioned. The name she had forgotten. Hoping that when she saw it she would remember.

Some ships looked empty. Stripped of cargo. On others, men hung in the web of rigging like hungry spiders. From the decks, raucous voices gave resonance to neither country nor county accents. While across the wharf, the smell of tar and linseed stirred in iron cauldrons drifted at nose height.

Emma wished she had not come.

The *Amelia Day* was the last. Its berth marked the end of the dock.

Ahead, the pier had collapsed leaving only the splintered seaweed-skirted piles protruding from shallow pools of seawater.

Emma looked across the bay. The sun had risen sufficiently to glance on the clay tiles of the newer houses at the other side. On the open water, small keels and cobles swayed idly from lines bearded in weed. The pumped chords of an accordion floated across the water. But behind her, the old buildings rising up from the wharf appeared even greyer than usual.

A voice called to her in a language she did not recognize. Men laughed. Faces peered. Fingers pointed. Emma quickened her pace. If only there was a rowboat to take her to the other side. She did not want to retrace her path. How foolish she had been.

A dappled grey snorted in the shafts. A pair of piglets, destined never again to see the light of day, squealed as they were lowered snout first into a ship's dark hold. A red-hot iron, dipped in a vat of seawater sizzled, alarming a scrawny cat which fled along the quay and found refuge under an upturned boat. Emma's breath quickened as seamen loitering on the wharf looked furtively at her from beneath their black felt hats.

'A shilling for your purse?' one called, as he stood and cupped his crotch in a vulgar gesture. 'Five minutes o' your time. All it'll take.'

Emma turned from the voice.

'Plenty o' life in Old Tom. You'll see.'

The narrow ghaut which ran up between the buildings was not far ahead.

'Slut!' he shouted after her.

Shop doorways tinkled to the sound of small brass bells. Matronly ladies stood outside gossiping, small girls in white aprons clinging to their skirts. Boys tired of pestering and tired of being ignored, climbed the metal railings of the yard opposite. Emma stopped in front of the confectioner's shop. She had to regain her breath.

Displayed in the bay window were rows of jars of assorted sweets: gum drops, toffees, licorice. Inside the shop, tin canisters lined the shelves. Emma gazed at the glass not looking through it.

What had been going on in her head? How embarrassing it would have been if she had found the Frenchman on the dock. Imagine what a chorus of cries would have been raised from the other men, jeering, deriding, taunting. What could she have said to justify her reason for being there? What if George had followed her?

She waited anxiously for the bridge to open. The old drawbridge was the only way across the harbour. It linked the old town on the east with the shops, houses and fish market on the western side of the valley.

Stepping from the bridge's weary timbers, Emma welcomed the stench of the Whitby fleet. Blue and white cobles floated on the shallow water or lay on their sides in the wet sand like sleeping seals. Blackened nets hung web-like from half buried oars as leaning towers of crab pots lined the quayside. No sooner were the wicker baskets stacked with crab and lobster than they were whisked away on the hawkers' carts. Fishermen, sorting their catch, tossed fish this way and that. Boards, set out in long rows, displayed trays of the North Sea's bounty. On them, hundreds of dead eyes glinted in the daylight.

The fishwives, their aprons daubed with oil and blood, spat and argued like common gulls. Emma regarded them wistfully. They were strong women. Not soft and foolish like she was. She envied them. Envied their courage. They were victims of a spiteful sea which provided their sustenance but claimed their men in exchange. They were wives without husbands, mothers without sons. But they survived. Emma admired their fortitude. Those women whose lives were ruled by the sea they never sailed.

'Penny for them?'

Emma smiled at the old man, his knobbed fingers weaving a length of twine through the torn fishing net.

Across the harbour, the cluster of ships cradled beneath the cliff presented a pleasing picture. The picket fence of masts supporting its lines of rigging reminded her of raspberry canes on a winter's morning decked with cobwebs.

'I was thinking how pretty the sailing ships looked from here,' she said.

The fisherman shrugged, then pulled another section of the net over his knee. He released a fish tangled by its gills and tossed it back to the sea. The birds responded quickly to the flash of silver.

Emma had seen the old salt many times before, always sitting in the same spot, surrounded by a mound of netting, or with a box of twigs beside him, busily bending the boughs of hazelwood into pots for crab and lobster.

'Pull up a pew and sit yourself down,' he said. 'Could do with a bit of company.'

Emma's feet ached. It would do no harm to sit for a moment. An upturned box made a convenient seat.

No sooner had she sat down than a female voice squawked in her ear, 'You're in me road there!' The smell of the previous night's haul wafted from the fishwife's apron. 'If you don't shift, you'll get a pail o' guts tipped o'er you.'

'I am sorry,' said Emma rising to her feet.

'Find somewhere else to chuck your slops,' the old salt shouted. 'You stay where you are, lass! Don't mind our Alice. Her bark's worse than her bite.'

The woman mumbled something which Emma did not hear.

'Relax yourself, lass.' The leathery skin of his weatherworn face was crinkled and dried. Emma's complexion was pale in comparison.

'It's a fine day,' she said.

'No wind,' he answered. Disappointed.

'Are you here everyday?' she asked. 'I believe I have noticed you before.'

'Aye, lass. Where else would I be?'

'You never sail with the fleet?'

'With this?' he said, thumping his fist on to his thigh. His leg ended at the knee. A turned peg leg sprouted from his trousers.

'I am sorry, I did not know.'

He cut another length of string and wound it into a knot.

'Do you miss the sea?'

'What sort of darn foolish question is that?' he said. 'If the sea's in a man's blood, he'd be lying if he said he didn't. Fishermen, sailors, seamen, they're all the same. The sea, she's like your mistress. Begging your pardon, miss, but once you get the taste, she won't let you go. Keeps pulling you back.'

He sighed. 'All I got is memories. And the tales the lads tell when they find the time to talk. I like to listen. Listen real good, I do.' His fingers stopped working as he stared across the water.

Emma followed his gaze. 'Perhaps then, you would have heard if a French ship is in the harbour?'

He scratched at the stubble on his chin. 'Not to my knowledge, lass. Not 'less she came in last night. What name she sail by?'

'I don't know.'

As the sun cleared the cliff top, tiny flecks of metal shone from the distant lattice of masts and spars.

'Pretty, aren't they?' Emma said.

'I suppose,' he said.

He lifted the stump of his thigh and shifted his position on the stool.

'Sailed when I was a lad,' he said, casting his eyes toward the sea. 'Whales and seals were all the go in them days. Most of Whitby chasing 'em. It stopped after the *Esk* went down on Saltscar Reef. September 1826.' He sighed. 'Not more than thirty miles from home. Sixty-five brave men lost,' he said. 'I was one of the lucky ones.'

He rested his hands on the net. 'Hard work it were, but was all a lad ever wanted. Aye, but that was a long while ago. Whitby ships not been chasing whales now for nigh on forty years, but that don't stop the lads from getting a hankering to sail away. Some of 'em don't want to follow the 'erring. Not exciting enough. So they sign themselves up on one of them cargo ships and away they go.'

On a strip of sand, not far from the bridge, two small boys were playing near an upturned boat. The old man watched for a moment then shook his head and returned to his work. 'Often breaks their mothers' hearts. Never see 'em again once they've gone.'

Emma thought about Joshua.

Having come to the edge of the net, the fisherman dragged the section he had checked over his knee and started again.

'Who knows what's best?' he said, as he sniffed the air. 'Fishing's not easy. North Sea's as cruel as any ocean. But I'd not swap it. Like I said afore, if the sea's in a man's blood, there's no getting away from it.'

A frenzied outburst by a mob of seagulls fighting over a pot of slimy fish-guts distracted the pair. It was over quickly.

'Do the ships stay in Whitby long?' she asked.

'Some do. Some don't. Depends what they're loading and where they're bound.'

'I once sailed on a ship,' Emma said cautiously.

'Like yon square riggers?'

'Yes,' she said. 'A clipper. When I was a girl.' The old man stopped and watched her as she gazed across the water. 'I sailed with my family from London to Le Havre, though I believe the ship was bound for the Orient. I remember how I enjoyed the voyage. How exciting it was. The ship seemed to fly across the water. And, I remember, when it was far from land, with only sea and the sky around it, I asked Papa if we could go all the way China. I will never forget it.'

The sailor laughed. 'Don't often hear a lady talk about the sea like that.'

The fishwife was standing over the pair, her fists resting squarely on her hips.

'I'm sorry,' Emma said, when she noticed her. 'I'll move out of your way.'

'Nay, stay as you are, lass. I haven't seen Dad's chin wag so much in weeks.'

The old man winked at Emma.

'Perhaps I can come back and talk another day?'

'Any time lass. Glad to have your company.'

The woman pushed a package into Emma's hand. "Ere. There's a couple of nice haddock. Cook 'em up for your man's tea.'

'I can't take that,' Emma said.

'There's now't wrong with 'em!'

'But I can pay you.'

'Take 'em before I change me mind!'

Emma smiled and thanked the woman and bade them both farewell, promising the fisherman that she would return and talk another day.

Behind where she had been sitting, not more than three paces away, François was leaning against a pile of crates. Emma stopped.

They regarded each other, their faces showing no emotion. She wondered how long he had been there. Wondered if perhaps he did not recognize her. But surely he must. Without wishing it, a smile curled the corner of her lips.

He acknowledged it with a twinkle from his dark eyes.

She spoke first. 'Good morning, *monsieur*. I was admiring the ships.'

'Ah,' he said. 'And what was it about them that took your fancy, may I ask?'

'Nothing in particular, I think.'

'I thought perhaps you may have been looking for a French ship?'

He had been listening. She lifted her skirt clear of the ground and walked along the wharf. He followed her, half a pace behind.

'If I can be of assistance, *madame*, I can tell you: there are no French ships in Whitby at this time.'

'But you are French, are you not, Monsieur le Fevre?'

'Ah!' he said quickly, coming alongside her. 'You came looking for me?'

'No! No! I came to purchase some fish.' She held out the package wrapped in paper. Her hand was shaking.

'*Naturellement!*' he replied. 'But tell me, *madame*, are you fully recovered?' A genuine expression replaced his smile.

'I am. And I thank you for your kindness.' She stopped and faced him. She had to ask. 'Where is your ship? What is its name?

He pointed. 'There,' he said. 'In the shipyard by the sand flats they call Belle Island. You can see it from here. It has only two masts. The main, it snapped in a storm. Took a good man to the bottom with it. It would have taken the ship too had we not cut the rigging.'

'So you must wait until it is repaired?'

'Yes, or sign on another ship. Some of the men have sailed already.'

'And you?'

'I think I will wait,' he said, adding with a sly smile, 'I am finding this port quite agreeable.'

With a respectable distance separating them they stood looking across the harbour to the cluster of grey houses running down to the wharfs on the east bank, some hanging over the water. Behind the rooftops, the long stone stairway ran diagonally across the steep hillside, up to the top of the cliff, to the parish church of St Mary, and behind that, to the ruined abbey silhouetted like a paper cut out against the sky.

'I have stayed too long. I must go,' said Emma.

'Will we meet again?'

'Perhaps,' she said, offering him her hand in a gesture of gratitude.

He inclined his head and held her fingers as he spoke. 'My ship is the *Morning Star*. It will be two weeks or more before she is ready to sail. I hope I will see you on the wharf another day.'

'Perhaps,' she said. 'Goodbye, *monsieur.*'

'*Au revoir, madame.*'

François watched as she wound her way between the fish stalls, around the queue of waiting carts and wagons, and across the road. He watched till she disappeared through the door of the butcher's shop.

'Nice bit o' skirt you got there, Frenchy!'

François wheeled around.

Old Tom leered at him from behind an upturned barrow.

'You mind your business!'

'Soft and warm, and tight as me fist, I reckon. Better than them loose sluts across the bay.'

François lunged toward the cart but the sailor overturned a tray of fish sending a shoal of dead herring slithering under his feet.

A gaggle of outraged fishwives scurried around, scolding and cursing.

'You touch her and I will kill you!' François yelled.

Thomas Barstow sneered. He fancied a bit of clean young flesh. What sailor wouldn't after months at sea? But this one took his fancy. Right pretty she was. Looked classy, too. But not too fine to talk to a seaman. He would bide his time, and whether the Frenchman liked it or not, he would have his way with this one. That was a promise.

# Chapter 5

'Spare a minute, luv, I've got something to show you.'

Emma laid down the rug she was beating. There was some urgency in Mrs Bradshaw's voice.

'Don't want to stop you doing your chores. Just thought you might like to see something.'

Emma followed her neighbour into the kitchen of number 26. The heavy damask curtains were only half drawn. A musty smell of scorched cloth, wet napkins and vinegar hung on the warm kitchen air. There was little space in the room. It was crowded with furniture, particularly chairs. High chairs, several stools and tall backed chairs in various states of dilapidation which provided additional flat surfaces for the piles of washing which were heaped everywhere. A thick felt pad covered one end of the large table where a pair of men's trousers lay half hidden under a damp cloth. A ball of wool and darning needles sat on top of a pile of assorted stockings. Vests in various sizes draped two large clothes horses which skirted the fender and hid the fire.

'Come in, lass. Don't be shy. Ignore the mess.'

Emma straightened her apron and brushed the dust from her face. Her nose was beginning to itch.

The matronly lady pulled a chair aside and pointed into a recess. 'There!' she said.

The corner smelled rank. A ginger cat, its fur matted into lumps, was sprawled flat against the wall. It reminded Emma of an old fox fur seasoned by moths and silverfish. As she leaned down, the cat turned its whiskers towards her, stood, arched its back, miaowed, then lay down again causing a burst of squeaks and wriggles. The kittens were little bigger than a nest of newborn rats.

53

'Born last night,' Mrs Bradshaw announced proudly. 'Though we didn't notice until this morning.'

'How many?' Emma asked.

'Five, our Fred said, but I think there may be six or eight.'

'That's nice.'

Emma glanced around her neighbour's kitchen. It was the first time she had been into the house.

'Thought you might like to take one. Keep you company. They'll only end up in a bucket if you don't.'

'Thank you, but Mr Quinlan is not partial to animals.'

'Aye, I noticed that. Never mind,' she said, 'seeing how you're 'ere, you'd best sit down and I'll make you a nice cup of tea.'

'But, I—'

'I won't take no for an answer,' she said, swinging one of the clothes horses back from the hearth. On the grill above the fire, a large dented kettle was already steaming. She pointed to one of the piles of laundry. 'Just pop them things on to that stool yonder and sit yourself down.'

The boiling water spurted and sizzled on the coals.

Emma shuffled the laundry and made herself a space. As she did, a small face surrounded by a mop of near white curls poked out from beneath the table. Large blue angelic eyes studied her cautiously before grasping the security of the table leg and retreating behind it. Mrs Bradshaw appeared not to notice.

'Go on, sit down, my dear.'

'Thank you.'

The washerwoman filled two tin mugs and gave one to Emma. 'Handle's a bit hot,' she said, as she settled herself. 'Now tell me, I ain't seen you getting out much lately. Nowt up with you, is there?'

It was obvious to Emma that Mrs Bradshaw missed little of what went on in Seal Street, especially the comings and goings directly across from her front door.

'I'll get out more when the weather warms a little,' said Emma. 'What about you, Mrs Bradshaw? Are you keeping well?'

'Can't grumble.' The girl crept to the woman's knee and tried to climb on. 'Go play outside with the others,' she said sharply. But the little one would not be prised from her skirt.

'And while I think on it, Mrs Cooper asked to be remembered to you, if I see'd you.'

'That's nice.'

Mrs Bradshaw folded her arms and leaned her elbows on to the table.

'That lad of yours – saw him with a barrow other day, coming from yard at back of Pie Shop. Working for Hepplethwaite, is he?' She lowered her voice and leaned forward. 'Not meaning to pry, of course!'

Emma knew that anything she said would be related to Mrs Cooper and possibly other neighbours in the street. But in this instance Emma saw little harm in satisfying the washerwoman's curiosity. 'He's been there for almost two weeks.'

'Thought that must be the case,' she said, satisfied. 'Said to Mrs Cooper, I did, I reckon Mrs Quinlan's lad is working at Pie Shop.' She blew the steam from her tea.

'Seems a shame, though, for an intelligent lad like yours to be working on't barrows. Still they've all got to start somewhere, 'aven't they?'

'Indeed,' said Emma.

'But I'd be right canny of that man.'

'Which man?'

'Hepplethwaite, of course. Makes out he's Mister High and Mighty. Anyone would think he owned half of Whitby the way he behaves.' She mopped her brow. 'I feel real sorry for his missus. Lovely lady, Mrs Hepplethwaite. Kind-hearted body, she is. But him. Wouldn't trust him further than I could throw him!'

Emma smiled politely.

'Haven't you ever noticed when you've been in his shop, fuss he makes of the girls and spinster ladies? Aye, and some of the married ones!'

'Is that so?'

'Sly, he is, too. I've watched 'im squeezing hands when he takes the money. Gives 'em a wry smile or a wink, or he talks to 'em real quiet like.' She leaned back. 'Wouldn't dare try that sort of palaver with me!'

'Joshua is coping just fine, and he'll learn to look out for himself. He's a bright boy, though, like all boys his age he's got a bee in his bonnet about going to sea. I find it hard to understand. No sailing blood in his veins, but it's like he's fixed on the idea and nothing is going to change his thinking.'

'Well, my dear, let me give you a bit of advice. If the lad has the bug in him to go to sea, there'll be no amount of tonic will cure 'im of it. It's something as gets into their blood like a sickness and eats away at 'em until you can do nothing but let 'em go. Don't do no good to hold 'em. No good at all. Ain't nothing to do with their upbringing, or what you've learned 'em, just part of 'em growing into men. It's like holding a candle in a fire, sooner or later you've got to let go. I tell you, if that's what he wants – let 'im go!'

Emma stared at the candle watching the wick curl like a pig's tail from the molten wax. The amber flame swayed on its vapour base of peacock blue and bowed towards the draught. A teardrop of hot wax trickled down the stem followed almost immediately by another. The second, faltered, stopped and hardened before it reached the holder.

The sheet of writing paper glowed in the light. Emma's hand rested beside it, the pen poised in her fingers. As she rolled the quill she watched the nib's shadow rotate on the paper. Her hand was quivering slightly. She pondered for a moment, stroked the crow's feather across her cheek, then dipped the sharpened nib into the ink. The writing flowed in fine copper-plate scroll:

*My dearest sister Anna*

*I trust you are well and Daniel and the boys. I send you all my fondest love and think of you often. How the years have flown since we were together. How I long to see you again but I know that cannot be. Perhaps one day I will see you again.*

*Two weeks ago, Elizabeth May was taken from me. Although she was very sickly I had prayed that she would survive. But that was not to be. Now I tell myself her death was a blessing. She was such a bonny baby.*

*George is well.*

*I am well also, though I am concerned for Joshua. He has the making of a fine young man but I fear he is becoming increasingly unhappy. George saw fit to organize a job for him as he is now almost thirteen. George said that we could no longer afford to pay for his schooling and that it was time for him to earn his keep.*

*I worry for him. He is growing so quickly into manhood and has a gentleness about him which reminds me of Papa. I fear the situation he has been placed into will teach him nothing – except perhaps bad habits. He is not suited to the work and already I see a change in him. He talks constantly of the ships which visit this port and yearns to sail away. I try to discourage him for my greatest fear is that he will run away and I will never see him again.*

*Sometimes I feel very lonely. But I have only myself to blame. I caused Mama and Papa so many worries and brought shame on the family. If only I could have been wise and strong like you.*

*My dearest Anna, how I wish to see you. To talk to you. If only it were*

*possible for me to visit you. That would be my fondest wish.*
  *But now I must close. May God bless you and care for you.*
  *Your loving sister*

                                    *Emma*

The armchair creaked as George changed his position. Saliva gurgled and
caught in his throat before he sucked loudly on the air and coughed.

Emma blew gently on the sheet of writing paper. Touched it lightly.
The ink was dry. Carefully, she folded her letter. From one of the
compartments in the writing desk she retrieved a bundle of papers tied
with a fraying ribbon. She unfastened the bow and placed her letter
amongst the others.

'Scribbling again?'

'Yes,' she said, as she tied the bundle and returned it to the desk.

'It'll do you no good. You mark my words!'

'It'll do you no good. You mark my words.' She meant to repeat the
words only in her head but they slipped quietly off her tongue before she
was able to stop them. She had mocked him. Within an instant he was
beside her.

'What was that you said?'

'Nothing,' she said, drawing her head back. 'It was nothing.'

'Nothing!' Only the pot of ink remained on the bureau. With a sweep
of his forearm the bottle skittled across the desk and settled in her lap.

'Pah! I said it would do you no good.' George hovered as if waiting for
an argument. Emma gave him no response.

It was a few seconds before she felt the wetness trickling between her
legs.

She rose carefully, holding the ink-stained skirt out in front of her.

'Excuse me,' she said politely. 'I will have to change.'

# Chapter 6

The clerk peered over the rim of his spectacles, blinked at the pair and continued writing. Joshua was about to speak but Emma nudged him to be silent.

'I'll attend to you in a minute,' the man said.

He continued copying details from a large journal on to a sheet of paper. When he finished, he opened the wooden shutter beside him and whistled, beckoning to one of the men on the wharfside.

A hand reached up to the sill and grasped the paper.

'*Lady Exeter* – and quick about it!' the clerk called. 'If she don't get a move on soon she'll be wallowing on the sand like a beached whale.'

Clogs clattered across the cobbles.

The clerk closed the shutter on the sea air and turned back to the desk. After running his finger down the page, he scratched his head, closed the ledger and placed it on top of an untidy pile of papers.

'Yes,' he said, looking first at Emma and then at Joshua. 'What can I do for you?'

'My son wants to go to sea. What must he do?'

The clerk pulled a rag from his pocket, spat on it, took off his spectacles and wiped them.

'Sailed before, lad?'

'No, sir.'

'Whitby lad?'

'Yes, sir.'

'Fishing?'

'No, sir but I—'

Emma interrupted. 'He is strong and intelligent and—'

'How old are you, lad?'

'Thirteen.'

The man reached for a flat box. Beneath its curling lid was an assortment of letters and notes. Some were flat, others crumpled or folded. A few carried only smudged words jotted on the back of hand bills or scraps torn from posters. One note was inscribed on a square of canvas, to Emma the writing looked illegible. A sheet of ivory writing paper, halfway down, looked out of place. It was embossed with a gold crest. The clerk fingered through the pile ignoring the ones at the bottom. They had obviously been there a long time.

'We ain't the Royal Navy 'ere, you know!' He started again from the top. 'Now, if you'd been a midshipman . . .' he said, after re-reading one. Then he closed the box and regarded the boy over the rim of his spectacles. 'Best ask around,' he said. 'That's my advice to you, lad. But if you've got a mind to go to sea' – he looked Joshua squarely in the eye – 'and I can see you 'ave, then you'd best spend some time around the ships . . . and the men.'

He recognized the concern in Emma's eyes.

'Though there's those you'd best be keeping well clear of,' he said, leaning forward across the counter. 'It helps if you know a bit about a ship, boy. I've heard tell of many a young sailor flogged for not following a call, only because he didn't know the name of the line or where he was supposed to be.'

As he spoke, the door to the shipping office opened. The old man who came in carried his back like the shell of turtle. His bare neck poked from his coat which hung in tatters. Emma had never seen such a stooped figure. From beneath a thatch of dirty hair, a weathered face, squinted upwards. Both man and clothing stank. The floorboards creaked as he shuffled towards the firebox in the corner.

'Out with you!' the clerk shouted. 'How many times do I have to tell you? There's nothing for you! Not last month, not this month, not next month! You wouldn't even get pressed into service!' He shook his head.

The old seaman sniffed and waddled out.

'We thank you for your advice,' said Emma. 'Come along, Josh.'

As they left, she slipped her hand into her son's. The wooden steps were rickety and the handrail loose. She held him firmly. At the bottom of the steps a group of seamen were loitering. One touched his knuckle to his brow.

'Fine day, ma'am,' he said.

Emma allowed herself to give a polite smile and glanced at Joshua. 'Are you all right?'

He nodded, a disconsolate look on his face.

Emma ignored his expression but accepted his arm for both comfort and support as they hurried away from the wharf area.

'I thought it would be easy,' Joshua said.

She didn't answer. 'You must get back to the shop as quick as you can. But, not one word to Mr Hepplethwaite about where you were or what you were doing.'

'But what will happen now, Mama?'

'In all honesty, I do not know, Son. We will talk tonight.'

'But, Father. . . ?'

'He is away for two nights.'

Joshua hesitated.

'Hurry now,' said Emma.

She saw him glance back only once as he ran ahead. The street was busy and he was soon lost amongst the pedestrians and carriages.

'Madame Emma Quinlan!'

Emma turned, recognizing the voice. '*Monsieur*,' she said.

He inclined his head respectfully. 'You were looking for that elusive French ship again? No?'

The glint in his eye belied the serious look on his face.

She could not hide her delight and smiled broadly. 'You have followed me?'

'I cannot deny it. But tell me truthfully, what were you looking for this time on the wharf?'

'My son Joshua, wants to go to sea. He wants to be like all Whitby boys and follow in the footsteps of James Cook.' She shook her head. 'I went with him to the shipping agent to enquire about a ship.'

'I will find him a ship if he wants one.'

'What do you mean?'

'I mean, *madame*, there are plenty of ships sailing in and out of Whitby all the time. I'm signed to sail on one this evening.'

Emma's brow furrowed. 'You are going already?'

'*Madame?*'

'I thought you said your ship was being repaired and it would be two weeks before it was ready to sail.'

The Frenchman looked into her eyes. 'Ah! You have not forgotten.'

She looked away.

'What you say is correct. My ship was waiting for a new mast. That has been floated across but it will be a few days before it can be fitted and then it must be rigged. As it will still take some time and I am becoming bored with doing nothing, I have signed on another vessel. It sails tonight for Rotterdam with a cargo of alum and leather.'

'Across the North Sea.'

'Of course! It is not far. If the wind is fair it will take a week and I will be back in time for my ship.'

She could not hide the disappointment she was feeling.

'You must understand,' he explained, 'a seaman goes crazy if he is on land too long. And besides, a man needs a little extra money – for ale and ... and other things.'

They walked in silence towards the fishing harbour.

'Tell me, François,' she said. 'What is the cost of a passage to North America?'

'That is long voyage!'

'I know it is a long way. What I wish to know is what would such a journey cost?'

'And may I ask who is hoping to make this journey?'

A wagon loaded with coal, veered towards the pair. As François pushed the horse's blinkered head away, a stream of French words, which Emma had never learned, issued from his mouth. The driver, whipping his nag, responded with a barrage of English curses. The voices were drowned in the rumble of wheels as the cart rolled past. The lumps of coal which had scattered on the road were quickly placed into shopping baskets or gathered in aprons and hurried away.

'Do you know the cost?' she asked again.

'No, I am sorry.'

Her skirt brushed his legs as they walked.

'These days many people go to the Americas in search of gold, looking for a new life. But I do not know what they pay for the passage. I have sailed around the globe more than once, but I sail on ships which carry cargo. I have seen ships in the Thames fitted to carry people. Too many people at times I fear.'

'But from Whitby? Do passenger ships sail from here?'

He hesitated choosing his words carefully. 'Sometimes a cargo ship carries a few passengers.'

Emma's pace slowed. 'Do you know if there is such a ship in the harbour?'

He looked out across the water to the tall ships tied up along the quay.

'There is a ship which may take a lad, but ...'

She stopped and waited. 'But, what?'

'It is not going to America.'

'But the man in the shipping office said there was nothing for my son.'

'What would he know? Every ship that sails needs men!' He paused. 'The ship I speak of will take him to Australia. From there he'll have to find another ship to take him to America. But if he is fit and strong and if he learns quickly and does what he is told, it will cost him nothing. Trust me,' he said. 'When I return, I will find your boy a ship.'

'And me?' she said cautiously. 'Will there be a ship for me?'

'You, also?'

'Yes, François. A ship for me!'

The folds of serge between them hid their hands. She felt his fingers touching hers and tingled to the pressure of his squeeze.

'When I get back,' he said, 'I will find a ship for you also, I promise.'

Dusk crept slowly down the hillside, sliding across the slate roofs to the anchorage in the valley below. The still water of the inner harbour reflected the gilt-edged clouds of evening. A ship, its dark sails loosely furled, drifted with the outgoing tide and river's current towards the sea, past Scotch Head and Collier Hope, the East Pier and rocks of The Scaur until it nosed beyond the West Pier wall and met the sea. It rolled, swinging its tall masts like an inverted pendulum.

Cold in the attic, Emma watched sailors, the size of ants, scrambling along the yards, releasing sails. On the deck she could see others scurrying round the rails. She watched the ship sway, then pitch, and almost stop, before a line of white water trailed from its bow. The sails luffed, flapped, then filled, the dull canvas turning gold as the ship sailed into the dying rays of day. Above the deck, the main yards moved in unison and slowly, almost imperceptibly at first, the vessel turned her head towards the east. The ship which carried the Frenchman was on its way. It was heading to the Continent. To Rotterdam.

It was a long week, though each day went quickly, filled with the preparations for going away. Emma sorted, mended, ironed. The tub was full for three whole days and she was aware her constant excursions to the washing line would have been noted by her neighbour, the news no doubt relayed to Mrs Cooper up the street. She didn't mind. Her only concern was George. But he showed no interest in the increase in her daily chores.

François had said he would be back in a week. Now the week was gone and everything was ready. Joshua's clothes were stored away, all neatly pressed and folded. His bag, made from a length of heavy calico, was finished too. Stitching it had made her fingers bleed, but as he had no sea chest, it had to be strong. She hoped it would suffice.

Her own clothes were ready too. Day dresses, washed and aired and hung up in the wardrobe. Her other things folded neatly in drawers perfumed with the scent of last year's lavender. George never noticed them or the large tapestry bag she had found beneath the blankets at the bottom of the wardrobe. The mice had chewed a hole in one corner but it was easily patched. She hoped it would be big enough as the wooden case was too heavy for her to carry.

Her hat box had been pushed against the wall on the top of the wardrobe but she had not forgotten it. She fetched a stool from the kitchen and lifted it down. A shower of dust particles floated down with it. As she untied the ribbon and lifted the lid, she sneezed.

Inside the round box was her apricot bonnet, rucked with cream frills and trimmed with feathers and long brown ribbons. She had forgotten how pretty it was. It had matched the dress she had worn to her sister's wedding. What a wonderful day that had been. She laid it on the bed. Beneath it was a lace veil, edged with tiny pearls, each delicate bead sewn so carefully the stitching could not be seen. It was her grandmother's wedding veil, handed down to her but she had never worn it.

At the bottom of the box was a pair of dancing shoes, the blue ones made from softest suede. As she turned them over in her hand they reminded her of her first ball. They had lain in the box since they had moved into the house in Seal Street and now her feet had grown too broad to wear them. Feeling around the box's satin lining she found a small silk purse. It was black and beaded with a drawstring cord. She neither opened it nor held it long, but sighed and returned it to the hat box. She replaced the shoes and veil and carefully laid the bonnet over them. After closing the lid, Emma tied the ribbon and returned the hat box to the top of the wardrobe.

When her passage was arranged, she must take only clothes that would be comfortable and practical. Her clothes were smart, respectable, though now showing signs of age. They were suited to the Yorkshire weather. She had heard it was hot in the new colony, but she was not aware of what the ladies wore.

Over the past week, apart from her dress, Emma had given no thought to her life in New South Wales. For the first time she wondered what she would do? How she would live if she were alone. How would she support herself? Had she imagined that François would be with her? Supporting her? How foolish! He said he would never leave the sea. Or would he? But surely in a country rich in gold, where land is cheap and plentiful, there would be ample opportunity for an intelligent woman. She could offer herself as a governess or teacher. She was not afraid.

She felt a cold dampness to her skin. Apprehension. Why had she not thought of these things before? Had she been blinded by her desire to get away and by her infatuation with the Frenchman? Perhaps! But the decision was made. She knew that if she stayed with George her life was over. She would become old before her years, and she would be lonely. At worst, her name would be daubed on a wooden cross which Mr Reginald G. Beckwith would hammer into the clay on the cliff top.

François had promised when he returned from Holland he would find Joshua a ship. It would break her heart, but as her neighbour said, she must let him go and pray one day they would meet again, somewhere. After that she would bide her time. François would find a ship for her and when he did, she would be ready. For Emma, waiting was the hardest. Waiting alone without Joshua would be even worse.

It was now more than two weeks since François had sailed to Holland and there was still no word from him. If Emma had known the name of this ship she would have asked at the agent's office. But she didn't know. She hadn't asked him and she was angry with herself. François had said it was bound for Rotterdam, but many ships sailed to ports across the North Sea. When she overhead talk on the street of a ship frozen in the Baltic ice, she grew anxious.

She did not even know if he had sailed on an English ship. What if it was Dutch and it was not returning to Whitby but sailing from Holland to the East Indies? It could be a year before François returned, if indeed he returned at all.

Despite trying to busy herself in the house, the stream of questions continued to mount. François had seemed kind, caring, but could she trust him? He had promised to help her, but could she believe his promises?

Joshua's frustrations made matters worse. Every day he pestered her about François' whereabouts asking why he had not come back. For the first time, their voices were raised against each other and Emma worried that George would overhear their conversations. Above all else, he must not find out what she was planning.

As the days went by, Emma found it hard to eat, to work or concentrate. She felt tired but could not sleep. She stayed in the house, not wanting to be drawn into conversation with anyone, especially her neighbour.

But despite the disappointment that François had not returned, Emma's resolve to leave Seal Street was still strong. If the French seaman was not back within a fortnight, she must find some other way to leave Whitby.

# Chapter 7

'Get a move on, boy! I ain't paying you for gas-bagging!' Hepplethwaite yelled.

Joshua dragged another bag of flour from the stack in the corner of the cellar, hoisted it to his shoulder and lumbered up the ramp into the daylight.

Zachary Solomon, a lanky youth, was waiting by the handcart in the alley. 'Fat, old get! Couldn't even lift one!' he said under his breath.

His employer was listening.

'What did you say? Don't give me any of your lip, boy! A good hiding is what you need!' As the boy stood up, the baker moved back into his doorway. 'You should think yourself lucky you got a job with me. As for you, Quinlan, with your hoity-toity ideas ... Perhaps you'd prefer to be polishing jet in one of them workshops, or spending all your day salting herrings down on the wharf. Mark my words, if it weren't for that pretty mother of yours, you'd not have a job with me.' He curled his finger through his whiskers and smirked. 'Tell me,' he said, 'When's your father going to have business away again?'

Joshua dropped the sack. 'You stay away from our house!' he shouted.

Albert Hepplethwaite sniggered, but as Joshua lunged towards him the shopkeeper hastily retreated up the steps into his bakery shop.

'Not worth cracking your knuckles on,' Zac said. 'Forget him!'

'I hate him and his job!' Josh said, planting the toe of his boot into the bag of flour.

The delivery consisted of ten bags of flour, five of sugar, five bags of oats, four of salt, one cheese, four pounds of butter and a seven pound jar of gooseberry jam.

'Where do I take it?' Joshua asked, when it was all loaded.

'Across the bridge. Mr Charlton's tea shop is on Sowerby Lane. Runs

up from Church Street. You'll find it. Go to the yard round the back, if
yer lucky, his missus might give you a bun or something for your trouble.'

Standing between the barrow's shafts, Joshua lifted and pushed. The
load rolled easily down the alley, one wheel on either side of the gutter.

As he started running he heard Zac calling, 'Don't be in rush. When
you get back tell old 'Epplethwaite the drawbridge was up and you 'ad to
wait. He'll be no wiser.'

The rumble of the wheels echoed between the tall buildings. At the
end of the alley the sun was shining. Round the corner and Joshua was on
the harbour front. With the tide flooding into the two harbours, a small
ketch took advantage of the flow and sailed with it upstream. It was close
to the wharf.

Dodging the other traffic, Joshua kept pace with it. Ahead was the old
drawbridge which divided the inner and outer harbours. The iron cogs
grated noisily as the heavy bridge timbers rose slowly to let the boat pass.
Joshua settled his cart at the back of the gathering crowd knowing he
would have to wait. It was the only bridge across the River Esk.

Leaning against his load, Joshua regarded the crowd: the group of
women chattering, their heads moving up and down like chickens pecking
grain. In contrast, a weathered fisherman hardly moved an inch, his eyes
staring straight ahead as if gazing across the sea. He watched a girl's frus-
trated efforts as she tried to spin a top and the nanny who seemed
oblivious to the baby screaming in the new perambulator.

An empty wagon cleared a track between the pedestrians. The blinkered horse was snorting. Joshua eyed it warily and moved aside, afraid the
animal might bolt.

'Whoa! Nellie. Quiet girl!' The driver secured the brake, jumped down
and eased a nosebag over the mare's head. The horse responded to the
oats, shaking the contents in the bag and chomping on them.

As soon as the bridge thudded down, the crowds who had congregated
on the banks were eager to cross. Children ran. Mothers shouted after
then. Women carrying wicker trays of fish clattered across in wooden
clogs. The drivers cursed.

Joshua waited till the wagon and a rig and pair had moved off before
he got behind his cart. He wasn't going to take a chance. The bridge
wasn't wide enough for all of them together.

But he must hurry. Now he had no excuse to offer Mr Hepplethwaite
if he was late. Head down, arms outs, he leaned into the cart and pushed.
He knew the tea shop. He had passed it many times. It wasn't far.

Mr Charlton was on the pavement outside his door. A flock of pigeons were cooing on the cobbles in front of him, pecking at the meal of crumbs he had thrown for them. As Joshua approached, a pair of sea-gulls dived, squawking aggressively, their necks and beaks extended, intimidating the smaller birds.

Mr Charlton lashed out at the pair with a broom, but each time he repelled one, the other bird swooped. From the safety of the rooftops the pigeons watched the battle. It continued until all the crumbs were gone.

Joshua didn't see the pothole in the road. One of the cart's wheels dropped into it. The cart stopped, wrenching the shaft from his hand. He fought to hold it as it began to topple and managed to save the load from going over. But the jolt had dislodged the stack. The jar which had been nestled on the top slid towards him. He grabbed, but missed. It fell. Broken into a dozen pieces, the yellow jam splattered in a sticky mess between his feet.

'You can't go throwing good jam around like that,' the fat man said.

'It just fell off! I swear.'

Mr Charlton didn't seem bothered by the loss. He certainly wasn't angry, but Joshua expected Mrs Charlton would be cross. Naturally, they would refuse to pay for the jam. There would be no reward for the delivery, and because of the delay at the bridge he was going to be late back to the Pie Shop. Mr Hepplethwaite would be angry with him for taking his time, and for breaking the jar. He would have to pay for the breakage and if he had no wages to take home on Friday, he would likely get a thrashing from his father.

Joshua's head was spinning. He hated the job. He hated Hepplethwaite. He hated his father. He wanted to sail away to the Indies or America and leave all this far behind.

'Damn! Damn! Damn!'

'Calm down, lad!' Mr Charlton cried. 'A paddy will get you nowhere. Follow me around to the back and we'll get this stuff unloaded. It will only take two ticks.'

'What about the gooseberry jam?' Joshua asked.

'Don't worry about that. You go round to the yard.'

Mr Charlton was an understanding man, but he was also pitifully slow. Joshua wanted to throw off the stores by the door and be gone as quickly as possible. But the shopkeeper insisted everything be carried inside under his supervision and stacked away carefully into its rightful place.

As soon as the job was finished, Joshua was off and running. Back to the river and the bridge, hanging on to the cart as it bounced along, lurching from side to side. The street, on the west side, was crowded with pedestrians. Joshua tried to snake his way between them but his pace was slowed, at times, almost to a stop.

'Stop, boy!' A hand tightened on his shoulder.

Joshua spun around.

The accent was foreign. 'Are you François?'

'Yes. And you are Joshua?'

'How did you know that?'

'I saw you once with your mother. Tell me where I find her. I must speak with you both. I have news of a ship.'

'She's at home,' Joshua panted. 'Number twenty-nine, Seal Street.' The sweat was running into his eyes.

'I see you are in a hurry,' François said. 'I will help you, then you will take me to your house.'

Joshua's legs dangled from the front of the barrow as the seaman ran along the street, pushing. Joshua, clinging to the sides, bounced up and down, urging the Frenchman to go faster.

The back alley was quiet and empty. There were no customers in the Pie Shop. Mrs Hepplethwaite said that her husband was out for the afternoon and Zac had just left with the day's last delivery. She had not missed Joshua and when François told her that he needed the boy urgently – a case of life or death – she was more than pleased to let him go.

Joshua said nothing about the gooseberry jam, but as they were about to leave, she called him back.

'Here,' Mrs Hepplethwaite said handing him a scone with a wedge of butter on the top. 'And take one for the man.'

Joshua thanked her and winked at François. The sailor's charm had worked a treat.

'Mama! It's me!'

Emma looked up from her needlework. 'Josh, don't shout! What is the matter?'

'The sailor wants to speak with you.'

Emma hesitated.

'The French sailor! François! He is waiting outside.'

'François has come back?' she cried, but her feeling of relief tinged with excitement was short-lived. 'But he cannot come in, Josh! Tell him he must go away! Tell him I will meet him somewhere.'

'But, Mama, there is a ship! And it is sailing on Wednesday!'

'But I dare not let him in . . .'

'Mama! He must speak with you urgently! Let me bring him in.'

Emma looked around the room trying to clear her thoughts. 'You are right, Josh. I'm sorry.'

Outside the window she heard a soft whistle, then footsteps and muffled voices. She glanced at herself in the mirror. Her hands were shaking.

François inclined his head politely as he walked into the room.

'Please come in, *monsieur*. Joshua, close the door quickly.'

Before having time to offer him a chair, François spoke, 'I did not know where to find you,' he said shaking his head. 'I have been looking for you for three days. On the fish wharf. In the markets. Even at the abbey up on the cliff. I thought perhaps you had changed your mind.'

'No. Not at all. But after all this time, I thought you were not coming back.' She could feel herself flushing. She sat down.

Joshua was watching her keenly.

'My son tells me you have news of a ship.'

'*Madame*—'

She interrupted him: 'My name is Emma.'

'Emma, my ship, the *Morning Star*, is sailing this week for New South Wales. I have spoken with the first mate and it is likely your boy can sign for the voyage.'

Joshua grabbed François' hand. 'Thank you, François! Thank you!'

Emma put a finger to her lips. 'One moment, Josh.'

François had not finished. He turned to Emma. 'You must write a letter for the boy stating his age and saying you permit him to join the vessel. You can write, can't you?'

Emma nodded.

François turned to Joshua. 'Wait for me by the drawbridge in the morning. I will find you and take you to the ship. You will speak with the mate and unless he finds you disagreeable, you can sign as one of the ship's boys. Do you understand?'

'Yes, sir.'

'Do you have a hammock?'

'No.'

'Then you will sleep on the deck.'

'A knife?'

'No.'

François shook his head. 'You must have a knife. A good knife. You cannot borrow another man's knife. But we will speak about that tomorrow. Now I must talk with your mother.'

Joshua's eyes glistened as he shook the Frenchman's hand. 'François, I cannot thank you enough. And you, Mama,' he said, as he hugged his mother. 'Now, I must get back to the Pie Shop. I must see Zac and tell him. Thank you, François. I will come to the wharf tomorrow.'

Emma stood beside the seaman as the boy dashed from house. The clap of his leather boots on the cobbles echoed down the street.

François reached out for Emma's hand. 'May I?' he said, before he laid a kiss upon it.

Her smile was sad. Soon Joshua would be gone. And François too.

Drawing her towards him, he slipped his arm around her waist and touched his lips to hers. It was a shy and gentle kiss. And then again, but full and deep. It stirred in Emma a memory of long ago. She smiled and cast it from her mind and closed her eyes.

How strong he felt. Protective. Reassuring. His smell was of the sea, his body firm and warm.

'And me?' she whispered, as he led her to the chair. 'Is there a place on your ship for me?'

In the hearth, the lumps of coal had broken and turned grey. She watched him as he gazed at the embers glowing in the ashes.

'Emma,' he began, 'the *Morning Star* is not built for passengers; it carries only cargo.'

She looked away.

'Besides,' he said, 'the ship is old and the passage can be hard for those who do not usually sail the oceans.'

'But will you carry some passengers on board or only crew and cargo?'

She waited for his reply.

'I cannot lie. This voyage we have one passenger. I only know this because his baggage arrived at the dock this morning. So many trunks and boxes. More luggage than all the crew together.'

'But if there is one passenger, why can't I also sail with the ship.'

'It would not be suitable. There will be no other ladies on board. Only men. It would not be right for you to travel alone.'

'But you and Joshua will be there. I would ask for nothing more. I require little space. And I can occupy myself during the voyage. I can take books and needlework.'

'Emma, you must hear what I am saying. I know something of the captain's nature. Enough to know he would not consider taking a woman on board for fear the trouble it may cause. The men could think you were a Jonah, come aboard to bring bad luck to the ship. And besides, seamen do not have the best of habits. There are things a lady should not have to see.'

She stirred the embers with a twig. It caught alight. 'Would you wish for me to sail with you, François?'

'That I would wish more than anything, but—'

'And tell me, does the captain not like women?'

'I expect he does. He is a man. A married man.'

'Then please,' she begged, 'if you have any feeling for me, speak with him and ask that he allows me to sail on his ship.' Her eyes were filled with tears. 'François, I cannot remain here. If I do, I fear I will die.'

He rested his face into her hair and held her to him.

'Tomorrow your boy will join the ship. The following day is Wednesday. We sail on the tide, at five o'clock. Come to the ship at four. Can you do that?'

'Yes,' she said, her breathing shallow. 'My husband is away and not expected to return until Thursday. I will come to the shipyard by Belle Island on Wednesday afternoon at four.'

He sighed. 'No. The ship will not be there. She is leaving the yard today when the water is high. She will dock on the wharf to the north of the drawbridge. Do you understand?'

Emma nodded.

'When you find the ship, the *Morning Star*, you must ask for me, Frenchy. That is the name the men call me by. I will be busy as we will be preparing to sail. You must wait on the wharf. Do not try to come on board. I will come to you.'

She nodded again.

'One more thing. I will not be free to help you with your baggage. Will you manage alone?'

'Yes. I will manage.' She smiled. 'I cannot thank you enough, for what you are doing for Joshua and for me.'

His smile had disappeared. His face was grave.

She put her hands on his but felt a tenseness in him. 'What is it, François? You are worried.'

'It is nothing,' he said. 'Remember, four o'clock on Wednesday. We sail at five.'

*

That evening Joshua was fired with excitement and talked non-stop. Emma had finished her meal while his plate was still full. As they sat together, they spoke of ships and ports and the Antipodes, and wondered what life would be like far from the bitterness of winter.

By the light of the lamp, Emma wrote a letter. She addressed it to the 'Captain of the Sailing Ship, *Morning Star*'. It would have been more respectful if she had known his name, but in her excitement she had failed to ask François for that detail.

In the letter, she stated she was the mother of Joshua Quinlan and that she gave permission for him to sail. That he was thirteen years of age and there was nothing which prohibited him from joining the crew. She thanked the captain for providing her son with the opportunity of going to sea, and assured him that he was a God-fearing boy, educated to a good standard in reading, writing, algebra and geometry and that he was willing and eager to work and learn. She added that he would follow the orders given to him.

She signed the letter Emma Quinlan, adding the title, Mrs, which she enclosed in brackets. She blotted it. Folded it in half, then half again and placed the letter in an envelope. She closed it with a dab of red sealing wax and handed it to her son.

'You must not forget to put it in your pocket in the morning.'

'Yes, Mama.'

From the chest of drawers in the attic bedroom she took the items she had prepared for Joshua. His clothes, all washed, ironed and folded neatly. Trousers steamed, jacket sponged and pressed. A muffler. Gloves. A spoon and fork and knife. A tin plate, mug, two slabs of soap, a comb.

Joshua stuffed the clothes into the calico bag. Emma had sewn it strongly.

She was concerned. The bag held so little. Did he have sufficient? What might he need? She was concerned for his welfare having heard tales about the men who worked on the merchant ships. She had heard they were hard, crude, sometimes cruel, and often dirty. She reminded Joshua about cleanliness. Manners. Reminded him that she would be there if he needed her.

'Mama!' he said. 'I am not a boy. Tomorrow when I join the ship, I become one of the men. A ship's boy maybe, but one of the crew.' He took his mother's hands in his. 'And if I am to get on, I must know the ship. I must learn the names of ropes and sheets and how to furl a sail. I can only learn this from the men. I must work like them and I must talk like them. But Mama,' he said, 'I will not become like them. You have taught me everything I know. You have taught me about many things. But the things I need to learn now, I can learn neither from you or books. Trust me, Mama; now I will learn as I see fit.'

The tears flowed down Emma's cheeks. He had grown up and she had not noticed. 'I love you, Joshua,' she said.

It was cold when he left the house. The sun had not yet come up. Emma hugged him. And cried again. It was as though he was leaving forever, yet she would see him again the following day.

'Take this,' she said, as she pressed something cold into his hand. Joshua's eyes widened to the half sovereign in his palm.

'Don't let anyone see it,' she said. 'You must buy a hammock and knife. François says every sailor must have a sound knife.'

Joshua looked at the gold coin. 'Mama, you will need this.'

'Take it, Joshua. Speak with François. He will help you. Ask him before the ship sails.'

'I will.'

'Now go.'

He pulled the cloth cap down over his ears and tucked the muffler underneath his collar.

'God speed,' she whispered, as they held each other close, then she watched as he strode proudly down the street, the new bag balancing on his shoulder.

Emma waited hoping he would turn and wave but his thoughts were on the ship. She watched as his step quickened and he turned down the hill towards the harbour and was gone.

The day was long. The evening even longer.

As Joshua had not returned, Emma presumed he had joined the *Morning Star*'s crew. She thought about him constantly. She thought about François too, and felt lonely.

Her clothes, sorted into neat piles covered the kitchen table. She had gone through them numerous times, choosing some, discarding others then changing her mind.

She had decided on two dresses. Pretty ones. Also the serge skirt and the blue merino. Three silk blouses, two frilled aprons, and a lace shawl. She would wear her everyday grey skirt and white linen blouse to travel in. And a bonnet of course. On her feet, the laced boots she wore for walking.

By the time everything was in the bag it was difficult to fasten. She was glad she had found the tapestry bag but even that would be heavy as it was a long walk to the ship. The wooden suitcase would have been unmanageable.

She decided to wear the plaid shawl. It kept her warm and no doubt evenings on the water would be cold. Besides, the shawl would serve as an extra blanket on the ship if she needed one.

As the fire died, she contemplated writing a letter, telling George she was going away. But what could she say except goodbye. He would discover soon enough that she was gone. And Joshua gone too.

She shuddered at the thought of her husband's temper. Fearful of his anger. But soon she would be far away and she was never coming back.

The staircase creaked as she paid her final visit to the attic. The empty cradle was standing against the wall. From the window she looked down upon the town. The moon had not yet risen. Lights twinkled from street lamps and kitchen windows. Across the valley, the East Cliff merged with the darkness of the sky. Beyond the cliffs the North Sea looked black and uninviting. If any sailing ships were out there, she could not see their lights. As she listened she could faintly hear the Whitby bell drumming out its warning.

The following evening she would be safely on the ship. She would hear the bell as the ship sailed beyond the stone piers. She would feel the ship surge forward as its sails filled. She would stand on deck and watch the Whitby lighthouses till they were but specks off the stern. And she knew she would rejoice.

The parlour clock chimed three. Emma paced the floor. It was almost time to leave. She had stoked the fire and now beneath all her clothes she was feeling very warm. But there was no time to change and she still had three things to attend to.

From the top of the wardrobe she retrieved the battered hat box. Feeling beneath the bonnet and beaded veil, she found the satin purse. Her fingers closed around it. Quickly she dropped it into her skirt pocket, replaced the hat box and returned to the kitchen. With the needle she had already threaded, she sewed a line of stitches across the opening in her pocket. The small bulge it made was hidden in the folds of skirt.

From above the writing desk she reached for the picture framed in oak and lifted it carefully from the nail. A ghostly outline, drawn by dust and insect webs, marked its hanging place. She laid the picture face down on the table. It was not difficult to slit the brown backing paper. It tore away easily. Beneath it a row of tiny nails secured the wooden backboard. When she lifted it, the drawing paper curled from the glass. She turned it over and looked at it. The pen and ink.

Using the brown paper to protect it, Emma rolled the picture and tied it with a piece of ribbon. Opening the tapestry bag for the final time, she eased the package beneath her clothes.

Finally, from within the bureau she took several sheets of writing paper and the pen. She would not chance the ink.

Now she was ready.

The air on the dock was dank and smelled of fish. There was little movement on the harbour. The bustle of the day was over. Some seamen lazed on the dockside, others on the decks of ships, talking, smoking, playing cards.

Her arms and shoulders burned from carrying the bag. She knew she must find François and his ship before it was too late. She did not feel afraid.

As she hurried along the wharf, she checked the name of each vessel hoping to see the words *Morning Star*. But the ship was not there and she had reached the end of the wharf. She turned, retraced her steps, conscious of the time.

Where was it? Still in the yard where it was repaired? Should she go there to look for it? But it was a long way and there was not enough time. The worry was tightening her throat. She was exhausted. The bag slipped from her shoulder and fell to the ground. A seaman leaning against the wall in the shadows called out: 'You looking for a ship?'

'Yes,' she said. 'The *Morning Star*.'

'Sorry, miss,' he said. 'The *Morning Star*'s not here. She sailed no more than an hour ago.'

# Chapter 8

It was a long walk home. The longest Emma could remember. The hill was steeper; the cobbles harder; the late afternoon chill, colder. The ship had gone. So too had François and Joshua. And with them her last chance for escape.

The bag weighed heavily on her arm.

When she passed a group of women gossiping in the alleyway she hid her face beneath the rim of her bonnet and hurried by. Although they were strangers to her, she felt sure their conversation was about her and sensed their eyes directed at her. Her imagination was playing tricks.

She worried. Had Mrs Bradshaw seen her leave? Would she be watching for her returning? Would she guess where she had been? Oh, what gossip she would be able to pass on!

Why had she allowed herself to be swept along on this fanciful infatuation? This whim? This hope to step out of the hum-drum of daily life and sail to the other side of the world? To live an idyllic life with a common sailor in some far away land? Happily ever after!

Thank goodness she had told no one. How they would laugh. Call her a fool. Thank goodness only François and Joshua knew her intentions. And now they were gone, no one else would know.

Two bare-foot urchins ran down the hill, knocking the bag from her arm.

'Slow down!' she called.

They ignored her, laughed and ran on, their feet padding along on the paving.

It's getting cold, she thought. I must get home. The kitchen will be warm. She had damped the fire before she left but if she was lucky it would still be alight.

When she got home she must unpack the tapestry bag. Put all the

77

clothes away. Hide away all signs of her misadventure.

Thank goodness George had gone away.

The steps up the ghaut from Pawson's Alley were steep but it was better to go that way than walk up the length of Seal Street. This way was quicker and she was less likely to be seen.

Her shoulders ached. Her legs were sore. She sniffed pipe tobacco swirling across the street. An old man was sitting on his doorstep.

He nodded, 'Evening.'

'Evening,' Emma replied.

The bowl of tobacco glowed as he drew on it.

She hurried along, shielding her face beneath her bonnet. Hoping her neighbours were indoors, hoping the children wouldn't tell, hoping this unfortunate venture would soon be forgotten.

She stopped when she noticed the house door was open. She remembered shutting it when she left. Perhaps Joshua had not sailed after all. Perhaps he had come home.

Her breathing quickened. Through the window she could see the lamp flickering. But the curtains were not drawn and Joshua always drew them before dark. And he always closed the door.

Her heart was pounding. George had returned a day early!

As she stood framed in the doorway, he eyed her, his features exaggerated by the dark shadows cast from the lamp. He was sitting at the dining-table, fists clenched, the knuckles criss-crossed with streaks of blood. Across the table, fragments of broken glass glinted in the yellow light. Scattered slivers of wood were all that remained of the oak picture frame.

'I didn't expect you home this evening,' she said.

His fist thumped the table bouncing the fragments of glass like hail on frozen ground.

'I can see that!'

She put the bag down.

'Tell me, woman, where do you think you were going?' His voice was low and controlled.

She closed the door quietly, unfastened her bonnet and hung it on the hallstand.

Both fists came crashing on to the table. She jumped.

George rose. The muscles in his jaw were twitching. 'Fetch that here!' he shouted pointing to her luggage.

' 'Tis only a few old things,' she said, trying to disguise the falter in her voice. 'I was taking them to the rag man. I thought I might get a few shillings for them. The extra money would be useful.'

Splinters of wood and broken glass flew from the table as he swept his forearm across it.

'Fetch it here!' he bellowed.

Emma did as she was bid but before she reached the table he grabbed it from her, tearing at its fastening.

'Old clothes,' she whispered.

George ripped out the contents, throwing her dresses on to the floor. His lips were quivering. 'Old clothes!' he shouted, flinging a silk blouse across the room. 'Old clothes!'

Emma's hand was on the chair. She was shaking. 'I was going to visit my sister.'

'Your sister? Huh! A moment ago it was the rag man!' The slap of his hands on the table scared her. 'You liar! You were running away!' He grabbed her nightdress and threw at her face. 'Where is he, this fancy man of yours?' His pitch was rising. His sneer contemptuous. 'Let you down, did he?'

Emma backed away. She was afraid. This time he was sober.

'How dare you try to leave me? Make me into a laughing stock! How dare you?'

She never saw his fist. Hardly felt it. It was the second blow which threw her backwards to the floor, thudding her head against the wall. Before she could move he was standing beside her kicking his boot into her ankles.

She curled her arms across her face, drew up her legs and waited. He stopped. Went back and tipped the remaining contents of the bag on to the table. A scroll of paper was amongst them.

Unrolling it, he held it out at arm's length, laughed sickeningly, then tore in half. Then again, and again, tossing the tiny pieces over her. They floated down like the petal from the dying rose.

The taste of blood was in her mouth. She licked it from her lips and dragged herself against the wall.

'You will go nowhere from now on! I will make sure of that!' Gathering the scattered items, he threw them into the hearth. Emma watched. One by one, slowly and deliberately, he poked her clothing in the smouldering embers. She watched the silks twist, then frizzle, in a burst of light. She smelt the cottons scorch before the rush of flames consumed them. The woollens smoked and shrivelled. They were slow to burn.

Everything went in. The satin gown, the black silk dress, blouses, petticoats and gloves. Finally the envelopes and paper. The fire flared and Emma closed her eyes.

It was over. His feet brushed past her skirt. She felt one final kick. The house door slammed. She listened to his footsteps die away and lay there long into the silence before she tried to move.

Her hand relaxed, her fingers stretched and reached a scrap of paper beside her on the floor. She lifted it and held it to the light. A man's face, etched in detail. The kindly eyes most striking. The pupils empty. His eyes were sightless. It was her father.

Emma's tears were silent.

'Wake up, Mama! Please, Mama, wake up!'

Emma tried to see but it was dark. The figures hovering were hazy. Was she dreaming?

'We need some light. Where is the lamp, Joshua?' It was François' voice.

She felt a hand on hers. Stroking. She turned her head. Only one eye would open. She touched her face. The skin was tight. It hurt. What had happened?

'Oh, Mama! I should not have gone!'

The lamp flared. She looked around. The fire had gone cold yet she was still dressed and sitting in the chair. François was kneeling by her side.

'Emma, I will not forgive myself knowing I caused this to happen to you.'

'Your ship,' she said. 'It was gone.'

'I will explain later. Now we must get you away from here.'

The voices sounded far away and anxious. Sleep seemed so easy.

'You must wake up, Mama!' said Joshua. 'You must get up and try to walk.'

She raised her head and smiled at him. Her boy had come home.

A cup was pressed against her lips. 'Some water,' François said. 'Please drink a little.'

She sipped, then pushed the cup away not listening to their quiet conversation.

'Mama, we cannot leave you here. François and I have spoken. We will take you with us. It will not be easy. Mama, you must get up! There is little time.'

François held her hands as she struggled to her feet.

'I could not find the ship,' she said.

'Hush,' said François. 'Where is your baggage?'

Emma looked towards the fireplace. 'There,' she said. 'He burned it. Everything.'

The seaman cursed, 'I'll kill him if I find him!'

Joshua grabbed the empty bag. 'Mama,' she heard him say, 'I'll find some clothes for you. There must be something.' She heard his footsteps on the stairs, the creaking of the bedroom floor.

Her shawl had fallen against the wall. François retrieved it and draped it round her neck. He took her bonnet and cape from the hallstand and helped her put them on. She couldn't tie the bows. He fastened them. 'How could I do this to you?'

'You are not to blame.'

He shook his head. 'We must get going!' Joshua appeared with the bag. 'There is no time to lose!'

Outside Seal Street was quiet. The houses were all in darkness. The only light spilling from the street lamp formed a pale circle on the paving beneath it.

Supporting her between them, the pair hurried from the house, down the hill to the harbour then along the wharf heading in the direction of the sea. Emma's feet barely touched the ground. She did not know what time it was, save that it was late. Everything was quiet. There was no one around.

They stopped at the end of the dock. The moon, glistening on the wet sand of Collier Hope, gave some light. Beneath the wall was a rowing boat. It was not a Whitby boat. It was moored to a rusted iron ring but the tide had gone out leaving it sitting on the sand. The steps from the wharf were crusted in cockle shells and wore a slippery coat of damp weed.

'Tread carefully,' François called.

Emma took his arm and leaned against him heavily. As she stepped down to the harbour floor she could feel her feet sinking in the sand and water seeping into her boots. François put his arm around her waist and helped her to the boat.

'Hold on to the sides,' he said. 'Do not try to stand.'

Emma clambered in and sat down in the middle.

The seaman quickly unfastened the line and with Joshua helping, slid the boat back across the sand and into the channel of the out-flowing River Esk. They needed little help from the oars as the river, swelled by

melt water and rain, was full, the current strong. It carried them passed
Scotch Head and the Bulmer Street Pier. Ahead were the high walls which
guarded the entrance to Whitby harbour. The old lighthouse, like a giant
Doric column, towered almost ninety feet on the West Pier, its bright light
directed far out over the sea. The newer lighthouse on the east side was
dwarfed against it.

As they passed between the stone walls Emma could feel the North
Sea's waves slapping the bow. The boat slowed.

'Row hard!' shouted François.

As they rounded the West Pier, Emma saw the ship, a black outline
against the dark sky.

The *Morning Star* was anchored to the east of the main pier, well away
from the flat rocks of The Scaur and less than 300 yards from a sandy
beach. Two lights on the ship, no more than pinpricks, swayed with the
swell. The seamen rowed hard towards it and though the sea was calm
their progress was slow.

'When we go on board, you must not say a word,' François whispered.

'But—?'

'Not a word!' he said. 'I will take you below and hide you somewhere
safe. Then Joshua and I must leave. We must return the boat for the men
who have gone ashore.

'But, François . . .'

He put his finger to his lips. 'Hush! Your voice will carry. You must be
silent. No one must know you are on board and you must remain hidden
for as long as I say. I will come to you later and explain. Trust me.'

Emma looked back at Joshua. She did not understand what was
happening.

'Mama, trust François,' he whispered. 'It is all that we could do. We
could not leave you there. It will be for the best.'

A rope ladder was dangling from the deck. François grabbed it. Their
boat bumped against the hull. A moment later a head peered down into
the darkness.

'Coming aboard!' François shouted.

'Who's there?'

'Frenchy and the lad.'

There was no answer. The face disappeared.

'I will go first,' François said. 'You must stand up. When the boat lifts
on a wave you must take hold of the ladder as high as you can reach. Pull
yourself on to it. Then climb. Do not look down. I will be at the top to

help you. Joshua will steady the ladder at the bottom. Do you understand?'

Emma nodded.

The ship heaved on the swell causing the small boat to rise and fall on
the passing waves. At times, despite their efforts, the boat banged against
the hull, at others it swung away from the ship and swayed perilously from
side to side. François gripped the ladder and climbed.

Emma was afraid to stand. Afraid to climb. The rope ladder was sliding on the ship's hull. What if she lost her grip and fell? She could not
swim.

On the next wave, she tucked her skirt between her thighs, grabbed the
ropes and held. Immediately, the boat dropped back into the trough and
left her hanging. She could not find a foothold. Her skirt was in the way.

'You must climb!' Joshua cried.

Her arms were stiff. She kicked and felt the rope against her toe. Her
legs were sore but she found a foothold and held fast. As she neared the
top François grasped her wrists and pulled her up on to the deck.

'Shh!' he whispered. 'Follow me!'

He guided her aft, to an open hatch which led below. A lantern on the
lower deck lit the companionway. The steps were steep. François held
Emma as she turned and climbed down backwards.

At the bottom of the stairs was an oblong room with several cabin
doors on either side. They were all closed. Through a hatch in the floor
was another ladder, even steeper, leading deeper into the ship. They went
down. It was dark. A distant pale glow barely illuminated the passageway.

François went first, bending his back near double. 'Mind your head,' he
said. Emma followed bowing her head and shoulders from the heavy
beams.

The air was thick. It smelled of food and men. But there was no sound
except the creak of timbers.

François stopped at a small door. It was no taller than the height of a
child.

'You must hide in here,' he said. 'At least for now.'

The room was black as pitch. There was no light. 'This is the best I can
provide,' he said. 'When we return I will bring you a bucket and some
food. You must stay in here until the ship is clear of England.'

No bigger than a bed, the sail locker was packed with folded canvas
topped with coils of heavy rope. The pile reached halfway up the door.
The space above it, no greater than an arm's length. Emma crawled in on

her hands and knees.

'But François, why?'

'I could not get permission for you to sail. But I had made a promise to you which I had to keep. This is the best I can do. I am sorry.'

'But what happens when the captain finds out?'

'Let me worry about that,' he said. 'Now I must return the boat to Whitby. Fasten the door from the inside,' he said. 'Do not open it for anyone!'

Before she had time to speak he closed the door leaving her in the darkness.

# Chapter 9

Emma pushed the ropes to one side so she could lie flat on the canvas. She could hear something banging on the outside of the ship. Like someone knocking. She listened, waiting for it to stop, counting the sounds, and drifted into sleep.

Loud voices startled her. Men's raucous voices with strange accents. Laughing. Cursing. And the sound of feet on wooden boards. A strip of light shone through the crack around the door.

She hardly dare to breathe. How long had she slept? Did they know she was on board? Were they looking for her? Then the footsteps faded and the voices died. She could feel her heart thumping. Her hands were wet. The light outside dimmed rapidly. The blackness returned and with it the silence broken only by the rhythmical banging.

Emma settled back on her pillow of hemp rope. It was comfortably warm in the sail locker, but the air was not good. She sniffed. Salt. Tar. The acrid smell of sulphur.

What was it that François had said? She must stay hidden until the ship was clear of England. Was that possible? How long was it since François had brought her to the ship? She had slept, but for how long she did not know. She must think clearly. Did he say when he would return? She thought about George. Where had he gone when he left her? Where did he go when he stayed away? Why was he so cruel? She tried to put all thoughts of him from her mind but they would not leave her.

There was a tap on the door. She started.

'Open the door,' a voice whispered. The voice was muffled but it sounded like François.

She untied the cord cautiously and let the door swing open. In the dim light a dark figure filled the doorway. Its back appeared hunched. She thought of the old tramp in the agent's office and caught her breath.

'Are you all right?'

'Yes,' she said.

The glow died as François closed the door and crawled on to the canvas beside her. He touched her hand. It was too dark for them to see each other.

'I have brought a bucket and a jug of water.' His voice was little more than a murmur. 'I am sorry there is no light. But no one must know you are here. It is terrible that I have caused this to happen to you.'

Emma reached out for him in the darkness. She touched his chest. He took her hand in his and pressed it to his lips.

'I could not come sooner. I had to wait. The captain has come back on board. And the crew also. Most of them are drunk. They will sleep for a few hours until first light. Then we sail. I will come to you when I can, but it will not be easy with the men around.'

'How is Joshua?'

'He is well. And he is concerned for you.'

She felt his arm slide across her hip.

'I cannot stay,' he sighed. 'Tomorrow, I will come to you and bring some food. Two days from now, we sail into the Channel, and two days after that the ship will be far from the coast of England. Until then you must make no sound. If you are discovered now, the captain will have you put ashore.'

'I cannot go back!' she cried.

'Trust me. In a few days all will be well.'

Emma pulled the twilled cape around herself and rested her cheek into the woollen shawl. The days would pass quicker if she could sleep. After four days the swelling round her eye would be gone. Four days and she would be far away from Whitby.

The ship rolled and heaved. A loose barrel on the deck banged against the rail.

Emma slept.

The distant clanging of a bell woke her. Was it the Whitby bell? She listened again but it stopped. The rhythmic banging she had heard before had also ceased. Her tiny room no longer rolled from side to side. Fearing the ship was tied up against the Whitby wharf, she listened in the blackness for harbour sound then realized her canvas bed was sloping to one side. The *Morning Star* was sailing with the wind.

*

The last of the staysails rattled up. Topmen, lying across the forecourse yard, unlashed the gaskets. The canvas thundered out. On deck, men hauled on sheets and eased the lines as yards of canvas fell loose, luffed then filled. The wind was strong. The deck a litter of tangled ropes waiting to be coiled and hung neatly along the pin rails. Flying a full complement of sail, the *Morning Star* was making almost seven knots.

'Man the braces!'

The seamen scuttled across the deck.

François took the forecourse brace on the port side and waited for the call. Another seaman came up behind him ready to haul with him.

'Haul port! Ease starboard!' When all hands were ready the mate made the call. 'Haul away!'

Their hands working in time, the two seamen hauled on the rope, pulling the forecourse yard slowly across the ship. The other yards above it moved in unison.

'Pretty package you brought on board, Frenchy!' The voice was gravely.

François craned his head around, his eyes glaring.

'Got it well hidden, 'ave you?'

François could not release his grip. He would lose control of the yard. But he knew the voice. And the smell.

'Like to give Old Tom a taste of your property?'

François clenched his teeth.

The call continued. 'Hold the t'gallant! Hold the mains'l! Haul the 'course!'

The main forecourse was lagging behind the other yards. François pulled.

'I'll not say a word to the capt'n,' the voice hissed.

'Hold the forecourse! Belay braces!'

As Tom Barstow wound the sheet around the belaying pin, François released the sheet and grabbed him by the throat forcing him back over the rail so his head was hanging out over the sea.

'I promise I will kill you one day!' the Frenchman shouted.

'You touch me and I'll squeal like a stuck pig!' Tom Barstow said.

François released his grip.

Tom straightened, sneered at François and spat into his face.

The wind carried his saliva out to sea.

'When I came to the wharf, the ship had gone.' Emma spoke in a whisper, her mouth almost touching François' ear. Their bodies were warm.

As he pushed the hair from their faces his finger caught in the knots.

'Why did you sail early?'

'I do not know,' he sighed. 'We were to sail on the outgoing tide, but around four o'clock the mate ordered the gangplank brought on deck. We made ready to cast off. By then it was too late to get a message to you. As the ship sailed through the harbour, I knew Joshua was alarmed. I was afraid he might speak to the mate or do something foolish. Lucky for him he held his tongue. Had he argued about the sailing it is likely he would have been tossed overboard.'

He held her to him.

'But why did the ship stop outside the harbour? I have never seen a ship anchored there before.'

'Again I do not know save for the fact the passenger had not joined the ship and the captain was prepared to wait for him. He is either a close friend of the captain or he paid good money for the voyage. Most ships would wait for no one.'

'But why did the ship put to sea instead of waiting on the wharf?'

'Perhaps the captain was eager to test the new mast and rigging. Or perhaps, like the men, he was anxious to feel the sea under him again. Perhaps the berth was needed for another ship, I don't know. All I know is that last night there was no wind. The air was dead. So we hung off the anchor. Then the captain announced he was going ashore. Some of the men went too. They dropped three boats over and ran them up on the beach to the west of the harbour. Josh and I were in the last one. We knew we had a few hours so when all was clear we took the boat into the harbour and came for you.'

'But what if you had been seen?'

'We were not seen. And the captain did not return until early this morning. I saw him come aboard and the passenger was with him.'

'And who is this man who caused fate to look kindly on me?'

'A man of some means, I would say. A gentleman by all appearances.' François released her hand as he slithered back towards the door. 'But now I must go.'

'Is it evening?'

'It is past midnight already. One day has gone already. I will be back before sunrise with some food.' He slid down from the bed of sails and held his ear to the door. With no sounds other than the ship's own, he opened it. As he crept out Emma fastened the cord on the inside as he had instructed.

*

In the mess, François had chosen a table away from the other men. A lump of bread was all that remained on his plate. Joshua slid along the bench opposite him.

'How is, Mama?' he whispered.

François' brow furrowed. 'She is faring well. I took her cheese and apples. This morning I gave her biscuits. She eats and sleeps. But two days stuck in that hole is a long time.' He breathed a long heaving sigh. 'She cannot sit or bathe. She cannot see. It is not right for her to be there. I think I should not have suggested that we do this. It was foolish.'

'But remember how she was when we found her, we could not leave her.'

'You are right.' He sighed as he broke his bread and ate. After finishing his drink he gazed into the bottom of the empty pot.

Joshua watched him. 'There's something more, isn't there, Frenchy?'

François eyed the other men in mess huddled over their plates. 'I worry,' he said. 'I worry about what will happen when your Mama is discovered. I cannot say what the captain will do.'

'But you said it would be all right. You told me that once we sailed beyond the English Channel the ship would not turn back to England. You promised everything would be all right.'

'Don't talk so loud! I had to promise because we had to get your mother from that place. I had to say all would be well or you would not have helped me. I had to promise to your mother or she would not have come.'

'Then you lied to us?'

'No. Do not think that. Like you, I trust and pray all will be well. But,' he said, 'now I fear there may be danger for her on this ship.'

'What danger, François? Tell me!'

'It is better you do not know. I will take care of it!'

'What can I do to help?'

'Pray for clear skies and good wind. Pray we are not grounded on the Goodwins. Pray that your mother is given safe passage. Pray, lad! That is what you can do.' François picked up his plate. 'I will take care of the rest.'

'Be careful,' Joshua said.

The seaman nodded.

# Chapter 10

Dragged like a worn sail from her hiding place, by a man she had never seen before, Emma's worst fears were being realized. As the seaman bullied her along the lower deck towards the companionway, she wanted to cry out for François but thought better of it. She did not know where she was being taken or what was to become of her.

Emma shuddered as the mate rapped on the door to the main cabin.

'What is it?' a voice replied.

'Begging your pardon, Capt'n. I've brought the woman.'

'Wait a minute!'

Emma pulled the woollen shawl tighter around her shoulders. The still air of the sail locker had been stuffy but not cold, its confined space warmed by the heat of her body and by its location deep in the ship. Standing beneath the open hatch, the sea air felt cold on her skin, but she welcomed its freshness and inhaled deeply. Her legs, weak from lack of standing made it difficult for her to accommodate the rolling motion of the ship. The mate regarded her suspiciously as she leaned against the wall.

The deck she was standing on appeared familiar. François had brought her down this way when they came onboard. She recognized the doors to the six private cabins and wondered if they were in use.

'Come in, Mr Thackray!'

The mate opened the door. 'Get inside!' he said to Emma, prodding her in the back. 'Hurry up! Capt'n ain't got all day!' As he stepped into the cabin, the Mate slipped the knitted hat from his head and tucked it under his arm.

The stateroom was broad and bright with windows set across the ship's stern. To the right of them was the captain's desk. He was writing, the quill in his hand quivering as the nib scratched across the paper. He had his back to his visitors and did not turn.

The mate cleared his throat. 'The men who were fighting are on deck.'

'Thank you, Mr Thackray. You may go.'

'Aye, Capt'n.' Touching two knuckles to his temple, the mate replaced his hat and closed the door.

Not knowing how she would be received, Emma remained silent. While she was waiting she feasted her eyes on the contents of the room. Through the windows she could see both sky and sea, grey sky on dark grey sea. It stretched to the horizon. There was no land in sight. They were far from the rugged Yorkshire coast.

The captain continued writing.

It was a grand stateroom in keeping with a ship of its age. It had a comfortable feel, like an old shoe. The bureau was set against the side wall with tall cupboards built in either side. A small library decked the shelves immediately above his desk. Thin fiddles of timber ran along the spines to prevent the books from falling out. The captain's chair, upholstered on the armrests, showed signs of age as did the other furnishings. The timber panelling was scratched and would have benefited from a coat of oil.

As the *Morning Star* slid from the top of the swell into a deep trough, Emma lost her balance. She grabbed the oak table in the centre of the room trying not to disturb the maps and charts lying on it. Despite the sound of shuffled papers, the captain appeared not to notice. Emma wondered if he had forgotten she was there.

When Nathaniel Preston finished his entry, he laid the quill on the desk, blotted his entry and carefully closed the inkpot.

'So,' he said, reading from his journal. 'The *Morning Star* sailed on Thursday. Today is Sunday and already I have a problem. I can tell you, I am not happy.'

Emma's toes clawed the teak boards.

'Goddamit, woman! How dare you have the audacity to stowaway on my vessel!' He forced the chair back noisily. 'If you were a man I would have you flogged!'

Emma dropped her chin. Her knotted ringlets fell across her face.

'But mark my words whoever helped you will be punished!'

She lifted her head and straightened. 'No one helped me. It was my doing,' she said.

He ignored her comment and went over to his charts. 'I intend to sail for Portsmouth. When we reach the harbour you will be taken from this ship and deposited on the wharf. Where you go from there is no concern of mine!'

'But, sir, I cannot go back.'

The captain stood up from his desk and faced her. 'Damn you, woman! You will not stay on my ship!'

Emma lifted her face.

It was the first time since she had stepped into the room that Captain Preston had regarded her. The bruises on her face and blood splattered on her bodice were a surprise. He had not been told she had been beaten. And she was younger than he had expected.

What had he imagined? An older woman – hard and worn from servicing the men who frequented the dockside taverns? A drunk? A thief? But the woman before him was quite young. Little older than his eldest daughter. But her hair. Her dress. Utterly disreputable. He considered she would smell if he were standing any closer.

'Your face!' he said, pointing to her forehead. 'Did this happen on my ship?'

'No, sir. Not on the ship. It was a fall.'

Captain Preston shook his head, the scowl of authority returning. 'I warn you, do not take me for a fool. I do not take kindly to liars.' He glared.

Emma stroked her cheek, as if to brush the offending bruises away. 'Captain,' she said cautiously, 'I am not seeking a free passage. I have some money, enough perhaps to pay my passage.' As she was speaking, she tore at the stitching in her skirt, ripping open the pocket she had sewn. From it she withdrew the beaded purse.

The captain watched.

Loosening the strings, she pulled from it a small bundle wrapped in a crumpled handkerchief. Emma laid it on her hand and lifted back the lace edges.

The yellow metal glinted. Sovereigns and half sovereigns.

'Now what do we have?' the captain scoffed. 'A harlot and a thief!'

The words hurt. 'Sir,' she said, 'I assure you, I am neither.'

'Then answer me this,' he demanded. 'How does a woman like you come to be in possession of such a substantial amount of gold?'

'My father gave it to me.'

'Oh, yes?' he said cynically. 'And how did he acquire it?'

'The money was for a portrait of a duke.'

'And that, no doubt, was stolen from some stately house in Yorkshire!'

'It was not stolen. My father sold the painting and gave me the money.'

'Poppycock! You expect me to believe that a woman of your sort would carry this amount of money in her pocket? Just look at the condition of you! I tell you, I have no respect for liars and no time for thieves.'

He paused, scrutinizing her intently. There was something about her that made him hesitate. Though her garb was frightful, her hair unkempt, she had bearing. Her voice was clear. Her manner polite. For a fleeting moment his mind strayed to his own daughters and he felt pity. But the thought was short-lived and, as the injuries she had suffered had not been inflicted by any of his men, her condition was none of his concern.

'Tell me,' he said, 'does anyone, besides us, know about this money?'

'No one.'

'Are you certain?'

'I am sure.'

Fastening the buttons of his coat, the captain leaned back on his desk. 'Good,' he said.

Nathaniel Preston had a reputation for running an efficient ship. François had told her so. He had no time for drunkards or insubordinates and, though master of a merchant ship, dealt with both in Royal Navy fashion. He had suffered stowaways before and even seen some become good seamen. But a young woman hiding on his ship was something Captain Preston had not been confronted with. He turned his chair and sat down facing Emma.

'You are the only female on this ship and that, in itself, is a recipe for disaster.' He paused, choosing his words carefully. 'And while it is possible you may not be the type of woman I would expect one of my men to bring on board, I nevertheless cannot allow you to stay on my ship irrespective of who or what you claim to be.'

Emma brushed the hair from her eyes.

'Madam,' he said, 'I will explain and I suggest you listen carefully to what I have to say. If my words sound blunt, they are meant to be! Your presence here puts my ship at risk. You also put yourself in danger.' He cleared his throat. 'I doubt, as a woman, you can comprehend the appetites which come over a man when he is at sea for long periods. And the men in my charge are at sea for many months, sometimes even years. You must pardon my candour when I say a man's need for a woman is often beyond his control. Some men become desperate and forget all moral values – that is if they ever had any in the first place!'

He looked across at the coins nestled in the kerchief.

'If I were to pander to your pleas and allow you to stay on board, I could not guarantee your safety. Neither the threat of flogging or worse would deter the appetite of a woman-hungry sailor.'

Emma rested against the table to keep her balance.

The captain leaned forward. 'I am told that your son is on my ship. Is this correct?'

Emma nodded. 'But he is not a stowaway. He has signed on for the voyage. And,' she added quickly, 'he is not responsible for me being here.' She held out her hand. 'Please take this. Let me pay my passage.'

The captain shook his head.

'At sea, a man must have his mind set on what he is doing. If he loses concentration for only a second he is in danger of becoming food for the fishes. A woman idling about on deck would be too much of a distraction.'

'But, sir, I would not "idle about" as you say. I can occupy myself.' She glanced across at the shelves of books. 'Read perhaps,' she said. 'If you allow me to stay, I promise I will keep away from the men. I will speak with no one. If necessary I will remain below decks. I beg you, sir, please reconsider. I cannot go back to Whitby.'

'Ma'am, Mrs. . . ?'

'My name is Emma Quinlan.'

'I have listened to what you have said. Now you listen to what I say. It is my intention to take this ship into Portsmouth. There you will be put ashore.' He glanced out of the window then examined the barometer hanging on the wall. 'Unless this weather breaks it will take us a week to make Portsmouth. But if the wind freshens we could be off the Isle of Wight in less than two days. Whichever is the case, I assure you, you will be leaving the ship. I suggest, therefore, you prepare yourself for that eventuality.'

There was a rap on the door.

'Begging your pardon, Capt'n. We're ready for you on deck.'

The captain raised his voice. 'One moment!' He fastened his jacket and continued.

'Seamen,' he explained 'are not like other men. They are a different breed. Crude. Unmannered. Illiterate. But they have one thing in common, they know the sea and respect it. They know its fickle nature and know it will probably get the better of them in the end. And if a job needs to be done, no matter how dangerous, they will do it. The men do not question my orders. They are men who lack any modicum of social demeanor but, believe me, they have courage surpassing that of any landlubber. And I wouldn't have them any other way. I am the captain of this ship and every man on board knows it. They must respect my command and follow my orders otherwise they will suffer the consequences.'

Captain Preston turned and reached for his hat. 'As I said, I could not teach the men the delicacies of moral virtue if they sailed with me for ten lifetimes.' He paused looking directly into Emma's eyes. 'And I include the seaman we call Frenchy, in this category. He is a man who may have impressed you with his foreign ways, but he is a seaman, no less, and a man of passion – perhaps more so than the others.'

Emma blinked.

'That is your concern, not mine and that brings me back to the coins you have in your hand.'

Emma uncurled her finger.

The captain's face was grave. 'If word passes around the ship that you are carrying gold, I assure you, it will be removed from your person in an instant. These men have no conscience. I have seen a man's throat cut for a bowl of tobacco.' He leaned on the table. 'For that reason, I will take the money from you, if only to prevent the same thing happening to you. And I will return it to you when in Portsmouth. In the meantime,' he said, 'I will consider whether or not I will hand you over to the authorities.'

'But, Captain, I beg you to listen to what I say. I do not lie. What I am telling you is the truth.'

The captain stood by the door. 'I do not have the time or inclination to argue the point. At this moment, I am required on deck. I have a ship to run.'

There was nothing more Emma could say. She folded the handkerchief around the money, squeezed the bundle into the purse and placed it on to the open palm of the ship's captain. In her estimation he was a reasonable man, she could appreciate his situation and he was probably right in what he said. At this point she had little alternative. She had to trust him.

'For the remainder of your time on board you will stay in the quarters where you were found. You will be allowed on the weather deck each day for a period of two hours, morning and afternoon. You will not talk to any of the men. You will behave with decorum at all times and not walk about unnecessarily. Finally, if I hear of any further incident which disrupts the running of this vessel, then, madam, be warned, you will be deposited on to the nearest beach. Failing that you will be secured in the hold under lock and key. Do you understand me?'

Emma nodded.

'So be it,' he said as he opened the door. 'Mr Thackray, escort Mrs Quinlan on deck!'

Emma lifted her skirt and stepped out of the cabin.

The mate led Emma up the companionway. She followed slowly. Her arms and legs lacked strength, and her skirt and petticoats made climbing difficult. From the hatch Emma stepped on to the after deck and though high cloud was covering the sun, the brightness hurt her eyes. She shielded them. The salt air felt fresh and brisk but there was little wind. The sails flapped but failed to fill, most of the squares hanging flaccidly. The *Morning Star* was wallowing, making no headway.

'Wait there!' the mate shouted, as he turned and went back below.

Emma waited turning away from the gaze of the seamen who were congregated further along the deck. All eyes were on her.

The interview with the captain had not been what she had expected. It left her confused, not knowing whether she should feel relieved or anxious. It also left her with many unanswered question. She wanted to speak with François, desperately, but now that would be impossible. One consolation was that the captain had not ordered the ship turned around and returned to Whitby. That had been her greatest fear. But she wondered if the captain could be trusted? He had taken her money but given no real guarantee he would not leave her stranded at some isolated cove on the south coast. When they arrived in Portsmouth, would he return the money to her or would he deny she ever gave it to him? It would be her word against his. And where would she go from there? She could not return to Whitby. No, she would make her way to Lincoln and her sister. But would she have money for the train? And would George be looking for her there? She tried to shake the thoughts from her head.

The captain appeared from the hatch. The mate followed him. On deck, the company of men quietened, stepping aside as the captain went forward.

Emma hadn't realized that there were so many men on board. Perhaps thirty. A rag-tag assortment. How could Joshua wish to belong to such company?

An uneasy feeling crept over her as if something were about to happen. Now all eyes were on the captain.

The mate tugged on her sleeve. 'Stay put! Right here!'

Emma stopped as he walked past. Gripped in his hand was a stout plaited handle from which hung long thongs of knotted leather. The tips were tailing on the bleached decking.

She felt sick inside.

As the captain walked between the men several gestured with knuckles to the forehead, others removed their hats. Joshua was there in a huddle with several other boys his age. He was the tallest of the group by almost three inches. Emma was afraid. Would he be punished for the part he played in helping her?

The mate moved forward. The men shuffled back. And she saw François. He was being held between two seamen. Bare to the waist. Emma's legs were weak. Across the deck, another man, dressed only in breeches, was flanked on either side. She had seen him on the dock. She recognized his face, his evil eyes. She knew immediately she did not like him.

The captain addressed the crew: 'For those who have sailed with me before, you know I will allow nothing to jeopardize the running of this ship. These men before you were fighting in the galley. For that they will receive a dozen lashes. Next time they'll find themselves in irons.' He looked towards the group of boys. 'For those who are new to my command, take heed.' Then he turned to the mate. 'Proceed with the punishment, Mr Thackray.'

The mate flicked out the whip as the two seamen were tied to the gratings.

Emma closed her eyes. But could not close her ears.

She heard each stroke, the murmurs from the men, the numbers counted under every breath. She heard the splash of water and the muffled groan of pain. Then it was over.

'Take them below!'

She heard feet tramp by and muffled voices. She opened her eyes. Her cheeks were wet. She dried them on her sleeve.

The captain's pale eyes were steady as he regarded her. 'The lesson your son has learnt today is perhaps the best lesson any boy can learn on his first voyage. He will not forget it quickly. It will stand him in good stead. You mark my words.'

'All done, Capt'n,' the mate reported.

'Thank you, Mr Thackray. Please return the cat to my cabin.'

'Aye, aye, Capt'n.'

'And, Mr Thackray, you can then make ready to set some sail.' He turned his face to the south-east. A line of dark cloud was forming on the horizon. He sniffed the air. 'If I am not mistaken, we will have some wind within the half-hour. A fresh breeze will do us all good.'

'Aye, aye!'

The deck was quiet. The wind had picked up as the captain had predicted, blowing from the east-south-east. For more than an hour Emma had watched the men as they climbed, like a column of ants, up the rigging and out along the yards. And like ants each man performed the same task as the man next to him, working in unison, without a single word being spoken. She heard the call from the deck and the sudden rush of noise as each sail fell, the crack, like a whip, as it luffed and filled. And with each new sail unfurled, the ship responded, leapt forward and sliced harder into the oncoming waves. Emma watched till all the sails were set, as the wind hammered the heavy canvas, smoothed out the cracks and turned each square into a billowing pillow of downy white.

From the stern, the wake swirled into eddies, pools spinning like tops, marking a pathway across the surface of the sea. For Emma every mile was a mile further from her home. But every mile was also a mile nearer Portsmouth. She watched as the trail of simmering water grew longer, stretching in a slow, curving line, pushing the horizon further and further from the ship.

Emma felt safe at the stern. The small barrel she had found that morning, wedged between two larger ones, provided a sheltered seat. Above her head the ropes securing the mizzen sail squeaked as it strained around the wooden block, thumping at times as the ship shifted on the swell.

She thought about François, wondering if he had recovered from the events of the previous day, unsure of what would happen to him now. In two day's time, depending on the wind, she would be put ashore and she would never see the Frenchman again.

As she ran her hand across her hair, her fingers caught in the greasy knots. What must she look like? Her skirt was ripped at the knee. There were stains on the bodice of her dress. It was no wonder the captain had taken her for a woman of the street. She must surely look like one.

Joshua's voice was comforting. 'Mama, a plate of food. The meat is good, and there is potato.'

Emma smiled at her son fighting back the tears. She took the plate in both hands and placed it on her lap.

He handed her a spoon.

'Are you all right?' she said.

'I'm fine, but I did not imagine that this would happen. François had said everything would be all right and I believed him.'

'Tell me, how is François?'

Before he had chance to answer a voice shouted his name.

'I must go. I will be back in fifteen minutes to take you below, but I will try to visit you later.'

'No, Joshua! The captain said that I should not speak to any of the crew and that includes you. I do not want you to get into trouble on my account.'

'But the mate told me it was the captain who said I should bring the food to you. Don't worry, Mama.'

Emma watched him as he ran from the after deck. He was no longer her boy of Seal Street. He looked tall, like a man. She felt proud. At least Joshua had got his wish.

A seagull dived, skimmed the water and without flapping its wings, glided upwards, high above the ship. Emma watched as it hovered above the ship wondering if it would settle on one of the masts. High in the rigging, a movement caught her eye. A seaman, sitting astride the topgallant yard, was watching her. She looked away. She knew the face. As she looked, the open mouth contorted into an evil laugh, but the only sound which reached the deck was the wind and the creek of timbers. When she dared to glance up again, the man had gone.

# Chapter 11

Emma opened her eyes to the blackness. Sleep was impossible. The pain in her belly would not go. She changed her position, rolled over on the coils of flaked rope, banging her elbow on the timbers a few inches above her head.

In the darkness, she thought of her father. Was this the hoodwink he had worn every day? The veil of pitch which shrouded even the faintest hint of a midsummer's day? Was this his world – a canvas of spilled ink blotted in chimney soot?

She thought of her child in the attic, of Elizabeth May, whose eyes, sealed with iced tears, would never see the pallid light of another snow-cold February morning.

The pain was worsening. She held her breath and curled her legs to her belly.

She did not know how long she had lain there, awake, waiting for some sound of morning, waiting for permission to be taken up on to the deck. She felt around for the bucket. She must use it. But it wasn't there. Someone must have removed it. She must get up to the deck. To the heads. She could wait no longer. She felt for the door and tapped lightly on it. If the seaman posted outside her door was not asleep, he would hear her. She waited, then knocked again, her ear pressed against the locker door. She listened but could hear nothing but the monotonous thudding which echoed through the body of the ship like a dull heartbeat.

Cautiously, Emma unfastened the door and pushed it open. It swung out wide on its hinges, creaking noisily. She looked left and right. The passage was empty.

A pale glow filtered back from the galley mess where the men slept, swaying in slung hammocks like bats hanging from tree branches in folded wings. The sounds of the sailors sleeping carried along the deck, as did the smells of night. Sweat, flat ale and salted meat-fat congealed in the pans.

She could not go through the mess, she must go back towards the stern. Up the two flights of steps closest to the captain's cabin. She prayed no one would see her.

To keep her balance, Emma slid her hands along the timbers above her head. She moved stealthily on bare feet. When she reached the first ladder she straightened herself, arched her back and looked up. A light was glowing from the deck above. She hoped when she reached the weather deck there would be sufficient moon for her to find her way to the bowsprit and the heads.

Pushing the folds of skirt and petticoat between her legs, Emma climbed. Her muscles were stiff but at least the pain in her stomach was subsiding. Crawling out on to her hands and knees, she sat for a moment. There was no one about.

The light was from the lantern hanging near the door to the main cabin. The shadows cast from it moved back and forth across the white doors of the private cabins. All was quiet. Everyone was sleeping.

Through the open hatch Emma could see the stars swinging rhythmically. It was as if the ship were standing still and the heavens swaying from side to side. The companionway leading up to the weather deck was wider than the previous one, less like a ladder and not as steep. She rolled her skirt to one side and climbed again. Halfway up, a length of knotted rope dangling from above, swung against her face. She grabbed it and cautiously climbed out on to the weather deck.

Silhouetted against the black sky a lanky seaman rested one hand on the double wheel, his only light from a pale, mottled moon. He did not appear to see her, though he was only a few yards away.

The wind caught her hair, trailing it around her face. She should have tied it back. Overhead, a sail cracked and rigging rattled. Emma knew she must tread warily. Finding a path along the deck would not be easy. It was littered like an obstacle course. Thick ropes seeped with oil and tar ran up to heavy blocks which swung dangerously above her head.

'Go steady, ma'am.' The voice came from the helm.

'I will,' she replied in a whisper, as she moved cautiously towards the bow.

The port side was leaning to the sea. Almost close enough to touch it. Foam whisked by the bow, churned along the hull. Beyond that the ocean was ink black and uninviting. Yet Emma felt no fear. Its vastness made her feel secure. So far from land. Perfect protection from threats and danger. She did not know what would become of her when she was put ashore, but for the first time she was glad she had run away.

The ship's heads were fixed precariously over the bow, on either side of the bowsprit. The two square seats each bore a large round hole. Though the timbers had once been sanded smooth, the wind and salt had dried them out. They were cracked and warped. Beneath the heads the bow waves crashed spraying white spume back on to the deck. Emma hoisted herself up from the gunnels and clambered on to the seat not daring to release her hold upon the ropes. She sat, her bare legs hanging over the sea.

The bow dipped. Salt water spray damped her skin. She caught her breath and held on gazing down at the sea turning from the bow. Something in the foam attracted her. Tiny pinpricks of light in the water like distant stars or silver dust! There were hundreds of them, darting up from the deep, dancing on the surface, then disappearing. Emma watched mesmerized. It was not the moon broken into a thousand fragments, nor the reflection of the heavens. Were her eyes playing tricks? Was it an illusion? Or was this a sample of the sea's seductive magic she had heard so much about?

A sound alerted her. She turned her head. Almost hidden by the ropes and headsails, a sailor was perched on the tip of the bowsprit. He was tapping his pipe on the baulk of timber, the sound carrying down its length. She hadn't noticed him when she had clambered out. Suddenly she was embarrassed for her situation. She felt vulnerable. If she fell overboard no one would know, and even if they did, François had told her the ship would not turn back if a seaman fell overboard. Her hand was shaking as she slid forward and dropped to the deck. She must get back to the sail locker.

From one object to another she balanced herself along the deck. She was thankful the ship was sailing well. The movement was smooth and there was no call for men on the deck. Apart for the man on the helm and the sailor on the bowsprit, she had seen no other. She shivered as she made her way below.

'Damn your eyes! Watch where you're standing!'

It was a man's leg not a rope she had stepped on. His body was half hidden beneath the upturned longboat. She had forgotten that some men slept on deck. She hurried. The helmsman's stance had not changed. The companionway was only a few yards ahead. For a moment she hesitated.

Turned her face into the wind. Tossed back her hair, opened her mouth and gulped the salty air wishing she did not have to go below – back to the sail room, back to the land, back to – she dare not think what!

Something touched her thigh. She swung around. It was the rope hanging over the companionway. Grasping it tightly, she stepped backwards into the darkness. Her toes felt for the wooden steps. The volume of her skirt made her descent awkward. She pulled the layers of folds up around her knees. The air rising from inside the ship warmed her bare legs. The dim glow from the lantern on the deck below was welcoming.

Suddenly a hand hooked her ankle and wrenched her down the ladder. Before she had time to cry out her chin bounced on the top step, snapping her teeth closed, her tongue sandwiched between. The force of the blow threw her neck back then, forward, bouncing her forehead on to the lower steps.

Emma's mind reeled into a near faint. Like an observer in a strange slow dream, she had no control. She could feel herself being dragged to her knees. She wanted to get up, to fight off the invading hands, but she could do neither.

A vice-like grip clamped over her face sending a searing pain through her jaw. Blood filled her mouth. Her right arm flailed the air. Her left hand hung limply by her side.

Words breathed into her ear. 'Ain't this my lucky day!' Matted hair, like greasy rope, draped down across her face.

'Couldn't sleep, could I? Then who should come looking for me but the fancy lady.' He grabbed Emma's hair and wrenched her head back. 'Came looking for Old Tom, did you? Well, now you found me, missy. But you don't look so fancy now.'

Emma's legs burned with the weight of his body upon her. She wanted to cry for help, but the words would not come out. Her mouth was hanging open. She could feel something running down her neck. A muffled moan was all she managed.

'Now listen, girl, and listen good. You and me's gunna have a little arrangement, as you might say.' He pressed his stubbly chin into her cheek, his lips squashed against her ear. 'Seems you got a boy on board, by the name o' Joshua.' He sniggered. 'Nice-mannered lad. I picked 'im out.'

Emma's heart thumped.

'Good mates now, 'im and me. Showed 'im a thing or two, I 'ave. Young Josh thinks Tom's all right,' he hissed, jerking his fingers in her hair. 'You listening to what I'm saying? You do what's right by me, and your lad'll be fine. I'll teach 'im all there is to know. You got me word.' He breathed into her face. 'But you make one murmur and mark my words I'll hang him from the yard and feed his innards to the fish, piece by slimy piece.' He rattled her head. 'Do you 'ear me?'

Emma could neither speak nor move.

'I said, do you 'ear me, woman? That ain't no idle jest. I done it before and on my oath, it'll give me pleasure to do it again.'

Letting out a faint moan and struggling against his grasp, she inclined her head to a nod.

'Good. Now you and me's got an understanding.'

He released his grip and fumbled with his breeches.

'Now you be a good girl and take what Old Tom gives you?' He poked his tar-stained fingers in her mouth, pushing open her sagging jaw.

Her cheeks burned with the pain. She wanted to think of Joshua. To pray no harm would come to him. But the pain was excruciating. A mat of wiry hair was thrust against her face. The rancid smell of greasy sweat was sickening. She could think of nothing.

'Open your mouth, you slut! Remember what I said.' Anchoring her by her hair, he pressed himself between her bloodied lips, deep into her throat.

She could not breathe. She gagged.

Her free hand grasped weakly at his wrist. Her strength had gone. In vain she tried to press her nails into his arms, but could not penetrate his leathered skin. Pain radiated across her cheeks, exquisite pain like she had never felt before. Frantic but helpless, she let out a soft moan. She could not have bitten down on the object invading her mouth even if she had wanted. She retched, the bitter fluid from her stomach burning into the back of her throat. It settled there. Swallowing was impossible.

Tom Barstow threw his head back, his eyes rolling as his whole body swayed back and forth exercising his bestial urge.

Suddenly Emma's pain stopped. She felt herself drifting. Succumbing to the sanctuary of unconsciousness. From the ship's deck the dull rhythmic banging echoed in her brain. She sensed herself falling backwards. Down. Down. Swaying back and forth. Back and forth.

Molly! Keep still! The stool is slipping.

She knew she would fall. The pail was slipping. She was hanging on, her forehead pressing hard into the moving flank. She could smell the barn. It was rank and warm and sickening.

Why won't she be still, Uncle? The stool is sinking. Please tell Molly to be still.

'Below!' a voice echoed.

It was a far away cry.

Uncle, is that you? Please help me. I'm falling!

Warm milk, thick and creamy, soothed her mouth. Flowed into her throat.

And with a final thrust the milking stool collapsed throwing the small girl backwards, tumbling over and over into a swirling mire of blackness.

Jack Mahoney was doing the last round of his watch. From the deck he glanced down the ladder into the dim glow of the afterdeck.

'Below! Who's that below?'

Illuminated only by the shadowy light of the lantern, he could see the seaman hunched over what appeared to be a heap of rags. 'What's your business there? Below, I say! Speak man!'

Having expelled every ounce of energy, Tom Barstow had collapsed exhausted on to Emma's crumpled body. Slowly he righted himself, his body shaking involuntarily. He staggered then lolled back against the wall, his flagging member hanging from beneath his blouse.

The pile of rags remained motionless on the floor.

'My, God! What's happened?' Mahoney muttered to himself, then, in a voice which would have carried to the royals in a roaring gale, 'Mr Piper! Call the captain! Now!'

The door to the private cabin door nearest the companionway swung open.

# Chapter 12

Soft pillows on either side prevented Emma's head from lolling over. The bed was warm and comfortable. The cotton sheets crisp and fresh. Sleep had come easily but had not been restful. It had been laced with strange and troubled dreams – confusing dreams which added to her tiredness.

Something touched her lips.

'Mrs Quinlan! You must try to take a drink.'

Her eyes opened to little more than narrow slits. Waking was not easy. It was hard to see. Above her head the ceiling was painted white. It puzzled her. The timbers were not far above her face. If she could lift her hand she could surely touch them. Where was she? Whose bed was she in? Her mind was playing tricks again. The bed was rocking like a cradle. Side to side. Something about the movement had made her faint but try as she might, she could not remember.

'You must drink a little. It will do you good.' It was an unfamiliar voice, a man's, but gentle.

A linen cloth was draped across her chest. A china dish was resting on it. Again she felt a touch upon her lips. Her mouth was parched. Her tongue dry. A little of the sweet warm liquid ran into her mouth. More spilled across her chin.

'That was good,' he said. 'Please try once more.' This time his hand slid behind her head and held her as she opened her lips and swallowed.

This man was kind. Like her father when she had been ill. She wanted to say thank you but her mouth would not respond. She wanted to ask where she was. But she was tired. And felt safe. Safe to sleep. And dream.

Emma woke to the lazy swaying. She remembered the ship. The sail locker. François. But where was she now?

106

She was in a bunk and it was light. There was a lantern hanging by the door. It was a small doorway. She sensed someone sitting beside her but she could not move her head. She tried to lift her arms but they were secured beneath the sheets. She closed her eyes again.

Emma could see the figure standing beside the bed. A man's face outlined but with no features. The light behind him was too bright.

'Well, I am pleased to see you are awake at last.' He moved closer as he spoke.

'Is that better?' he said, realizing the light shone in her face. 'Tell me, how do you feel?'

Emma opened her lips but her answer was inaudible. She tried again.

'Perhaps now is not the time for questions. But let me introduce myself. I am Charles Witton.'

Emma's right arm was fixed by her side. She could move her left arm. She wanted to extend it to him. He helped her lift it from the linen and rested it on his own soft hand. His head inclined in a respectful gesture.

'And you, I gather, are Mrs Emma Quinlan.'

Who was this man she had never met before? Was he a doctor? The gold pin glinting in his silk cravat indicated he was a man of means, a gentleman. How old he was she could not guess. Perhaps almost ten years her senior. His hair was dark but thinning at the temples. Well groomed. Yet his face, furrowed with lines and his cheeks sunken beneath the bones, resembled that of a man deprived of food and shelter. He slid his hand away.

There were many questions she wanted to ask. Was this the *Morning Star*? Or was she on another ship? She wondered how long she had been there. What was wrong with her? She sighed, puffing the air across her swollen lips. She touched her chin and found a line of bandage encircling her face from chin to crown. But why?

'I thought it necessary,' he said apologetically. 'Please do not try to talk.'

She thought of George. Had he done this? Had he discovered where she was?

'You are quite safe here. There is nothing to worry about.'

She touched her nose.

'Nothing broken,' he said. 'Nothing that will not heal with time and a little rest.' He picked up a mug from the cabinet beside the bed. 'I will ensure you get plenty of both. But,' he said, 'if you are to get well, you must take plenty of fluid. This is some of my best tea. Please drink a little then I will leave you.'

He leaned forward and fed the liquid to her. She swallowed half. Sleep was trying hard to overcome her.

'Thank you,' she whispered.

'Get well. That is all I ask.'

'You are a doctor?'

'No,' he said. 'Though I studied medicine for some years, I cannot claim to be a physician.' He suddenly looked old and tired. 'But I am the nearest thing on this ship.'

Emma relaxed back into the pillow. Her eyes closed.

'Mama, it's me, Joshua.'

Emma was not asleep. She turned her head slightly towards her son and the man standing beside him.

'I wasn't allowed to see you before. I was worried.' He held her hand.

'I'm getting better,' she said. 'I think it is all the Chinese tea Mr Witton makes me drink.' Her bruised skin felt taught as she smiled.

'But what of your face? Your eye is black. You've been fighting!'

'I hit a man. He said things I did not like. So I hit him.'

'And he hit you back, I would say. Have I not told you about brawling?'

'Mama!'

'I'm sorry. Tell me about yourself.'

Joshua hesitated and looked around.

'Five minutes, lad!' Mr Witton said. 'No more or you will tire your mother. I will leave you for the present.'

'Mama, I don't know what to say – seeing you here like this – it is terrible – like Seal Street.'

'Don't talk of that, Joshua. But tell me, are you happy? Is this what you wanted?'

'Mama, you do not know how good it is to be on the ship, to be away from Whitby.' He shook his head in disbelief. 'To watch the sea. The waves. The sky. The wind on the clouds. It is like no feeling I have ever had before. Far better than I ever dreamed.'

'Go on,' she said.

'At first I was a little afraid. When we sailed around the Goodwin Sands I was told of ships that had gone aground, and of ghost ships which sail those waters. The stories scared me. And when we sailed by and I saw the waves breaking in the middle of the sea, breaking on the shifting sands and I thought the stories must be real. But when we sailed past Dover I climbed the mast and I could see the cliffs of England and the coast of France at the same time. And while I sat there, the ship heeled over and from where I sat, I looked down as the sea was coming up to meet me and it was like I was a gull diving down from the cliff top. Oh, Mama. I felt free as the seabird. You cannot imagine how good that feeling is.'

Emma smiled.

'But, Mama, when we get to Australia you will be free too. And I will make sure no one hurts you ever again.'

Emma's voice was soft. 'But I will not be sailing with you, son. The captain will have me put ashore in Portsmouth.'

'But, Mama—'

'Hush, I must abide by what he says.'

'But, Mama—'

'Don't worry, Josh, I will travel to Lincoln and stay with my sister, Anna. She will be happy to see me.'

'But Mama, haven't you heard? We sailed south of Portsmouth three days ago. We are no longer in the Channel. We are heading south!'

Emma tried to raise herself in the bunk. 'But why did the ship not go to Portsmouth?'

'It was the fog. It was thick and damp and cold – like a Whitby sea fret but worse. There was no wind at all and I think the crew was worried, though not a word was said. There was nothing for them to do, they just sat around all day. When the wind blew in it came off the land and was bitter cold. It made the sea steam. And the captain set a new course, due south towards the coast of France. I heard one seamen say it was fool-hardy sailing that way, that we would likely hit another ship. We lit the lanterns and had them burning bright all through the day. And I was given duty on the for'ard deck to toll the bell. You must have heard it ringing.'

Emma shook her head.

'And it was mighty cold. But we neither saw nor heard another ship. And when we sailed out of the fog it was like someone had opened a curtain on the day. On the outside was bright sunshine and clear sky, and the sea was bluer than I have ever seen before. And behind us you could see the fog, sitting like a huge ball of cloud on the sea. And not more than five miles ahead was France. Cherbourg. And as the wind picked up we headed west following the coastline for a time.' Joshua looked kindly at his mother. 'Trust me, Mama,' he said. 'We are far from Portsmouth, and we are not going back.'

The thoughts tumbled so fast through Emma's brain she could not hold one long enough to grasp it. 'Tell me, Joshua, how long have I been here?'

'Five or six days.'

'And you say I will not be put ashore?'

From the doorway Charles Witton answered the question. 'No, ma'am. What your boy says is correct. The *Morning Star* is in the North Atlantic and heading south-south-west. The captain tells me our first port of call is the island of Madeira. It may take us a week to get there and we will not stay long. Only sufficient time to take on water and some fresh provision.'

Relief welled in Emma's eyes. Joshua squeezed her hand and bent his face down to hers. She felt his cheek brush hers.

'I will look after you, Mama. Please don't worry.'

'Enough for now, lad. Your mother needs some rest.'

'Yes, sir.' Joshua laid his mother's hand on to the bed, leaned towards her and whispered, 'François asked me to convey his good wishes.'

'Tell him, thank you,' she said quietly. 'Now go, Josh. I am in good hands.'

She watched as he bent his head to get through the door. 'Thank you for allowing that,' she said.

'A good-looking boy,' Charles Witton said, inclining his head as he looked into her face. 'You both have the same eyes.'

'You mean we both have bruises?'

He laughed. 'That is not what I meant, Mrs Quinlan.'

'My name is Emma,' she said, as she smiled and wondered about this man who had nursed her for the past week, attending to her every need while she slept. 'I do not remember hearing mention of your name before and cannot recall seeing you on the deck when I was there. May I ask your position on the ship?'

'But I have noticed you on the deck on more than one occasion – but I will not dwell on that. Let me explain.' He thought for a moment. 'Unfortunately the ship does not carry a surgeon, much to the chagrin of the men. This, I gather, is not unusual on small merchant vessels, quite unlike the Royal Navy ships.' He cleared his throat. 'I am sailing at the invitation of the captain, as a passenger. As for my profession, I study insects and, if I am fortunate, I will be able to discover some new species in the Antipodes previously unidentified.'

Emma's eyes were closed.

Perhaps his answer had disappointed her. He could not be sure.

'Sadly, my dear, I cannot claim to be a physician though it would be my greatest wish.'

As he spoke he saw Emma's eyelids flickering. He continued talking softly as if for his own benefit. 'In the last six months I have lost both my wife and daughter and there was nothing I could do to help either of them. If only they had accompanied me on my last voyage to Sydney,' he said with a sigh. 'I begged my wife to come. I felt sure the climate would improve her health.' He paused. 'She died in October when the weather was beginning to turn cold. She hated the English winter and in her heart I think she knew that she would not see another Christmas. My daughter died several weeks ago.'

Looking down at his charge, he knew she was asleep. 'And so, my dear, like you, I am running away. Turning my back on the past and hoping that in Australia life will be somewhat kinder to me than it has been.'

# Chapter 13

A strip of pale light outlined the cabin door.

Emma sat up, swung her legs over the edge of the bunk and slid her toes to the timber deck. She steadied herself, waiting until she felt comfortable with the roll of the ship, aware she must learn to move with it. She lit the lantern.

The private cabin was little more than two paces long with hardly width to turn around. It was smaller than her pantry at Seal Street. Wedged between the wall and the head of the boxed bunk was a compact cabinet, comprising one drawer and a tiny cupboard below it. On it was a silver handled brush, a slab of soap in a china dish and linen cloth. A straight backed chair just fitted into the other end. On that, a tin jug and bowl. The water in the jug slopped back and forth but the narrow neck prevented it from spilling. Under the chair, covered with a piece of Hessian, the wooden night bucket. Next to that, her boots. Built into the front of the bunk, two drawers. Emma opened them with difficulty as the timber frame had warped. They squeaked. It was the first time she had examined the contents.

The clothes she had worn when she came aboard were in the top drawer. Neatly folded, though ragged and dirty. The line of broken threads on the skirt pocket reminded her of her conversation with the captain. As she had not been put ashore, then the coins would have to pay for the voyage. She thought it unlikely she would get any back in Sydney. She wondered where her bag was. The tapestry bag and the clothes she had selected. Then she remembered the fire. The smell of burning and George's face.

The second drawer was deeper than the first. It contained the clothes Joshua had collected for her when they left. She examined each garment in turn.

The skirt. Good quality, but with an inkstain the size of a dinner plate across the front. It was clean and warm and the stain could be hidden beneath an apron. It would suffice. Two blouses. One clean, but old and fraying at the collar. The second needed stitching and had no buttons. She would tear it into strips to use for rags.

There was little else. No dresses, hose or handkerchiefs. But she was relieved to find some underwear and a pinafore. The nightshirt she was wearing was a man's, but it belonged neither to George nor Joshua.

Hanging from the coat peg on the cabin door were her bonnet and cape. The plaid shawl covered the foot of the bed. It was a poor selection, drab but serviceable. No satin, silk or fine wool. No dress or gloves. Certainly nothing elegant. But sufficient for a change of clothes while the others were washed. And suitable for wearing on the ship. Joshua would understand and possibly François would never notice. She would not worry about her dress until the ship arrived in Sydney.

She looked again at the nightshirt. Mr Witton must have dressed her in it. He must have washed her, and attended to her toilet. He was the only one who had fed her and had nursed her back to health. He had been very kind and she had not thanked him properly.

Making sure the bolt was securely shot, Emma undressed. She winced to the pain in her arm as she slipped the nightshirt from her head and let it drop around her feet. Kneeling beside the chair, she poured an inch of water into the bowl. The cabin was warm, the water tepid. It slid lazily as it had done in the jug, but it did not spill.

The soap was greasy but after it she felt clean, much fresher than she had for several days. Untangling her hair was hard. Her arm ached when she lifted it and her hair was badly knotted. She brushed it out and left it hanging loose around her shoulders.

When she had completed her toilet, she dressed, and sat back pondering what would happen when she was well again. Would the captain send her back to the sail locker or allow her to remain in the cabin? The sound of bare feet on the boards outside startled her. They stopped. She listened but could hear nothing. No doors opening. No voices. The bolt on the door was secure. No one could get in. The teak boards creaked. Was someone was out there, or was it her imagination?

'Take my hand. I will not let you fall.'

Emma grasped the outstretched arm and allowed herself to be helped through the hatchway and out on to the deck.

Mr Witton wrapped the cloak around her shoulders. 'We do not want you to get a chill.'

'Thank you. You are very kind.'

'This way,' he said, as he guided her along the deck. 'I have found a place where you can sit. It is sheltered from the wind.'

The deck was wet and cold beneath her feet. Her cloak did not keep out the wind. But Emma was pleased to be outside. She filled her lungs with the sea air.

Two seamen standing by the braces watched her progress. One nodded sympathetically. She was conscious of them watching her. Did her face still bear the colour of the bruises? Hiding her eyes beneath her bonnet, she refrained from returning the gesture.

'Here,' he said, indicating a stool squeezed between two packing boxes. 'You can sit here.'

The wind blowing from the north east was fresh and cold, and strong enough to ruffle the wave tips turning them white. But her seat was sheltered by the longboat lashed behind it. She wondered if this stool was used by the sailors or if Mr Witton had placed it there for her.

'Will you be all right on your own? If you prefer, I can stay with you.'

'I will be fine here. I will enjoy sitting out for a while.'

'In that case, I will leave you and come back shortly.' He lifted the end of her cloak from the deck and draped it over her lap. She thanked him and watched as he made his way back toward the stern, struggling at times to keep his balance.

Most of the men on deck she had not seen before. She recognized the mate, Mr Thackray and the helmsman, the lanky young sailor. Two seamen were leaning against the gunnels smoking. Another man appeared to be asleep. A seaman jumped down from the rigging, unfastened a hessian tool bag from his waist and stored it in one of the deck lockers. He smelled of tar.

As she watched, a big wave battered the bow, crashed across the forward deck and delivered a mist of spray which carried the length of the weather deck. Sea foam swilled across the forward deck before running along the ship and sluicing out through the scuppers. Emma wiped the dampness from her face.

She could understand Josh's feelings. The sea was exhilarating. From the top of a swell the ship slid into a trough, fast as a leaf down a rain-swollen gutter, thrilling as a sledge ride after the first fall of snow.

'Emma!' It was François' voice. Behind her. He was leaning over the upturned boat. 'Are you better?'

'François,' she cried, somewhat afraid to turn for fear of being seen talking with him. 'I am well. But you – you are the one who—'

'Do not worry about me. That is not important. What is important is that I brought you here and caused this to happen to you. My God, you could have died and for this I make a promise: I will kill the man who did this to you.' The venom in his voice was real.

'Please, François, you must not speak that way. I am getting stronger everyday.'

There was no reply. Emma turned around but the Frenchman was gone. She looked up into the rigging.

From the crosstrees, a pair of eyes had been observing their conversation. Thomas Barstow leaned back against the mast. With his feet spread, his body swayed with the lilt of the ship. With one hand on the ship he buried his other into the crotch of his breeches in an ugly gesture. A trickle of brown saliva oozed from the corner of his lip. After a while he spat out the bolus of chewed leaf. The wind carried it far out to sea.

The Bay of Biscay was predictably rough. The winds gusted into squalls whipping sheets of spray from the wave crests. Troughs opened in the sea and competed against the roll of the swell. Clouds gathered on the horizon, closed and converged releasing stabbing rain which bounced headlong across the sea's surface turning it into a boiling menace. On deck, the sound of the wind was deafening. Canvas cracked as the ship shuddered from end to end and water thundered against the bow.

For two days Emma remained below. At first she was afraid. Afraid of the noises as every joint of the ship heaved and strained; afraid of the jolts and shudders fearing the ship had hit rock or collided with another; afraid of the motion which continually tried to tip her from her chair or throw her from her bunk. While the storm blew she felt unwell at times and tried to sleep on the floor. But as the sea settled she found herself becoming bored and restless with her limited surroundings.

Joshua visited each day and spent as much time as he was allowed. He told her about his duties and was proud to name the sails and tell her the location of the running gear. He spoke of the men. He said Mr Thackray, the first mate, was hard on the boys, but fair. The boatswain, a Norwegian, spoke little English and would tolerate no one around his store, flaring into a rage at the slightest provocation. He had quickly learned most of the men did not take kindly to questions and he had learned to watch and listen. He said the other three lads did the same and in the evenings they shared what they had learned. Knowledge, skills, even the ribald jokes. He said there were a few men on board whom he had not met. Some of the topmen and those on the other watch. He added that there were some sailors he would cross the deck to avoid.

Emma listened and spared him her motherly concerns. She left her questions about François until last. Joshua said he had recovered quickly and rejoined his watch.

Charles Witton visited her little during those two days. She wondered if it was something she had said or done which made him stay away. She had enjoyed his company and missed the opportunity to speak with him. The hours passed slowly.

On the afternoon of the third day, he knocked on her door. Emma slid back the bolt.

He looked tired as though he was unwell. She invited him to sit but he declined insisting she use the chair. He said he had been deprived of sleep. There had been an accident; two men injured when the halyard on the foremast topgallant yard had snapped. It had brought the yard crashing on to the heads of the sailors furling the mainsail below it. Though none of the men had fallen, it had taken a deal of time to lower the two injured men to the deck and even longer to sort out the tangle of ropes and sheets left dangling from the mast. He said it was fortunate that the yard had not broken or fallen into the sea. That could have brought the top of the foremast down with it. Three of the men received deep cuts to their heads, a fourth mangled his arm.

'It does not look good,' Mr Witton said. 'The arm is broken. The bone has pierced the skin. I have done all I can but that is not enough. His pain is terrible.'

Since the accident he had spent much time sitting with the seaman.

'The arm is infected,' he said, 'and as he will take neither food nor water, I fear he will not survive.'

There was a deep sadness in his pale eyes. It was the heaviness of frustration caused by his lack of knowledge to save the man. He admitted he could do no more than watch him die and would no doubt see his body committed to the deep.

After the brief visit, he excused himself saying he must rest. Emma was disappointed to see him go but saddened by his appearance. But she had barely time to lock the door before he returned. In his hand he had a book.

'You may enjoy glancing though this,' he said. 'It is only a child's book of verse, but it is one which never ceases to delight me. Perhaps it may help you pass the time. There are some excellent illustrations in it.' Without waiting for an answer, he pressed the book into her hand and left.

The yellowed paper and worn binding told Emma the book had been well used. She turned each page with care, reading verses her mother had sung to her when she was young, admiring the lithographs which illustrated each rhyme.

Before she laid it down she turned to the words written on the first leaf:

*This book is presented to Charles Aislaby Witton*
*on the occasion of his Fifth Birthday*
*Your loving Mama and Papa 3rd October 1823*

As she read the words a second time she heard the patter of light footsteps outside her door. The handle turned. Emma put the book down and slid to the floor. As her hand reached for the bolt to open it she felt pressure being laid against it.

'Mr Witton is that you?'

There was no answer. Emma held her breath.

'Who's there?' she called. Her heart began to pound. A sickening odour was coming through the door. She knew it instantly: it was the smell of Thomas Barstow.

# Chapter 14

Through the night Emma listened to the ship, its creaks and groans. Scraping, banging noises which stopped at times and then started up again. Sleep came eventually. Troubled, restless sleep.

A knock on the door woke her.

'Mrs Quinlan!' It was Mr Thackray's voice. 'Mrs Quinlan! Captain says he wants a word.'

'Thank you,' she said. 'I will be there in a moment.'

It was dark in the cabin. She had no idea of the time whether it was night or day. She lit the lamp, splashed her face with cold water and dressed quickly. She had no mirror.

The captain opened his door and was cordial. 'Good morning. I trust you are feeling better. Mr Witton told me you have made a good and speedy recovery.'

'Yes. He has been very considerate.'

Emma hovered at the door.

'Come in. It is time we spoke. There are some matters I need to make clear.'

Emma waited. 'Sit down,' he said, gesturing to the chair by the writing desk.

Captain Preston stared through the window. 'Mrs Quinlan, I am sure you are aware of my feelings towards . . . stowaways. I feel I discussed that at length the last time you were in this room.'

Emma nodded but did not reply.

'And you are also aware it was my decision to have you put ashore in Portsmouth.'

'Yes.'

'Believe me, ma'am, had it not been for circumstances over which I had

118

no control, that is the course of action which I would have taken. As I said to you a week ago, the running of this ship and the welfare of the crew are my prime concerns. Do not doubt that.'

He turned and faced her. 'However, to that I will add that I am not the unfeeling man you may think, and the treatment which you received at the hands of one of my men grieved me. As master of this ship I must take responsibility for whatever transpires on board.' He sighed. 'So be it. Where was I? Yes – circumstances beyond my control. You may be aware we met with inclement weather in the Channel. Thick fog made it impossible for us to sail into Portsmouth and for that reason and also the fact that you were' – he hesitated – 'unwell, I had little choice but to go back on the decision I had made.'

He looked to the sea. 'Perhaps for your sake, the fog was fortuitous. However, that is enough on that matter. Now, as to the present. I have been kept informed of your progress. You are obviously not aware that it was Mr Witton who insisted you be moved to the cabin on this deck. He also volunteered to take care of you.' He looked at her curiously. 'He seems to have taken an interest in your welfare.'

'May I say—?'

'Let me continue. On any vessel, be it a naval or merchant ship the captain must maintain discipline. Sometimes it is not a pleasant task but it has to be done.' His tone changed. 'The man who did this thing to you has been punished, and I hope that is an end to the matter. But . . .'

He hesitated again. 'But, be aware, the seaman, one Thomas Barstow, has returned to his watch and may still be a danger to you. I say to you, be very careful. Barstow is a man with no conscience, we are all aware of that, yet I cannot have him held below indefinitely when we need every able-bodied man on deck. However, he has been warned that if he misbehaves again he will be put in irons.'

Emma acknowledged what was being said.

'Now,' he continued, 'regarding your position on this ship for the duration of the voyage. After giving the matter considerable thought I have come to the following conclusion. From this point on, I will regard you as a passenger on the *Morning Star*. But mark my words, you will receive no special treatment or privileges.'

Emma listened.

'As a passenger, I cannot deny you the right to be on deck whenever you wish or to speak to whomsoever you choose. *But*,' he stressed the word, 'I would strongly advise you to be very wary and to keep your wits

about you at all times. I suggest that after dark you remain in your cabin
and keep the door bolted.'

Emma nodded.

'And when you are on deck, be in a place where you can be seen by
more than one of the men. Finally, I insist you restrict your movements
to the weather deck and do not, I repeat, do not venture into the mess, or
the hold, or any of the areas which the men use. That would be very foolish. Do you understand?'

'I understand.'

'I believe from what Mr Witton tells me you are an intelligent woman.
He has vigorously appealed your case, at times, I must admit, against my
better judgement. But I trust him implicitly. I am therefore granting this
compromise. I feel that my offer is exceedingly fair and trust that you will
abide by my stipulations.'

'You can be assured I will,' she said. 'And I thank you sincerely.'

With nothing more to add, the captain moved to the cabin door and
held it open. 'So be it,' he said.

The smell of woodsmoke and tar drifted across the deck. The cooper
sweated as he pumped the brazier's bellows, even though the wind blowing across the deck was keeping the flames alight. The resonance of his
hammer on the heated metal was accompanied by the cracking of a
poorly trimmed sail. A seaman sent to check the shroud, took up the
slack, waited for the canvas to respond then wound the hessian rope into
a neat figure of eight around the belaying pin.

Emma looked out from the rail. The *Morning Star* was sailing away from
the early sun. The sky was blue. The Islands of Madeira lay somewhere in
the ocean ahead and Mr Witton was taking a morning stroll around the
deck.

'You are looking much better this morning,' he said.

Emma smiled. 'Thank you,' she said. 'The sea air must be doing me
good.' As she spoke she thought of the conversation she had had with the
captain on the previous evening. It was Mr Witton who had spoken for
her. It was he who had arranged for her to be moved into her present
quarters. And it was he alone who had nursed her. She felt the flush of
blood in her cheeks.

The pair stood in silence for a moment looking at the sea and the day-
to-day activities of the ship. On the platform high above the deck two
men worked on either side of the main mast with brush and pot daubing

a treacle-like mixture on to the heavy ropes.

Emma cleared her throat. 'Mr Witton.'

He turned his face towards her. 'Charles,' he said.

'Charles, I wanted to thank you – for the loan of the book. There are some delightful illustrations. May I keep it with me for a little while?'

'But of course. And if there is anything else I can do, anything at all, please feel at liberty to ask.'

'I will.'

'Now if you will excuse me I will continue my morning exercise.'

Emma watched him as he continued his walk, zigzagging along the deck unlike the sailors whose gait at most times accommodated the movement of the ship. Beneath her bare feet the deck was holystone-smooth. Its teak timbers almost white from sun and salt. Across the water a slender fish flew fifty yards from one wave ridge to another ignoring several smaller waves between. Its silver body glistened as it left its habitat and darted bird-like through the air. Above her head the square sails stuffed with wind, hung from the yards like bed sheets on a Monday washing line. How far she was from Seal Street!

She didn't notice the tiny bird until it fell. Without opening its wings, it dropped from the yard, slid down the filled forecourse and landed on the deck with barely a sound. It was so small. Smaller than a robin. Sandy brown but with a hint of green, like the tits she would watch flitting through bare hawthorn before the new leaves of spring blocked its path.

Instinctively she squatted down and lifted it to the cup of her palm.

'It's gone, missus,' the sailor said, not lifting his eyes from the rope he was splicing.

'But why?'

'Not his place,' he said. 'Shouldn't be 'ere.'

She watched as he twisted the thick end of the hemp, forcing a hole between the coils and pushing the loose ends back upon themselves.

'But birds fly from one country to another,' she said.

'Aye, some do. But there's others are meant to stay put.' He slapped the rope on his knee. 'Sometimes they follow the ship, then one day they find themselves too far from home and they can't get back. Then it's too late so they just give up and die.'

Emma stroked the tiny head, cupped the bird in her hands and held it on her lap.

'No point hanging on to something that's dead, missus. Cat could make a meal of that.' The sailor tucked the last of the fraying fibres into the thick knob.

'I think I will keep it, if you don't mind.'

He shrugged his shoulder. 'Suit yourself, missus.'

Slipping the bird into her pocket, she smiled apologetically and made her way aft.

In the cabin she lifted the bird from her pocket and placed it on the locker beside her bunk. It could not sit upright. Its head lolled to one side. Its legs poked out like bare twigs – thin and brittle.

Running her finger up its chest she felt the softness of its breast, examined its delicate feathers, soft, downy, each perfectly patterned like the edges of a snowflake, grey white on the inside, tinted with soft brown at the tips. Quite beautiful. Carefully she opened its wings. Its miniature quill feathers were tinged with the hue of spring – fresh green, almost yellow in the glow of the lamp. Emma sat on her bunk gazing at the bird. Poor little mite.

From the locker, the glistening dead eyes stared back at her.

# Chapter 15

'Land ho!'

Emma woke to the call conveyed from aloft.

'Land! One point off starboard bow!'

She felt around for her skirt and blouse and dressed quickly in the darkness. Outside her door, the pale light spilling down from the companionway indicated it was almost dawn.

From the bow, Emma watched the morning's events with interest. The deck was a hive of activity. The daily work had started early. The brasses had lost their tarnish. The decking had been scrubbed and was still wet in patches. Some of the squares were furled while a line of men, leaning across the foremast yards, were fisting in another and lashing gaskets. Once the morning chores had been completed, the men sat around eagerly awaiting the opportunity to go ashore. The captain observed the activity from the rail.

To the south-west the fading night melded in a haze of mauve and blue. On the horizon a faint grey outline hovered like a long thin cloud above the sea. As the ship sailed closer, the image changed, transforming slowly into a line of purple mountains rising from the seabed.

'Is one of those islands, Madeira?' Emma asked a seaman.

'Sure is, missus.'

She turned and looked back. With the sunrise, the whole expanse of the eastern sky burned with an orange fire born of the Sahara. And like the shiny trail left by the early garden slug, the ship's wake glistened on the face of the sea. The breeze blowing in from the south east was warm. Emma dropped the shawl from her shoulders.

Charles had been watching her, studying her expression. 'It blows off the African continent,' he said. 'Though it is a little unusual for this time of the year.'

Together they watched as the land drew closer and the ship skirted the island. To the north, a line of peaks, ragged like a dragon's tail, drifted into the sea while along the coast, the cliffs, folded into giant rock waves, rose up like a petrified sea. On the hillsides, deep gorges furrowing the forests captured pockets of cloud in their crevices, while above the tree-line, streams, shining like silver threads, tumbled over the polished mountain rock.

'The *Morning Star* will be off Funchal in a few hours,' Charles said. 'The captain plans to drop anchor and stay at least one night. He has friends living in the town.'

'Will you be going on shore?'

'Yes, that is my intention. But,' he added, 'the captain feels it would be unwise for you to venture ashore.'

'But if you and the captain are leaving. . . ?'

'I spoke to Nathaniel about that and though, he says, the Portuguese are very hospitable and assures me this port is safer than most, we agree you will be safer on the ship – providing you remain on the weather deck. Most of the crew will be going ashore. A few will stay.' He paused. 'Foreign ports are no place for a . . .' he paused, 'a woman alone.'

Emma had not considered going ashore until he mentioned the idea. How she would love to leave the ship, to smell the moist mountain air, to drink from a free-flowing brook, feel the earth under her feet, collect seashells on the beach. But she could not go alone. She thanked him and agreed. She would stay on the ship.

The heavy chain thundered from the locker as the anchor dragged it to the seabed. Midships, the long boat was secured to the davits, swung out over the side and lowered into the sea. Several fishing boats, bearing fresh fruits and flower garlands, sailed close in, but until the mast was raised on the longboat and the other boats launched, the locals were warned to keep their distance. Unperturbed by the sailors' curses the colourful craft bobbed on the water no more than a stone's throw from the *Morning Star*'s hull.

The longboat carried a dozen men. Nine on the thwarts, two in the bow and another man on the rudder. The second boat took only six. When it was time for the ship's boys to go, they scrambled down the ropes and hung from the ship's side, dropping into the boat as it floated beneath them much to the aggravation of the boat's skipper. Joshua was among them. For the boys it was great sport, pushing and elbowing each other for the seat in the bow. For a few there was the anticipation of stepping on foreign soil and a chance to sample the exotic tastes of a new country, its fruits, its drinks, its scenery. For the seasoned seamen, their sights were set on the island's fine Verdelho, or the fleeting comforts of a real bed whose movement was not caused by the sea.

As the rope splashed from the *Morning Star*, and an oar pushed off from the ship's side, the boat floated free. The helmsman growled at the boys, threatening to throw them overboard if they were not still. The triangle of cloth filled on the short mast, carrying the boat into the broad bay. Emma watched Joshua hoping he would turn and wave, but his back was to the ship and besides, he was more interested in the port.

François left in the same boat as Tom Barstow. The sight of the seaman she despised made Emma nervous. A few times recently when her mind had been occupied, she had forgotten about him. Other times she had jumped at the slightest sound, imagined the noises of the night were the sailor loitering outside her cabin. At times she had sensed his eyes peering at her, though he was nowhere to be seen. Even seeing him sail away made her feel uncomfortable.

As she watched, the sailor turned. His eyes narrowed and his mouth curled in a menacing grin. Emma quickly looked away but his gaze remained clinging to her like a leach. Blood drained from her skin. Her flesh became cold. Despite the balmy breeze, she shivered, and wished she had never looked. Thomas Barstow was evil. His threats scared her. She feared him more than she had ever feared any man and she had no way of escaping from him. They would be together on the ship for the remainder of the voyage.

The captain and Mr Witton left on the longboat's second trip. The boatswain accompanied them, the second mate on the rudder. Emma acknowledged a wave as the boat headed across the sheltered bay. The smaller boat followed half empty. They would not return until late afternoon.

Though the deck was quiet Emma was slightly ill at ease. The men she trusted had gone ashore leaving her alone with sailors she hardly knew. She looked around. A couple of older salts were on deck, the others had stayed below. She told herself there was nothing to fear and settled down to watch the day go by.

The sun rose rapidly. The wind warmed considerably. Apart from the cries of inquisitive gulls, the deck was silent. Across the water, to the west of Funchal Bay, a huge cliff face rose from sea. Waves rolling in from the south broke all along the rocky shore, edging the island with a rim of white. Behind the town, nestled around the bay, the hillside rose in steep ridges broken by deep valleys. Waterfalls glistened like streaks of silver. It was a lovely sight.

The cook, a Chinaman, was a tall, yellow-skinned man with a mop of black hair which, when unplaited, reached below his waist. Emma had seen him on deck before, tossing slops or scraps into the sea or scrubbing out the galley buckets. The first time she saw him she had thought him to be a fearsome man, wielding a metal ladle over his head, chasing one of the sailors along the deck, screaming in his own language. The rest of the crew had been unconcerned, finding the cook's antics a source of amusement.

Whenever Emma had seen him he had always been wearing the same baggy breeches rolled up to the knee and a striped jumper with sleeves cut off at the shoulders. This morning, however, when he appeared from the galley hatch, he was wearing a kimono. It was the colour of crabmeat, edged with emerald green and tied with a sash. It reflected the light like sun on water. It was either silk or satin. A large stained apron wrapped around his middle spoiled his appearance.

Emma observed him from a distance as he performed his chores, scrubbing and scraping the blackened cooking pots. At times he lowered a pail over the side and drew fresh seawater. As he worked he hummed a strange disjointed melody.

'You want breakfast?' he shouted, when he had finished.

Emma looked around. She was alone at the stern.

'I get you good breakfast,' he said. 'You stay there.'

Apart from the Chinaman's verbal outburst, this was the first time she had heard the man speak English. Though his face and dress was oriental, his accent was that of an American.

When he presented Emma with the plate, he smiled and bowed several times. She was hungry as she had not been eating well.

'You like? You eat!' he said, as she glanced at her meal. Two pieces of bony pork and three eggs swimming in a greasy juice. A large chunk of bread on the side of the plate was rapidly soaking up the bronze liquid.

She smiled and thanked him, nodding her head in response every time he bowed. When he disappeared down the galley hatch she sat on the boards and rested the plate on her legs. The eggs were good and though the pork had a strange smell she ate most of it and all the bread and dip.

When satisfied, she slipped the remaining meat over the side and left her plate by the galley's companionway. After shouting the words, 'Thank you', through the opening, the cook emerged, reached for the plate and dropped back into the hole.

Jack Burns, the sailmaker was sitting not far from the hatch surrounded by folds of canvas. He was sewing a patch on a sail. Beside him was a large bag from which he had selected a piece suitable for the repair. Other pieces were scattered on the deck nearby. Some big, some small, assorted shapes and textures, some yellowed and hardened by salt.

'May I?' said Emma, leaning down and touching the material.

'Help yourself,' he said, continuing his work.

Emma watched.

'It'll be good and strong when I've done with it. Strong as the rest of the jib. Maybe stronger.'

She tested its texture. 'It is quite stiff.'

'Has to be. Wind is mighty powerful. I've seen new sails ripped to shreds like they were made from paper.'

'Could you spare a small piece?'

The man looked up. It was a strange request. 'Take what you want. I got enough in me locker to make a set of royals.' He scratched his head. 'Here!' he said, pushing the bag towards her. 'Take your pick. Darned if I know what you want it for.' He pushed the needle against the leather pad on his palm, pulled it through the layers of canvas and secured it firmly at the other side.

From the sail bag, Emma selected three pieces each the size of a man's handkerchief. 'Thank you,' she said.

With the canvas in one hand she wandered along the deck to the hatch which led down to the seamen's mess and galley. The captain had given her strict instructions not go there, but she needed to see the cook and he appeared kindly. The seaman she feared was ashore.

Emma descended cautiously, feeling for each step with her bare feet. The air rising from the galley fire was warm. It smelled of the pork mixed with woodsmoke and tar. Above the tables three hammocks swayed gently. Two contained the rounded outline of men's bodies. Three seamen were sitting at one of the tables. She had not realized there were so many men still on the ship.

They stared at her as she climbed down. She had interrupted a game of cards. Another man lay with his head resting on his arms. He did not stir. The cook was sitting by the stove eating from one of the large cooking pots. When he saw Emma, he stopped and rubbed his hands across his apron.

'Excuse me,' said Emma, not moving far from the bottom of the stairs. 'Do you have any charcoal?'

The cook looked at the large square stove, its chimney running up through the deck above. 'No, missy. That fire keep going all time. He burn low in the night but he never go out.'

Emma was disappointed but thanked him and climbed back to the fresh air. She was followed by one of the seamen. He had been watching her.

'You want some charcoal?' he said in a husky voice.

She nodded.

'Come with me!'

Emma followed him along the deck. The brazier was cold and empty, but from the bucket of ash he had cleaned from the previous fire, the cooper picked a handful of charcoal.

'Grind it fine,' he said. 'It'll stop the poison in your belly.'

Emma smiled. 'So I have heard. Thank you.'


The sun was dropping towards the mountains on the western end of the island when the first boat returned. The handful of seamen who clamoured noisily on board quickly disappeared below. Joshua was not amongst them, nor François, nor Thomas Barstow.

The early evening air was pleasant and though Emma was tired, she did not want to go below while the aft quarters were empty. She was happy to see the boats returning. The mood on deck was jovial.

Joshua and the other boys were crowded in the longboat, brimful of youthful energy. The taste of local wine no doubt contributed to their animated excitement, their voices louder and coarser than she had ever noticed before.

'Mama,' Joshua shouted, as he scrambled back on to the deck.

Emma greeted him from the rail.

'For you, Mama,' he said, as he pulled a handful of white flowers from beneath his shirt. Though some of the petals were crushed the sweet scent was strong.

Emma was delighted. 'They are beautiful,' she said, resisting the temptation to kiss her son. 'Tell me about the island. What is it like?'

'It is a pretty place. You would like it. Sam and I followed a track up the hill. It was very steep and it led to a church. It was very old and very different from St Mary's.'

'Did you see François?'

Joshua's answer was hesitant. 'We passed him in the town when we were coming back.'

'Was he heading for the ship?'

'No,' he said cautiously. 'I think not.' He looked towards Funchal. 'Samuel has a bag of oranges. They were growing along the roadside. I will bring you some later.'

Emma sniffed the flowers and smiled as Joshua hurried along the deck calling for his mate, Sam, to wait.

The wind was failing by the time the next boat returned. In place of the small sail, four seamen pulled on oars. As the boat neared the *Morning Star*, they shipped the oars spraying a stream of seawater across the captain and Mr Witton sitting in the bow. Before anyone climbed on deck several items were hoisted from the boat's hull. Two small barrels and several bottles of wine, a basket of fruit, several bags, and a large carcass wrapped in linen. The last item was a black box with brass hinges. It appeared to be fairly heavy and its handling was supervised by Mr Witton. When all the goods were off-loaded, the captain and his passenger were assisted from the boat.

On deck, instructions were given. The barrels were hastily despatched to the hold, the carcass to the care of the cook, the bottles of wine and the basket of fruit to the captain's cabin and the black box to Mr Witton's day cabin.

By the time the last boat approached, the sun was low in the western sky. The sailors' return was heralded by the sound of jocular voices which carried across the water. A day in port had raised the men's spirits. As they stumbled on to the deck the tell-tale smells of the taverns came with them. Thomas Barstow was amongst them. Emma hid behind the rigging so he would not see her. She could hear his curses as he pushed another man aside to get down to the lower deck. Her uneasiness returned. But, as the boats were hauled dripping on to the deck, and the rope ladder hoisted from the ship's side, Emma's uneasiness turned to worry.

François had not returned.

# Chapter 16

'Surely not all the men are on board,' Emma said to the mate, as the boat was upturned and secured to the deck.

Another seaman answered. 'Three short!' he called, unconcerned.

'But – the ship won't sail without them, will it?'

'Don't worry, miss,' the sailor said. 'He'll be back.' As he was speaking, he pointed towards the harbour. A local fishing boat similar to the ones which had visited in the morning was heading towards the *Morning Star*. The metal on the mast glinted in the rays of the late afternoon sun. On the boat's deck flashes of red and black appeared to slide beneath the luffing sail.

Emma watched as it approached, hoping it was carrying the three seamen. Praying that François was on board.

A drunken voice drawled across the water. 'Ahoy there! *Morning Star*!' As the distance between the two vessels closed, the boat dropped its sail and with it Emma's heart sank. She moved back from the rail and again slid herself behind the rigging.

François was reclining amidships, his head nestled in the bosom of a dark-haired woman. Another girl was leaning against his legs, her head on the thwart beside him. Emma took little notice of who the other two seamen were but their female companions were young and swarthily attractive, their long hair flowing loose across shoulders tinged amber by the setting sun. The men's necks were draped in slender arms, bare save for their gaudy trinket bracelets.

Cries from the deck were rude and raucous. In comparison, the women's tones were mellow and inviting, and though the language was quite foreign, their words needed little interpretation.

As the fishing boat thudded alongside, the rope ladder was rolled down again.

Emma shrank back. The seamen were obviously drunk. Her heart was thumping and a sickening feeling invaded her belly.

Peering cautiously over the rail, she could see François' hand on the ladder. He leaned back across one of the women, his mouth pressed on hers.

As the swell heaved the boat up the side of the *Morning Star* he was pulled from the woman's grasp. She reached out to him. He reached and grabbed her hand, not wanting to let go. The girl overbalanced, falling backwards against her companion. Arms and legs lashed the air. The men on deck jeered. The man on the rudder cursed his passengers.

'Jump, man!' a voice cried. 'Climb, you fool!'

The little craft slewed out then bumped again.

With both hands on the ladder, François secured his grip and slipped his foot on to the rope.

'Climb, Frenchy!'

He climbed. High enough for the seamen to grab his jacket and pull him headlong on to the deck. His eyes were glistening with excitement – his expression that of a young sailor at his first foreign port. He rolled over on to his back and lay there, grinning.

The two other men were dragged on board in similar fashion. One was forced to the deck when he tried to jump back into the boat. A bucket of seawater dampened the spirits of all three.

François pulled himself up to the gunnels and shouted to the women. Emma heard but did not understand the words. The girls understood and waved their reply. As the fishing boat drifted away, François delivered the contents of his belly to the fishes and with a satisfied expression, dropped back to the deck and closed his eyes.

Emma slid away, back along the deck, down the companionway, to her cabin. She closed the door, slid the bolt and waited. But the tears did not flow. She was angry.

How could she have liked this man? Been so infatuated to imagine she could share a future with him? She had been warned of the nature of sailors, of men like François, by both her neighbour and the old fisherman on the wharf, but she had taken no heed. She had fallen under his charms. She had followed him to the docks. Now she was with him on his ship. Had he enticed other women in distress and received their thanks in kind? Did this behaviour happen in every port?

But he had not tried to woo her. Had not taken advantage of her on the cliff top when he had the chance. He had been kind. Sympathetic.

Could he perhaps love her? A little? Was it his looks, his French manner and lilting accent which had beguiled her? Blinded her to the truth? Even he had tried to warn her he was a wanderer, but she had not listened.

François le Fevre was nothing but a common seaman. A maritime itin-erant. A man aligned to the sea who could not, or would not, escape its clutches. He was a sailor whose life would never change. But he had changed her life and nothing would be the same again. Now she wished she had never met him. Wished she had never agreed to come aboard his ship. Wished the *Morning Star* had sailed and left him in Madeira.

'Emma!' The cry was loud followed by a thump on the cabin door.

'Who is it?' she called, though she recognized the voice.

'It is François! Open the door!'

Her hands were trembling. 'Go away!'

'Open the door! I want to speak with you.'

'Go away!'

He thumped again.

Dropping down from her bunk, Emma slid back the bolt. François was leaning against the wall, his head resting on his forearm.

She could see that the door of the main cabin was slightly open.

'Here,' he said. 'This is for you.' He pressed something into her hand. It was a piece of folded cloth.

She stared up at him.

'Take it! It is a gift,' he said, and without waiting for a response, sniffed and turned away.

Charles Witton stepped out of his cabin. 'Is that man bothering you?'

'No,' Emma replied. 'He brought me this.' She let the folds of cloth fall open. It was a blouse. Tiny flowers of fine embroidery decorated the yoke and cuffs. The same coloured silks were plaited into a braid threaded around the neck. She held it out and shook her head. 'It is a gift.'

Charles Witton stood for a moment, his look uncomfortable. 'Then I will bid you good evening,' he said.

'Very nice indeed,' François said, as he swung himself down from the rigging and walked a full circle around Emma. She smiled unashamedly. His dark eyes responded.

'I did not thank you last night,' she said.

'Last night is a long time ago,' he said. 'Let us forget about last night. The shirt is new, in case you thought maybe it was not. The women on the island—' He cleared his throat. 'The old ones that is, they sit on their doorsteps and do this fancy work. You suit it very well. Do you like it?'

'It is beautiful, François.' She looked across to her old blouse which she had hung on the rigging to dry. 'Now I have two blouses.'

'Then I'm pleased I make you happy. Now, I must get back aloft.'

'François,' she called.

He turned and looked down.

She shook her head. 'It is nothing.'

'Your gift, if I am not mistaken,' Charles observed, when he joined Emma on deck. 'May I say that it is very becoming?'

'Thank you,' she sighed. 'François is thoughtful. He is good to me.'

The man looked disappointed. 'Yes,' he said. 'I see he is, and I now realize that this seaman means something to you.'

She looked at him closely. The early signs of age masked sadness in his face. 'Please understand I am grateful to François. I would not be here if it were not for him.'

'I understand,' he said gently, pulling her aside as a pair of empty barrels was trundled along the deck. 'We will be sailing early in the morning,' he said looking up to check the wind.

'So be it,' she said. The words she spoke had little meaning. They were the words the captain often used, though she was never sure what meaning was behind them. Was it acceptance? Resentment? Cynicism? Or appreciation?

For Emma the ship was her sanctuary. Save for the presence of one man, she felt secure. The crew, both officers and men treated her with politeness, or ignored her. Either way she felt no threat. She had a bunk – something the sailors did not have – and ample rations. When she had been sick, she had been nursed to health, and cared for as if she were a child. On the *Morning Star* she felt free, without any undue pressure.

But when the ship reached Australia all that would change. So far she had given little thought to what her future held. She had few clothes to wear and no accommodation to go to. She knew of no one in Sydney and, despite her schooling, had no professional qualifications. Though well schooled, she had not been brought up to work. She did not know where she would go. What she would do. She had no money: the captain had that. She had no claim on François and her relationship with him was of no consequence. And if Joshua remained at sea, she would have no one to lean upon.

Perhaps, after all, she should have gone to her sister's home. Perhaps

she should have remained in Whitby with George, and accepted her life
and whatever fortune that brought with it. But she had made her choice
to run away and now she must stand by it.

'So be it,' she repeated softly.

From between a pile of barrels on the deck, Emma caught sight of him.
He was standing near the bowsprit, his hand buried in his breeches,
thrusting at himself, relentlessly. How pathetic he was, this decrepit old
seaman. The man she hated and despised.

As she watched, his shoulders slumped forward, his knees faltered. He
grabbed the rail for support. After a few moments he righted himself,
rubbed his crotch and went back to his work. He was unaware and unconcerned that anyone was watching him.

Emma shuddered. What was it about these seamen? Was it the sea that
made them the way they were? The movement of that black body of
water swaying beneath them? All day. Every day. Teasing like the tides. In
and out. Back and forth. Luring them to her but giving nothing in return.
And in the end how many would be sucked down into her darkness.
Emma thought of the mothers of men who succumbed to her clutches.
Names merely entered in a log as: *Lost at Sea.*

She shook her head knowing she should not have witnessed such a
thing. Surely she should be shocked or afraid, or alarmed at what she saw,
but on this occasion she had been compelled to watch, not out of fear or
anger, but out of pity.

# Chapter 17

'Mr Witton, you said I should ask if there was anything I wanted.'
He pushed himself from his chair and fastened his cravat. 'Yes.
What can I get for you?'

'A pen and paper please. A few sheets if you could spare them.'

A look of satisfaction warmed his face dispelling a little of the tiredness his eyes were hiding. 'That is not a problem,' he said. 'In fact it
pleases me you feel well enough to write. I will get those immediately.'

'Thank you,' said Emma. 'But there is no real urgency.'

'Perhaps you would let me be the judge,' he said. 'If this wind holds
I am told we will be arriving in Santa de la Cruz on Friday. It is a busy
port and we will no doubt find some other English vessels in the dock.
I have correspondence of my own. If you will permit me,' he said,
'when you have written your letters, I will seal them for you and they
can be delivered with mine to a reputable ship which is returning
home.'

Emma smiled timidly but did not answer.

He hesitated. 'Perhaps, on the other hand, you would prefer to seal
your own letters. I will supply you with the wax.'

'Oh no! That is not necessary. I would have nothing which is private.
You have already been kind and now I find myself again indulging in your
generosity.'

'Then allow me to satisfy that indulgence,' he said. 'You will have your
writing materials immediately.'

'Missus!'

Emma didn't recognize the voice, but opened her cabin door.

'Water,' the seaman said, placing a wooden pail on the floor. The water slopped from one side to another but being only half full it did not splash over the sides.

'It's hot and it's not salt!' he announced.

'Thank you,' she said, wondering why she had been afforded this luxury.

'Cook says that you are to make sure the bucket comes back to the galley.'

'Would you please tell Mr Sung, I will, and also tell him I said thank you.'

The man nodded and shuffled away.

She lifted the pail into her cabin and closed the door. The rope was coarse and slightly greasy. The wooden slats, though scrubbed clean, were black around the lip with stains of various colours engrained below the waterline. Dipping her hand, Emma was delighted to feel the hot water swirl between her fingers.

Before she had chance to undress, there was another knock on the cabin door. Charles Witton's hands were full. Sheets of paper, blotter, ink, knife and quill.

Emma accepted the items, thanked him, but spoke only briefly. She did not want the water to go cold. As she closed the door, she was conscious of the heaviness which had returned to his face.

That evening, the lamp in her cabin remained lit until late.

'I did not see you on the deck this morning. I trust you are not unwell.'

Emma was embarrassed by the gentleman's attention. 'No, on the contrary,' she said. 'The writing materials you provided for me kept me occupied for a considerable time, both last evening and this morning.'

'Then I am happy. And if there is anything else I can do, please ask.' He inclined his head and wandered back towards the helm where the captain was standing watching them.

'Mama!' shouted Joshua. 'Are you all right?' He climbed down the ratlines and jumped on to the deck.

'I am very well,' she said, breathing deeply on the sea air. 'And I can think of nothing better than being here on this ship. I don't know what life in Sydney will bring, but it can be no worse than what we left behind.'

'But Mama, I will not be—' Their conversation was cut short.

'All hands!' the call went out. 'To the braces! Look lively, lad! Port side! Ease the main!'

Joshua jumped to the order. The deck came alive as men descended from the rigging. Others appeared from the hatches. Emma knew to keep away from the lengths of rope snaked out on the deck. She had heard when a rope started to run, it could strip the skin from a man's hands if he tried to hold it. With both watches on deck and busy, she returned below. For the second night her lamp burned long into the silent hours.

Leaning over the rail, François watched the water curl as the bow cut cleanly through the near flat sea. He did not look at Emma as he spoke. 'You have been trying to ignore me, I think.'

'No, I have been busy. I am sorry if you think I have been rude.'

'Perhaps you have found better company amongst the gentlemen.' His words were cutting.

'That is not true.'

'But you have the passenger to attend to you. The word amongst the men is that he has taken a liking to you.' His look was cold as stone. 'I have seen you on deck laughing with him.'

'Mr Witton has been good to me. He cared for me when I was sick. He shows concern. But there is nothing between us, and I have done nothing to encourage him in any way.'

'But you spend much time below. I thought you hated being in your cabin.'

'Charles brought me pen and paper. It kept me occupied. And cook, he sent me water. Hot water. Not salt. And I washed my blouse and skirt.' She spoke slowly trying to control the sense of irritation she was feeling. 'I am grateful to them both. François, you have been good to me and I would not be here were it not for you.' Her voice had mellowed. 'It is I who have caused you pain and it grieves me to think I would cause you more.'

He shrugged. 'Time will tell!' he said, and walked away.

Why did he make it so hard for her? Why was he jealous? He was strong, good-looking, youthful. And he had stirred in her feelings which she had thought were lost forever. Her feelings for Charles were born out of gratitude. He had nursed her to health. He was gentle and soft, intelligent and kind. Kind like a father. She liked both men but was committed to neither. She stared ahead not looking up into the rigging.

A pleasured smirk snaked across Tom Barstow's face as he dropped

*Margaret Muir*

lightly to the deck in front of her. She started. Looked back for François but he was nowhere to be seen. 'Please, let me pass,' she said.

'Please,' he laughed. 'Saying please to Old Tom. I like that.'

Emma looked about. No one was watching them.

'Tonight I'll come and visit you. Not a word to anyone mind. You and me's got unfinished business. Remember?' His tongue flapped like a rutting goat's.

'Get out of my way!' she shouted.

'Tonight!' he hissed.

His forced laughter rang in her ears as she hurried back below. She shot the bolt hard, and stood in the darkness with her back to the door, her body shaking.

During the long evening she slid from her bunk several times to check that the door was still locked. Though it was black as pitch, she was afraid to undress, afraid to sleep, afraid of every sound, especially the sound of feet and creaking boards outside her cabin door.

The men appeared from the two forward hatchways. No one hurried. No one spoke. Burials at sea were always met with uncomfortable familiarity. The cloudless sky and sun lifting over the starboard side did nothing to raise the feeling of heaviness which was hanging like a wet sail over the ship.

Captain Preston paced the deck. He was in a black mood and becoming increasing impatient by the minute. The mate suffered the brunt of his agitation.

'Let's get these proceedings over and done with,' he snarled. 'What's keeping those bloody men?'

The second mate, Will Wortley, yelled down the stairs: 'All hands on deck! Now!'

The seamen congregated slowly, shuffling around the corpse stitched into its canvas wrapping. The cabin door on which it lay was at least eighteen inches shorter than the length of the man.

'Bloody waste of a good hammock, if you ask me!' a seaman mumbled as he tapped his pipe against his knee. 'Bloody waste!'

The captain scowled at the line of faces. 'Who said that? Mr Thackray, find out who said that and make sure when it's his turn to go over, his hammock is weighted with salt pork for the sharks!'

'What's got into him?' one of the young seamen whispered. 'I never seen the captain in a mood as black as this before.'

'Always like this if someone dies. Gets angry as a bull seal at breeding time. Takes it to heart, he does. Like they did it just to spite him.' The talking stopped as the captain approached.

'Get these men in order! Let's get on with this!'

'All right you lot!' Wortley shouted. 'Up straight. You! Take your hat off! Show a bit of respect! You 'eard the capt'n.'

The ragged crew formed into two loose lines. Joshua and the younger boys were unwillingly pushed to the front. Emma could see François standing behind them. Because of his lack of height, Tom Barstow's face was hidden behind the other men, but Emma knew exactly where he was. On the narrow deck, a margin of only a man's stride was left between the row of seamen and the body sewn in its canvas envelope.

From the bow, Emma could not hear all the captain's words. She had not known the man. Yorkie, he was called. Ben Yorke of Whitby. Charles had described him to her. Blond. Nineteen. Long-legged and fine-looking, save for a cast in his left eye. A good topmast man. Perhaps that was the reason she had seen little of him on the deck before his accident. Even though Charles had described him in detail, she could not remember him. That made her feel guilty, disrespectful. She knew that somewhere in the North Yorkshire port there was a mother who would not know her son had died. A mother who might learn his fate – in six months' time – or in a year – or perhaps she may never hear what happened to her boy. One thing was certain: she would never see her son again.

In the front row, one of the boys giggled nervously. A sharp poke in the back took the smile from his face. He cursed the man standing behind him.

Joshua did not look up.

Mr Witton appeared preoccupied. He had his back turned against the morning's proceedings. He was gazing across the water as if watching a ship sailing by.

Nathaniel Preston held a worn black book in his hands though it was never opened. The words which commended the body of Benjamin Yorke to the deep were recited by rote, not read. The burial service was in accordance with the proceedings set out for Her Majesty's naval ships. As it concluded two of the older sailors lifted the cabin door. It tilted and the body of the boy from the fishing port slipped over the side and was received by the passing sea.

The captain tapped the book on his leg. Like the men he had a hankering to get away.

'Dismiss the men, sir?' the mate asked quietly.

The captain was staring at the cabin door on the deck. Staring at the holes where the hinges had been. Staring at the stain left on the wood. He glared at his officer. 'What are you waiting for, Mr Thackray? Get on with it! And get this deck swabbed!'

'You heard the captain! Move! Now! Get on with it!'

The lines broke. The men who were not on watch scuttled below before any further duties were handed out.

Emma ran to the side. She was the only one to look back along the ship's wake in an attempt to see the spot which marked where the seaman had been buried. But the sea bore no mark and already the small disturbance his weighted body had caused had disappeared. No evidence remained of what had taken place and young Ben Yorke would quickly be forgotten.

'I could not help him,' Charles murmured sadly. His cheeks bore the stain of tears.

'His death was no fault of yours.'

'I tried,' he said. 'But I lacked the skill. His arm should have been removed. I bound it but beneath the bandages it turned bad and then it was too late. I know I should not blame myself, but if only . . .'

Emma sensed his depth of grief which went beyond the loss of the young seaman. 'Can I be of any help?'

'Not now.'

They walked in silence towards the helm.

'I must go below. The captain may need some company at this time.'

'Is there anything wrong?' Emma asked, as he stepped back down the steps.

'No,' he said pensively. 'Nothing anyone can change.' He stood for a moment looking along the deck. 'I don't know what it is about a ship and a man's relationship with the sea, but when things happen on board somehow they seem to get magnified. Perhaps it is because it is a confined space and for those who live on board it is their whole world. Small. Claustrophobic. They know no better. The sea is their life. They live it, twenty-four hours every day and seven days every week. It is all they want to live for and when they die it is the sea they want to return to. I find it hard to understand.'

Emma waited not knowing what to say.

He paused. 'The ship will dock on the island of Tenerife the day after tomorrow. I understand the crew will be given time to go ashore. I wondered...' He sighed. 'Would you care to take a drive with me into the town? I will hire a carriage. There are several places, quite respectable, where we can purchase a cup of coffee or tea.' He looked for Emma's response. 'Or I can ask cook to make up a picnic basket which we can take with us. Santa Cruz is an interesting port and I would be happy to show you a little of it, if you would agree to accompany me.'

Emma smiled and thanked him, but her smile quickly faded into disappointment.

'What is it?' he said. 'Have I offended you?'

'No,' she said, looking down at herself. 'How can I accompany you, a fine gentleman in a carriage dressed this way? I neither look nor feel presentable and I dare say my presence with you may raise some eyebrows.'

'I am not concerned how you are dressed.'

'But I am. I would not go into town dressed like this.' She held out the front of her skirt which bore the stain of ink the size of a dinner plate. 'And the only good blouse I have—'

'The one François gave you?'

'Yes.'

He sighed and shook his head. 'I have said before, I am a thoughtless man. My head is filled with past events. At times I think I have forgotten how to care for the present. Forgive me, Emma. Say yes. Come with me, if only for a carriage ride to enjoy the sights. It will do us both good.'

'I will think about it,' she said.

'So be it,' he said.

She watched as he stepped back through the hatchway and climbed down to the lower deck. She knew he was weary.

Suddenly cold water swirled around her feet. It startled her.

'Like to tease, don't you?' Old Tom hissed, as he scrubbed the deck around her.

She turned her head from his rancid smell.

'I'm sure you ain't forgotten your promise.' The toothless mouth gaped open as he dowsed the remaining water towards her legs.

Emma turned and felt for the companionway steps beneath her feet.

'Your boy got a good fitting hammock, has he?'

As she climbed backwards through the hatch, his leathery foot stamped down on her hand clamping her fingers like a rat caught in a trap. Tom Barstow lowered his head to hers and breathed in her face. 'Now I'm feeling ready for you. Mark my words, in a few days you're gunna get what's coming to you!'

# Chapter 18

A seagull sat on the end of the bowsprit content as a duck on a clutch of eggs. It looked as much a part of the *Morning Star* as the brass bell engraved with the same name. Though the bell swung rhythmically to the ocean's pulse, the gull showed no inclination to change its position. It was oblivious to the sweeping motion of the bow, carried up one moment like a rising shuttlecock, then crashing back to the sea like a sack of lead shot. Perched at the tip of the ship, the seagull sat proudly like a feathered figurehead.

'Been there since morning,' the sailmaker said.

'Is that unusual?'

'They like to take a ride sometimes. But he's cunning that one. I've seen him before. He was in that same spot the day before yesterday.' The old man got up and took Emma's elbow. 'Look there,' he pointed. 'On his chest. You can make out a sprig of yellow. I thought it was a daub of tar or paint but I've watched him cleaning himself. It's a feather all right. And bright yellow. A bit of cross blood in him, I reckon.'

'Could you ask him to stay for a while?'

'Won't take no notice of me, missus,' he answered seriously.

'Never mind,' she said. 'I'll be back in a moment.'

Emma hurried back along the deck, jumping over the lengths of rope waiting to be coiled and returned to the pin rails. After collecting the items from the cabin which she required, she returned on deck and was pleased to find that the bird had not flown away.

Though the wind occasionally fluffed its feathers, the gull did not move.

Sitting cross-legged on the deck and resting her paper on a piece of board Emma dipped her pen in the ink and started to sketch. Jack Burns eyed her curiously.

As the ocean turned beneath the hull, rolling and turning like a body in a restless sleep, she worked; completely absorbed; her mind blocked off to everything but the subject posing for her. She heard nothing of the cries for sails to be trimmed. Heard nothing of the whispers from the men whose curiosity brought them to lean over as they passed. Never noticed them as they hovered round and pointed.

The seagull was copied in fine detail, from the hook of its beak, to the distinctive tip of its tail quills, each blackened as if dipped in a pot of pitch. Even the twisted feather bursting from its chest was etched lightly. She could add a dab of colour to it later.

Throughout the sitting, the bird's eye remained half open as if regarding the artist inquisitively.

Occasionally she stopped to examine her work. The proportions were sound, yet in her opinion the sketch was poor. The position of the eye was correct and its gaze was lifelike. She had caught the correct curvature of the beak and had shaded the subtle variations in the grey feather tones without difficulty. Yet, something about it was wrong. The legs. She attempted them again in the corner of the page.

'I'll give a shilling for it,' the sailmaker said.

'It is yours when I have finished.'

A half circle had formed around her. Watching.

'Stone me dead!' a voice cried. 'I ain't seen now't like that before. Like she's got the bird and stuck it on the paper if you ask me.'

The gull had been an ideal model.

'Here you are,' she said, as she handed the drawing to the old man.

The small gathering on the foredeck attracted the mate. 'Give me a look!' he said, as he saw what the attraction was.

Jack Burns, reluctant to hand over his property, held it at arm's length. 'Here. Take a gawk!' As the wind fluttered the paper, he gripped it firmly as if afraid the disturbance might cause the bird to fly away.

Len Thackray studied it, running his fingers along the line of wing feathers. Emma feared if he rubbed too hard, the ink would smudge.

'Get your dirty paws off it!' the old man yelled. 'Nobody touches!' As he shuffled away to deposit his possession in his sea chest, Emma picked up her materials and the crowd broke up.

'I see you have been busy this morning,' François said.

Emma wondered how long he had been there.

'A little silly sketching to pass the time.'

'You enjoy doing that, I see.'

'Yes.'

'I think you are very clever.'

'No.'

'I think you are very good at what you do.'

Emma smiled. 'It is far from perfect. It should be better. But it amused me.'


That evening Emma ate her meal on deck. The days were longer in these latitudes and the evening air warm. She had not forgotten the captain's advice about staying below after dark, but a big white moon was rising and with several sailors lazing around she felt relaxed. This evening she did not want to go below.

Leaning against the rail, Emma watched the sea as it curled along the side of the ship creating its own small waves in its wake. She was pleased to see François when he stepped up on deck and joined her. He read the greeting in her eyes.

They spoke of the sunset and the sea and she asked him about his life. About Brittany and what the French countryside was like. About why he had run away from home as a boy to become a sailor. Throughout the conversation she made no mention of Madeira.

'Enough of my past,' he said, with a flick of the hand as if wafting his words to the wind. 'Tell me about yourself. What you have done. Where you have been.' He inclined his head to one side and looked into Emma's eyes. 'I once overheard you telling an old fisherman you sailed to France. Tell me about that. When you were a small girl.'

'You have a good memory,' she said.

The Frenchman smiled cheekily.

'Some things in the past one can never forget,' she mused. 'Because they are printed on the mind like words in a book. When I was a child life was wonderful. How can I ever forget that time?'

She could feel his eyes on her as she looked out across the water, to the ripples shimmering in the moonlight.

'You sailed to Le Havre, if I am not mistaken?'

'Yes. From the docks in London, on a clipper. When we arrived in France we were met by a coach and taken to a château – not far from Paris.'

'A château! That sounds very grand.'

'It was grand indeed. I was just a girl. I thought it was a palace.'

His eyes sparkled. 'Tell me about this palace you went to.'

'I remember it clearly. There were lots of rooms and broad staircases. And covering every wall were paintings in gilded frames. Portraits of ladies in elegant gowns and of the French countryside in springtime.'

'And?'

'And in the dining-hall there was a table long enough to seat every sailor on this ship. And on it were silver candelabras shining with dozens of candles.'

'And it was there you learned to speak French?' François said, with a glint in his eye.

Emma smiled broadly and nodded.

'How long did you stay?'

'For more than six months,' she said. 'My papa had been invited to paint a portrait of a lady. She was a widow and, I think, very rich. My papa was a very good artist and well respected. He had painted several English lords and ladies, but it was the first time he had been commissioned to paint in Europe.'

François raised his eyebrows.

'When the picture was finished *madame* was delighted. To celebrate, she arranged a big party and invited many important guests. But despite their rank, she insisted that Papa was the only *célébrité*.'

'Your father enjoyed his popularity, no doubt?'

'Alas, no. He never wished for that. But his work was popular and his services sought after. He was invited to stay in France, but Mama was not happy there. She wanted to go home. It was strange for her. Poor, dear Mama, she felt uncomfortable in so grand a place.'

Emma closed her eyes and swayed against the rail. 'But I am boring you,' she said. 'You do not want to listen to this childish talk.'

'You are not boring me. And I can see from your eyes these things make you happy. I think in the past you have seen much sadness. These memories are good. Continue.'

Emma glanced at François' tar-stained shirt and the shock of unruly hair tied with a strip of greasy leather. 'The estate covered many acres like a great park. And from the ornamental gardens flowering with a full palette of colour, a mosaic path led between two rows of marble statues to a lake with a fountain in the centre. The water pattered from it like heavy rain on paving slabs.

'In the afternoons, my sister and I would wander down to the lake. We would chase butterflies, or weave daisy chains, or make boats out of leaves and sail them on the water. We would pretend we were sailing to the

Indies or America.' She laughed. 'I never thought I would sail to Australia.'

As the shadows of the square sails swayed across the ship's deck, Emma smiled and breathed the night. In her mind it was filled with the fragrance of the château's gardens: scents of rose, jasmine and honeysuckle, and memories of a boy she had met beside the pattering fountain.

François interrupted her dreaming. 'And when your father's work was finished, you went back to England?'

'Yes,' Emma said, as she looked down to the spume turning from the ship's bow. In the frothy foam tiny pinpricks of light shone and faded. 'I do not know why I am telling you these things. I have not spoken about them for many years.'

She pushed the hair from her eyes. The moon was high and it was late.

'I must go,' she said.

'No,' he begged. 'Stay a little longer. For me. Please.'

# Chapter 19

'Would you step into my cabin for a moment? There are two things I want to speak with you about.'

Charles Witton's tone was out of character. Emma accepted politely, but was unsure if his demeanour was masking embarrassment or hiding an underlying feeling of annoyance. She followed him into his day cabin.

'Please take a seat.'

Emma perched on the edge of the straight chair as she allowed her eyes to feast on both the cabin and its contents. It was the first time she had been into his day quarters.

It was a small stateroom, half the size of the captain's, but still spacious enough for a narrow table and two chairs. On the built-in desk lay several large leather-bound books, their spines adorned with gold embossed characters and roman numerals. A vacant space on the shelf above the desk indicated where the volumes usually resided. The adjacent cupboards fixed to the hull, ran from ceiling to floor save for a small round window. The natural light it provided, though limited, was a great improvement on the glow from an oil lamp.

Sitting in the centre of the table was the box Emma had seen hoisted aboard in Funchal Bay. Black-stained wood with shiny brass corners and hinges, it was set on its end, the lid open like a door. Fitted inside was a microscope, its brasses also brightly polished. An ocular lens lay on a piece of blue velvet.

Mr Witton closed the lid of the instrument box. 'A gift from an old friend,' he said as he squeezed awkwardly between the table and a large cabin trunk which was taking up most of the floor space. A scrap of white cloth was protruding from beneath the lid of the chest. The padlock complete with its key lay on the table.

Facing Emma, Charles appeared uncomfortable. She cupped her hands

148

on her lap and waited.

'I must know,' he said gravely, as he turned and reached for a piece of paper from his desk, 'are you responsible for this?' He handed it to Emma. It was the drawing of the seagull.

'Yes,' she replied cautiously. 'I did not think that you would mind that I used your writing paper to draw on.'

'No! No! Just tell me, did you really draw this?'

'Yes.'

He leaned forward as Emma looked down at the picture. 'This is one of the most observant drawings I have seen since my visits to the Society's rooms some years ago. It reminds me of the fine work of an unfortunate young artist, Sydney Parkinson. He sailed with Cook to the South Seas. You may have heard of him.'

Emma shook her head.

'It is anatomically correct and quite exquisite.'

Emma smiled and handed the paper back to him.

'I gave it to the sailmaker. I believe his name is Jack Burns.'

'Yes, yes. He showed it to me and I could not resist asking him if I might borrow it.' His face and tone relaxed. 'I must say he was reticent at first, and I can understand why. I had to promise I would return it to him this afternoon.' He studied the picture and shook his head. 'Though it seems such a waste. This quality of work should be set in a frame.'

She acknowledged his compliment with a smile.

'But tell me, where did you learn? Which school did you study at? Do you have any more?'

'My father taught me,' she said, allowing herself to relax against the chair back. 'Both my sister and I learnt at home.' She digressed. 'She is far better with oils. I have always been more comfortable with pen and ink.'

'Do you have any more of these?' he repeated. 'Could you do some more?'

'I have four or five sketches in the cabin. They have kept me occupied lately.'

'And I thought . . .' He placed the picture beneath one of the books on his desk. 'No matter,' he said. 'I want to ask a favour. Would you permit me to supply you with whatever materials you require so that you can pursue your art whenever you feel inclined?'

'That would be very kind of you. It is a pastime which gives me a great deal of pleasure.' She smiled. 'It also keeps me out of harm's way.'

'But where do you draw? I have not seen you working.'

'Sometimes on the deck, but mostly in the cabin.'

'But the light must be poor and you have no proper bench to work on. Oh, Emma,' he said, 'why am I so blind and inconsiderate. You must forgive my failings. From now on,' he said, 'I insist, you work in here.' He hesitated. 'That is if you would not object to sharing these surroundings. You may use the table and you are welcome to come whenever you wish. It would give me great pleasure.'

'That is a very kind offer, but the captain—'

'Do not concern yourself about the captain. I will speak with him. He will understand, I assure you. But I ask your permission to show this drawing to him. I am sure he will be as impressed as I am, and I guarantee he will be surprised to learn that you are the artist.'

Emma blushed. 'As you wish.'

'That brings me to my second question.' He edged around the table and leaned down to the cabin trunk. His voice again adopted a serious tone. 'I find this matter a little difficult to broach as I do not want to cause you embarrassment.' He lifted the hasp on the chest and opened the lid.

From where she sat Emma was unable to see the contents of the trunk.

Charles looked directly at her. 'I understand that due to unforseen circumstances you boarded the ship without luggage. You told me in your own words, you have few clothes apart from those you are wearing now.' He breathed deeply and gazed down to the contents of the chest. 'This chest contains the personal effects of my wife and daughter, God rest their souls. I have no use for them.' He sat back into the chair.

'I am truly sorry.'

'I did not know what to do with them,' he said, gazing through the window. Across the sky, fine lines of parallel cloud stretched out like warp threads on a giant loom. 'But I could not dispose of them so I had them consigned with me on the ship.' He looked at Emma. 'If there are any items here which could be of use to you, you are welcome to them.'

Response was not easy, but before Emma could speak, he held up his hand. 'I know nothing of the fickleness of ladies' fashions, but I assure you the garments are of best quality materials and workmanship, and if you will excuse me for saying, they will be far more becoming than the attire you are currently wearing.'

Emma fingered the stain on her lap.

'Please,' he said, without waiting, 'you would be doing me a favour if you would at least accept some of these things. And if the dresses do not fit I will find a dressmaker to make the alterations when we are in port.

Please,' he said, as he held out his hand to help Emma to her feet, 'take a little time. Examine them. I will leave you alone.'

As he stood beside the door, she could see the tension had vanished from his face. The lines around his eyes fanned into a caring smile.

'Perhaps, later this afternoon, you will show me your other drawings.'

'Yes,' she said.

'I will look forward to that.'


The cooper touched the knuckle of his index finger to his forehead. 'Enjoy your day, miss.' The seamen rolling the empty water barrels across lashed planks stopped and gawped at Emma as she disembarked. The captain watched from the quarterdeck.

With layers of fine cotton clouding her legs, Emma was unable to see her feet. Fortunately the laced boots she was wearing were made from the softest suede and easily moulded to the shape of her feet. After padding the deck bare-foot for three weeks, she was pleased they did not pinch her toes. With her gloved hand held firmly by Mr Witton, Emma tripped lightly across the gangplank and on to the noisy quay at Santa Cruz de Tenerife.

A carriage was waiting for them. 'Let me help you,' Charles said, as he took her arm. She swayed against him as she climbed the two small steps.

'I am sorry,' she said. 'I feel I am still moving with the ship.'

'That is not unusual,' he said 'It is good to go ashore whenever in port. I like to reclaim my land legs, even if only for a short time.'

From the busy wharf the rig rumbled slowly through the sprawling town. As Emma's eyes flitted butterfly-like, Charles Witton regarded her closely. She scanned the streets, houses, stalls and shops, indulging herself in all Santa Cruz had to offer.

'It is place of contrasts,' she said. 'The ugly black beaches. The white houses. The pale turquoise sea. And the great grey mountain ugly and plain yet caped in ermine. And the colours of the flowers, magenta, yellow, indigo – so vibrant. I had not imagined it to be like this. It is charming.'

'And may I say, you are charming too.'

Emma smiled coyly.

'Let us find somewhere to sit for a while. May I suggest a short drive out of the town and into the hills? I guarantee the air there will be cool and fresh.' He turned and spoke to the driver.

Emma was surprised at his command of the Spanish language.

*

From the garden of a small café they looked down to the ocean, a sea of blues, greens and aquamarine dotted with flecks of white – the single sails of local fishing boats.

'It looks so smooth from here,' said Emma. 'Yet we experienced so much turbulence on the way.'

'Yes,' he said. 'Life can be unkind.' He reached across the table. 'May I?' he said, as he took her hand and lifted it into his. 'I think you are a remarkable woman, Emma Quinlan. And, if I may say, you look lovely today.'

'It is the clothes,' she said, looking down at the layers of frills which decorated her dress. 'The clothes are lovely.' She unfastened the bow from under her chin and laid her bonnet on the table. 'I trust it does not bring back too many sad memories seeing me wearing them.'

'On the contrary,' he said. 'It upset me to see them locked away.'

'Please tell me of your family, if it is not too painful.'

Charles smiled sadly as he gazed along the rugged coastline. 'My wife died of consumption, October last year. She had been ailing for several years but her death came as a shock. I felt guilty that I had neglected her. I had just returned from Australia and had not been aware how ill she was. I had always wanted her to go overseas with me. Begged her. But she would not leave England. She loved the English countryside and I think she was afraid of the sea voyage.'

He turned to Emma. 'After her death I did not want to stay in England, and as Charlotte, our daughter, was eager to see the colonies, I booked a passage for us both. The Royal Society offered me the opportunity to join a scientific expedition. I accepted. I thought it would be good to keep myself occupied. My intention was that, when we arrived, Charlotte could stay with our friends in Sydney. She was looking forward to it.

'She was unlike her mother,' he said. 'She was afraid of nothing. She had my enthusiasm for travel and a zest and confidence not usually seen in young ladies her age. Alas, perhaps, too much. Six weeks ago she fell from her horse.' He sighed heavily. 'She clung to life for a week, but never woke once in that time. I spoke to her while she lay unconscious but I do not know if she could hear me. On the seventh night she died. She was seventeen.'

Emma waited a while before speaking. 'What will you do now when you get to Sydney?'

'I will catch up with the expedition. They will not be too far ahead. I should have been with the main party when they sailed from London three weeks ago but the arrangements which had to be made delayed me. Then I had difficulty finding another ship and thought I would have to abort my journey.

'When Nathaniel offered me a berth on the *Morning Star*, I was pleased to accept. It was fortunate for me, he too had been delayed. I know you do not know him as I do, but the captain is a good man. He, too, has been confronted with considerable trauma in his life, though of a different nature.' He looked at Emma. 'Nathaniel Preston is my brother-in-law. My wife was his youngest sister.'

A girl appeared from the house carrying a jug of fresh lemonade. She refilled their glasses. As they drank the conversation flowed easily. Charles spoke enthusiastically of his books, the first editions he had collected which were travelling with him, carefully packed in one of his trunks, and the countries he had visited. They watched a pair of butterflies flitting between the flowers and listened to the hum of bees which swarmed past them swirling like a column of chimney smoke. In turn, Emma spoke of her sister. Her childhood. Of Lincolnshire and cows and memories. They shared the patchwork snippets which create a lasting picture.

'Would you care to walk a little?' he said.

The verdant grass, a product of the rich volcanic soil, was soft beneath their feet. Overhead, trees rustled in the light breeze. Multi-coloured flowers cascaded from stone walls and arches while in the fields twisted old vines, thick and nobbled, crept along fences or stood with arms extended like drooping scarecrows, the leaves dancing lightly from the wood. Above them the snow-capped peak of the sleeping mountain glistened in the sun.

'So peaceful,' Charles said. 'If only it could always be this way.'

As the sun was shielded by the line of mountains, dusk fell on the streets of Santa Cruz. Night clouds rolling in from the west looked ominous.

'Damn them!' the captain cried. He could wait no longer. 'Damn them!' he murmured.

'Cast off!'

The aft line splashed in to the sea and the last seaman stepped aboard before the gap between ship and jetty widened. Will Wortley and two other men slid the gangplank back on to the deck as the *Morning Star*'s bow nudged along the jetty, timber squealing on timber. The wharf recoiled under the pressure but the boys who were fishing from its decking were unconcerned.

For a moment the ship remained motionless, as if not knowing which way to head, then slowly, creating only the lightest ripples, it drifted from the wharf, floating seaward on the placid harbour like a piece of flotsam. Without a call, the heavy mooring ropes were hauled on board to bask on the open deck like sleeping serpents. With the helm hard over, the canvas dropped and the *Morning Star* sailed from Santa Cruz de Tenerife, gliding silently between other ships anchored in the busy port.

As it met the ocean's swell it rolled. The wind lifted the sails.

'Take her out, Mr Thackray.'

With little light left the *Morning Star* sailed towards the south east.

'How many?' the captain asked impatiently.

'Two.'

Nathaniel Preston looked back towards Tenerife. Pinpricks of light flickered from windows in the old town. The white buildings looked black, and the grey mountain which dominated the island by day had disappeared into the clouds.

'Damn them!' the captain cried. 'Damn their ungrateful souls!'

# Chapter 20

Captain Preston handed the telescope to the mate. 'What do you make of that, Mr Thackray?'

The mate scanned the sea but saw nothing. No ships, no land, not even white caps. He put the piece to his eye, adjusted it and searched again.

'A column of smoke?'

'That is what I thought.'

'A ship on fire?'

'I think not.' The captain blinked his right eye and massaged it gently. 'If I am not mistaken what we are seeing is coming from Fogo!'

The mate handed back the telescope. 'But ain't we still a day's sailing from Cape Verde, Captain?'

'By my calculations, fifty nautical miles.' Captain Preston stepped up on to the boatswain's locker balancing himself against the rigging. 'If my assumption is correct and if what we are seeing is smoke, then what we are looking at is something mighty big,' he said cautiously. 'I fear that is a cloud of ash which is extremely tall and is being carried this way.'

'But doesn't our bearing take us well to the west of the islands? You had no intention of sailing in there, had you?'

'Correct, Mr Thackray. A place best to be avoided. But a volcanic erup-tion . . . that is a worry.' The captain swung himself up on to the rigging but without the telescope the ominous cloud was not visible. 'I want you to reduce sail, Mr Thackray. Keep the same bearing but get a good man up top with a glass. Tell him to keep a close watch on that cloud but tell him to also give a good eye to the sea. I want to be informed of the slight-est change in either.'

'Aye, Captain.'

'And get the men to look sharp about furling the sails. I want everything lashed down tight and double checked and the main hatches locked down.'

Len Thackray called for all hands but the response was slow, the men grumbled as they filtered on to the deck and climbed slowly. As the calls went out, the two largest square sails were hauled up to their yards and gasketed. The men on the downhauls moved steadily, stepping over the tangled mess of sheets and lines.

Muttered grumbles were heard from the crew who were unaware of the reason for reducing sail. The sky showed no inclination to storm. There was no damage to the ship and there were no other vessels bearing down. And besides, the *Morning Star* had been struggling to make four knots in the light conditions. In the opinion of the men there was no justification for reducing sail further.

'Tidy those lines!' the mate shouted. 'And quick about it! I've seen lubbers do a better job!' But the men still worked grudgingly, cursing the captain's orders which had taken them from their relaxation.

'What's happening, Nathaniel?' Charles asked, as he joined his brother-in-law near the helm.

The captain indicated the direction of the possible problem and handed him the glass. 'Very low on the horizon. Take a look.'

'Looks like a speck of grey fluff to me.'

'If I'm not wrong it's smoke from a volcano. Fogo in the Verde Islands. What concerns me is that we were not advised of it before we left Tenerife. My assumption therefore can only be that it has just exploded.'

'Does that put us in any danger?'

'I can't be sure,' he said. 'It's a mountain that erupts every few years. I remember hearing about it in '52 when I was on the *Lord Clarence*, and again in '54. What concerns me is its size. That cloud is way beyond the horizon, yet we can see it from here. That means it is huge and it is rising to a great height. If the explosion was only recent and a big one, it could have stirred up a tidal wave that hasn't yet reached us. All I know is that since we left the Canaries we have not experienced any big waves.' He paused. 'What we do not know is when the explosion happened.'

'Perhaps the volcano is only grumbling. Could that be possible? I gather some smoke constantly.'

'It is possible.'

'Do you intend to sail close in?'

'No. I will chart a wide course. Unfortunately that will take us further west than I had originally planned. The only hope then is that we do not get ourselves becalmed in the process.'

'What can I do?'

'I suggest you batten down anything in your cabin which is loose or fragile. If the sea builds up it could become a little damp and lumpy.'

'You have a delightful way of understating the obvious, Nathan.'

The captain winked. 'Then, perhaps I should have said, it could be like a dam when the wall breaks.'

'Much better,' Charles said. 'Now I understand.'

It was a wearying afternoon. Sailing with only its topgallants before the wind, the ship made slow headway. The men on deck, now aware of the possible danger, observed the progress of the creeping cloud which had loomed up from the horizon and was advancing across the sky, broadening and deepening with each mile that was covered. Opinions as to its origin and significance were argued by the men at the rails. From her favourite place in the bow, Emma found herself more interested in a pod of dolphins which was accompanying the ship on its slow south-westerly bearing.

'I have not seen you on deck much these days.' François' tone was cynical. 'Not since you went ashore on the arm of the gentleman. I hear you now spend your time in his cabin. Perhaps you have become too fancy to speak with a common seaman.'

'François, that is not so. I have been drawing.'

'Ah! I remember,' he said. 'The artist!'

'François, I believe you are jealous. But you have no reason to be. And I have no reason to feel guilty.'

'Of course.' The disparaging tone was still evident.

'The dresses! That is what you do not like, that he has given some things to me. Is it that which has upset you?'

'I am not upset. Why should I be?' He turned away from her, his arms folded across his chest.

'François,' she said firmly. 'I like to draw and Mr Witton has generously allowed me to use his day cabin. I am alone when I am working. He goes on deck. I don't know why it makes you annoyed.'

His voice mellowed. 'I am not! I am pleased for you,' he said. 'But I admit, when I saw you leaving the ship and going with him on the island I was angry. I had forgotten you were born a lady. And Mr Witton is a gentleman.'

'But François, when we get to Sydney . . .'

'Ah! Sydney. When we get there…' He laughed a strange laugh. 'You wish to gaze into the crystal ball? You want to know what the future holds?' He looked at her, his eyes questioning hers. 'Tell me this, what is it you want to see? What is it you wish for? Deep inside your heart?'

'I do not know what I wish for!'

'Then let me guess. I would suggest that you do not wish to live your life alone. That you would wish to take another husband. And, if I dare suggest, since we first met by the abbey, you may have wished that man to be me. Am I right? Was that your wish?'

Emma looked confused. 'I don't know.'

'Tell me truthfully, would you like it if I were to leave the ship in Sydney? I have some money you know. I could buy a piece of land and work each day from dawn till dusk till I was an old man.' The smile had left his eyes. 'I can tell you that is not what I would wish. Being tied to one place would be an anchor around my neck. As I told you, I've been at sea since I was a boy. And even now, when we are in port, I hanker for the day we leave. I wander the wharfs looking at the water, wishing for nothing better than to be back on it.' He shook his head. 'There is salt in my veins and my place is here. I would rather drown in the bosom of the ocean, than die a rich man on the streets of Sydney, and that is the truth.'

His tone relaxed. 'I made only one promise to you, Emma, and that I will keep. But I made no promise to you that I would leave the sea. When the *Morning Star* docks in Sydney, you will go ashore alone. As for me, I will sail with the ship. It is better you do not waste any of your thoughts and wishes on me.'

A cry from the mainmast brought the crew hurrying to the port side. 'Boat! Four points off the starboard bow!'

A small boat was bobbing on the swell. It carried no sail and the sea was in control of its rudder. The red and white clinkered hull looked empty, adrift, then a man clambered to his feet and supported himself against the mast. He was half naked. Black. His hair was white.

'What do you make of it, Capt'n?'

As the *Morning Star* sailed closer, the bodies of half-a-dozen other men, all black skinned could be seen lying in the boat's hull. There was nothing to protect them from the glaring sun.

'Trouble,' answered the captain shaking his head.

'Pirates?' the helmsman asked.

'Two skins of water,' the captain ordered. 'Be ready to toss them overboard and quick about it.'

'Do we lose some sail, Captain?'

'No! Make sail, Mr Thackray!'

'Aye, aye, sir.'

The crew responded quickly to the call for sail. From the bobbing boat the man's cries went unheeded.

When Emma realized the *Morning Star* was about to sail past the boat she dashed along deck. 'Captain! Captain!' she shouted, pointing to the man who was waving his arms desperately. 'You must stop the ship!'

The boat was no more than twenty yards away.

'Stop! Stop!' she cried.

The captain turned his back towards her.

Before she reached the quarterdeck, Charles grabbed her by the arms. She struggled against his grip. 'Those men!' she shouted to the captain. 'Why will you not help them? They will perish out there!'

'Emma, please stop it!' Charles begged.

'No!' she cried. 'You must stop him. Tell him to stop this ship. You must help them! Are you blind?' she cried out again. 'Can't you see they are dying?'

From the stern, Nathaniel Preston scowled at her as Charles led her by the arm to the companionway.

'It is best if you go below, Emma. At least until this incident is over.'

'But why does he not help them? They will die!'

'The captain knows best. It is a decision he alone must make. Please, let me take you below. To my cabin . . .'

'No, I can manage, thank you.'

As the small boat slid by the side of the *Morning Star*, the man held up his arms in supplication. The two goatskins, tossed overboard, landed close beside the boat but no effort was made to retrieve them. It was not long before the man's cries were left behind. The only sound on deck was the wind in the sails and the creak of the ship's timbers. Even the crew was silent. The red and white hull was soon a speck on the sea. A piece of drifting flotsam.

Emma lay back on her bunk unable to dispel thoughts of the scene she had witnessed. The expression on the black man's face was fixed in her mind. The anguish, anger, desperation and despair were unforgettable. She felt them all.

What manner of man was Nathaniel Preston who could turn his back on a human being pleading for help? And the other men, already dead or close to death lying in the bottom of the boat. How could he leave them to perish adrift in an open boat under a blazing sun? How could François and Charles describe the captain as a good man? His actions were incomprehensible and unforgivable.

Outside her door, the boards creaked. She sat up cradling her knees in her arms. She held her breath and listened. The doorknob rattled. She watched it turn around and back. She had slid the bolt across. No one could get in. Her heartbeat quickened. Thomas Barstow? Perhaps. She did not move. Hardly breathed. The boards creaked. Then it was quiet.

That night an eerie yellow gloom veiled the moon. The pungent smell of sulphur seeped deep into the ship. The bell rang out. Clang-*clang*, clang-*clang*, clang-*clang*. At dawn a burning sunrise heralded the day. And on the deck, the tiny particles of ash which had rained down throughout the night lay like a carpet of grey snow, broken only by the bare footprints of the men on watch.

It had been an uneventful night. No sound had been detected from the Verde Islands and the surface of the sea had not risen. The *Morning Star* was heading south. It would change course before it reached the Doldrums.

# Chapter 21

'He is cruel and without a soul!'

'Emma! Listen to me! The captain is not without feeling and he is a man with a conscience. The decision he made was hard enough without your wild outburst.'

'But his decision was cruel. He made it without stopping. Without helping. He condemned those men without even listening to them.'

'The captain was well aware he was sentencing those men to their death. But their fate was already sealed' – he sighed – 'probably even before they left their island.'

He pulled his chair closer. 'Nathaniel knew those men would perish. He also knew if he brought them on board they would share their fate with many of his crew.' Charles drew a long breath. 'Cape Verde is not a good place,' he said. 'Those men, God rest their souls, were probably slaves trying to escape. Escape!' he mused. 'Escape from their overseers, escape from an island beset by drought and famine, and escape from a mountain that had just exploded. But sadly there was nowhere for them to escape to. And they had nothing to take with them except disease.

'This group of islands is smitten with cholera and in recent years the disease has killed hundreds. Yes,' he said, 'the captain condemned those unfortunate souls and they will perish, but what he did was right. He had no choice.'

Joshua's hands were tied. As the spikes of a pitchfork poked at his bare back he slumped forward and crawled along the deck on his hands and knees. The deriding cries, jeers and taunts from the seamen echoed across the ship. There was no escape.

But he was not alone. As he was pulled to his feet, four others were lined up beside him. Two were topmast men, Irish lads in their twenties,

161

experienced seamen who had served time on an American route, but had only ever sailed in the North Atlantic. There was the boatswain's apprentice and a Whitby boy who had sailed north to Greenland but never been south of the Thames. The ritual they were to be submitted to was mandatory, irrespective of age. No seaman was exempt if it was the first time he had crossed the Line.

From the quarterdeck the haunting sound blown from a large conch shell echoed around the deck. The ship had been turned into the wind. It was rolling but holding fairly still. The breeze was catching the back of his sails.

'What will happen?' asked Emma, concerned for her son.

'Watch,' said Charles.

Len Thackray, the first mate appeared from below deck – King Neptune, escorted by his entourage. His face, arms and chest were painted blue. His immediate helpers and his *wife* were also daubed in colour. A length of sacking tied around his loins satisfactorily represented his tail. He held a pitchfork and on his head wore a wig of fresh seaweed, wet and shiny. A small hoop honed to the size of his head, made an adequate crown. As he paraded the deck he was greeted with cheers and whistles, some men bowing, others dropping to their knees.

Enthroned on an empty water barrel, the king listened to the charges brought against the five men and delivered his maritime judgement accordingly.

As the ceremony proceeded, Charles could read an increasing concern on Emma's face. 'It is the tradition,' he said. 'The boys must go through it. And believe me they enjoy it. Ask any of them when it is over and they will tell you they would not miss it.'

Emma looked sceptical.

'Believe me. Even I was put though the ordeal when I first crossed the equator. Although,' he added, 'I think they were kind to me. But I am pleased they have excluded you from their games.'

Emma watched as Neptune's new subjects were shaved, their heads then smeared with a foul looking substance and dusted with flour. With the addition of feathers from a recently plucked chicken, the victims were placed, in turn, astride a plank balanced over a large barrel.

'What is in it?' Emma asked, sensing what was about to happen.

'It is better you do not know. The contents will not kill anyone but I imagine it is not pleasant. When I was put thought my initiation I was daubed with the blue, but I was excused from being taunted over the barrel. At least there are some advantages in being a gentleman!'

With the extra ration of rum in their bellies, the crew's shrieks and yells grew steadily louder. One by one the boys were summonsed to pay the required forfeit to the king. Unable to comply with the request, they succumbed to the barrel's sloppy contents and after near drowning in it, each initiate was run headlong to the gunnels and tossed overboard to the cheers of the assembled company.

When Joshua was dragged dripping back on to the deck, relief showed on Emma's face. The white of his teeth and broad smile showed through the layer of muck and grease sticking to his face. He waved to his mother then helped haul out the boatswain's young mate who, being unable to swim, had almost drowned. The boy's spluttering and coughing was greeted with thunderous applause from the crew.

'Sailors are a strange breed,' Emma said.

'You think so?'

'They are fit and fearless and at times seem intelligent and kind. But at other times they seem cruel and cold-hearted.'

'No different from men anywhere, I think.'

'What are you looking at?' Charles asked.

Emma drew herself back from the rail and stared back into the darkness. Waiting for the moon to rise, the sails hung like leaden clouds against the black sky.

'You have been here for over an hour and hardly moved. I thought perhaps you were sick.'

'There,' she said, pointing down to the waves curling from the ship's bow. 'I am watching the stars in the sea. See them,' she said. 'They sparkle like tiny diamonds. So many of them. They seem to dance in the foam. I think they are attracted to the ship as I cannot see them where the water is calm.'

'You are observant, Emma,' said Charles, as he leaned against the rail beside her. 'Those diamonds, as you call them, have puzzled men for centuries. Long ago, men thought they were the sun's rays which had dived into the sea. At night, they said the fiery spirits would try to escape the water, to fly back to the heavens. Some said the troubled sea created sparks like those emitted when a flint strikes a stone. Some said they were small fish or insects which could glow like firefly. Some say that sometimes they can come alive and swirl together in a shining mist of colour which floats across the sea turning like a spinning top. Some say it is an aurora. Some say an illusion.'

'And what do you say?'

'I say the sparkling in the sea is a wonder. I say we have so much to learn and so little time to do it.' He sighed to the twinkling water cascading along the hull. 'Each flash of light,' he said, 'is from an animalcule, a minute organism. It only glows when turbulence disturbs it. The *Morning Star* is causing it to shine.' He looked at her but her eyes were not distracted from the sea. 'Your tiny stars are no illusion, Emma. They are real. Millions upon millions of them. And perhaps, as you suggest, they lie in wait for ships to pass to come to life and dance together in the foam.'

They stood by the rail, shoulders resting together, listening as the bow pounded the sea, watching as the churning water glittered with flecks of light.

'Quiet tonight.' Will Wortley said, as he joined them on the foredeck. The watch had changed. The evening had slipped by without them noticing.

'Nothing out there?' the seaman asked.

'Nothing,' Charles replied. 'Emma, would you care to go below?'

Her back had stiffened. She straightened. 'Thank you.'

'Good night, Will.'

'G'night.'

'Take my hand, Emma, I do not want you to fall.' His palm was soft. Uncalloused. Secure. He supported her as they ambled slowly back along the swaying deck.

'One last look,' she said. They stopped to gaze at the sea and stars and stayed on deck till late.

The great baulk of timber which pointed the ship's way, rose and fell like a painted horse on a merry-go-round. The sailor whose knees gripped the bowsprit rode it while not lifting his eyes from the sea. Other keen eyes scanned the water from the top of the foremast. Men scoured the sea's surface from the gunnels, each fleck of white, curl of wave, even a landing seagull, was viewed with suspicion.

'One point to starboard,' a voice cried out, several arms shot out in unison indicating the direction. The ship sailed slowly.

From the port side, seamen darted across the deck to watch as they passed a tall single stake, draped in a coat of dull green, protruding from the water. They watched in silence. The sunken ship was unmoved by the swirling water, the mast standing upright, like the topmost branch of some ancient forest drowned in a flooded valley.

As the *Morning Star* glided past, not a word was spoken. Ears were pricked as the lifting waves carried the ship over more than twenty wrecks scattered haphazardly across that section of the bay. Not far beneath the surface, hemp ropes plaited with seaweed waved from the skeleton ships whose arched claws extended upwards to scratch, score or gouge the barnacled hulls of unwary vessels sailing above.

This ship's graveyard was Cape Town Bay. It was a product of the Atlantic's contrary currents and the off-shore winds which in winter blew down from the north-west and made it an unsafe anchorage for any ship.

'Damn this place,' the captain hissed.

The helmsman's eyes were on the topgallants as the wind spilled from the canvas.

'I understood you said we would be going into harbour in the morning,' Charles said.

Captain Preston's attention was on the remaining square sails as they were dragged up. After the flapping jibs were dropped, he answered the question as though no time had elapsed since Charles had spoken.

'Correct,' he said. 'I will take the boat and go ashore this evening to arrange for us to be towed into the wharf at first light.' He glanced back at his friend and lowered his voice. 'It's a course of action I dislike, but I have suffered this port before. Too much congestion on the dock. You will witness it yourself in the morning, ships jostling for position like bulls in the cattle market. Some of the foreign captains have neither patience nor manners.' He glanced down at the slowing pace of the sea. 'Away anchor, Mr Thackray!'

The call was echoed at the bow followed by a loud splash and the rumble of iron. Giant links of chain thundered out of the locker and spewed from the ship's port bow following the iron pick down to the seabed.

'It is about time this port had a better wharf. It gets busier every year.' Nathaniel Preston was talking to no one in particular. 'It's already difficult to navigate the maze of wrecks which block the bay. If many more ships sink it will be downright impossible to get in here.'

Charles was gazing at the flat-topped mountain shrouded in its covering of cloud considering if now was the appropriate time to pose a favour of his brother-in-law. 'I would like to go ashore and make a trek up into those hills,' he said. 'I have not sampled this area before.'

Captain Preston thought for a moment. 'Not wise to go alone,' he said.

'Take one of the men. A reliable fellow. And perhaps a couple of the boys.'

'How much time do I have?'

'Two days. Time for one hundred tons of water, fresh fruit, vegetables and some fresh meat. And I will make you a promise,' he said, as he looked towards the town nestled under the mountains. 'Come back alive and when we leave here we will celebrate with a dinner of roast beef and Yorkshire pudding.'

Charles smiled. 'I will hold you to that.'

Emma watched the two men from her usual seat in the bow. She noticed the difference a smile made to the captain's visage even though it did not last. He smiled so infrequently. Perhaps it was a luxury he did not allow himself. No doubt his position deemed that he should maintain an air of superiority and authority. Yet, she noted, how kindly his appearance was, when the stern features softened and melded within the curls of his side whiskers, if only for a fleeting time.

As Charles walked towards her along the deck, she could see by his bearing he was pleased with the outcome of his conversation.

'Will you go ashore?' she asked.

'Yes. And I will ask Joshua if he would like to accompany me. The captain prefers I do not go alone.'

'Is it better I stay on the ship?'

'Indeed,' he said. 'I trust you will be safe! The captain will be going ashore and apart from the man on harbour watch, I expect most of the men will want to . . .' He stopped and regarded her closely. 'You know what the crew are like when they are in port. No doubt they will head straight for the taverns and relieve themselves of whatever money they have left. But let me warn you, Cape Town is a place of some unrest,' he said shaking his head. 'And poverty. And there are hundreds of slaves, both black and white. I would advise you to be careful who you speak to from the deck. And do not go ashore.' His brow furrowed as he thought for moment. 'Perhaps I should not go.'

Emma smiled. 'Enjoy your visit and do not worry about me. I will be all right,' she said.

# Chapter 22

Charles Witton and his party left soon after the ship had docked. It was still early and the wind gusting from Table Mountain was surprisingly cold. Joshua, the boy from Whitby, and the two seamen were quietly pleased to be excused from the morning chores. The idea of a two day trek into the mountains excited the boys.

From the deck, the cooper supervised the stream of barrels as they were rolled off the ship and loaded on to the wagons pulled by heavy oxen. Large baskets and trays woven from leaves were returned on board. Green, orange, yellow, exotic fruits, some smooth skinned, some large and angular, others small and prickly. The strange smells were a welcome change from the odours which escaped the bowels of the *Morning Star*.

As the routine of taking on stores proceeded, little was said. Emma watched the activity on the wharf with interest listening to the voices speaking in Dutch, Portuguese and German, and languages she had never heard before. She studied the black faces, shiny as hot pitch, broad flattened noses, and hair, shrivelled into tiny tight curls. Watched ragged men, their shirts hanging like shredded sails, struggling under heavy burdens. Black women, some slovenly and indolent, others wrapped in vibrant hand-dyed cloths balancing yellow baskets of woven raffia on their heads.

From the rail she noticed babies riding cocooned on their mother's backs and admired the rows of beads decorating a few of the women's slender necks and wrists. Even their ankles tinkled with coloured trinkets. Emma smiled occasionally but her gesture was not returned. She wanted to copy their faces on paper, capture the lines and expressions, the lips, the assortment of teeth which flashed as they smiled to each other.

And the sounds which vibrated along the wharf intrigued her ears. The tame monkeys chattering, bright coloured birds screeching. The workers' voices singing, humming, harmonizing. How different, she thought, these melodies from the raucous cackling of the ship's crew, no doubt their lyrics were far removed from the shanty songs the sailors sang. For Emma these voices were like the chorus at the opera but they had neither orchestra, nor conductor and they performed to no audience but themselves.

For Emma, Cape Town had a special atmosphere. It throbbed with the heart of the people and was richer in colour than anywhere she had ever seen before. She liked it.

She had never climbed the ship's standing rigging. Never wanted to. Never even considered it. Now she had a sudden desire to do so. She would take her drawing materials up to the platform above the forecourse yard. From there she would be able to see from the harbour, over the buildings and have a clear view to the mountains running down the sea.

With some sharpened charcoal and several pieces of writing paper rolled into a scroll, Emma pressed them into her apron pocket and pulled herself on to the rail. Gripping the ropes she started to climb.

She had never considered the forecourse yard to be high above the deck. The men ran up and down the rigging without fear, in wind and rain, even when the ship was lurching and threatening to throw them in the sea. They made it look easy, but it was not. Halfway up, she stopped and lay against the ropes. The hemp ladder was swaying. She had not expected any movement as the ship was close against the wharf. The rope was cutting across her feet. She was afraid she may lose her grip and fall.

But she was determined to climb. If she did not look down she could climb to the top. It was no higher than the attic window in Seal Street and she had stood there many times looking at the street below. Emma climbed. Pulling herself up, one step at a time.

When she reached the platform she pulled herself on to it and quickly sat down. Her legs and arms felt weak and her heart was beating fast. But the effort had been worth it. She remembered what Joshua had said about climbing the mast. She felt exhilarated. Her fear had gone.

To either side was the criss-crossed rigging of other ships – a cat's cradle of wood and hemp. Ahead was Table Mountain. Since morning, the mist had melted and slithered into the sea. Now its flattened top was clearly visible. To the side the other mountains rolled to the ocean like giant arms offering protection to the settlement.

From her vantage point Emma could see the town, its regular streets set out spaciously. Neat houses gleamed white. The black rushes which thatched the roofs stood out in sharp contrast.

The charcoal Emma had brought was brittle. It broke easily, littering her apron with black crumbs but she ignored them. With her back against the ropes she sketched contentedly. As the ship swayed on the harbour water she was reminded of the swing she had swung on as a child. From the wharf below she was lulled by the rhythmic humming of the natives.

A hand clamped around her ankle. 'Not a word or I'll toss you over!'

Pieces of charcoal dropped to the deck like black hailstones. The sheets of paper floated down like autumn leaves.

'Ain't it a pity all ya' fancy men have gone ashore?'

Emma froze. Her fingers gripped the ropes. She had no escape. She was afraid to go higher, and if she attempted to climb down he could easily peel her from the rigging. She had no option; she must stay where she was.

'I ain't never had a woman on the yard before. Not that I ain't imagined one laid out on it.'

Tom Barstow was too big to squeeze through the hole in the platform she was on. The only way he could get on to it was by climbing around the rigging on the outside. To do that he must release his grip on her leg. Emma sat still and said nothing. Reaching down into her apron pocket she crushed the remaining pieces of charcoal in her hand. He released his grip and poked his hand beneath her skirt. She shuffled from it closer to the mast.

He turned and spat out towards the sea. 'Now!' he cried, grabbing the rails with both hands. Emma leaned forward and as his face reached the level of the platform she shot the handful of black power at him landing a deal in his eyes and some in his throat.

His head flicked. His eyes screwed. He spat much of the dust from his throat but some lodged in his wind pipe. He coughed, spat and sneezed at the irritation.

'Bitch!' he yelled. His face resembled that of a chimney sweep. His eyes the colour of fire. 'You will pay for this, you slut! You will pay!'

Emma kicked at him with her feet.

He caught her ankle. Pulled her towards him. She tried to kick, to stop herself from sliding. She was being dragged down. She knew if she fell from that height she would die. She dug her heels between the slats and held on.

It was the boom of musket fire which stopped him. He had ignored the cries from the deck, the threats of punishment, the pleadings from the handful of crew who had gathered below.

Emma heard the gun re-cocked.

'Come down, sailor! Now!'

Tom Barstow released Emma's leg and, holding the rigging with one hand leaned out and grabbed the nearest shroud. For a moment he hung suspended then as agile as an ape, swung himself from the rigging, wrapped his leg around the rope and slid down to the deck.

Before the mate had time to have him held and shackled, the seaman jumped from the gunnels on to the wharf. The crowd of spectators ducked as the musket boomed again. From the mast Emma could see it did not hit its target. The man she hated was running, weaving across the quayside, his red eyes flashing back at his pursuers, his black face bursting like a slave running from the dogs.

'I should not have gone. I felt it when we were away. I was afraid something like this would happen.'

'I am fine, but I am worried what will happen now? Has the captain been told?'

'Of course,' said Charles. 'And he was not impressed.'

Emma's brow tightened.

'No,' he said. 'You misunderstand. He has always disliked that seaman, despised him with a vengeance. I gather he has had trouble with him before. But the captain says Barstow is a good topmast man and he does not want to lose any more men. Tomorrow, at first light he intends to send a few of the crew into town to search for him.'

'You mean they will bring him back to the ship?'

'Yes. But if that is the case, I guarantee he will be spending his time in the hold and not in the rigging.'

'And if they do not find him?'

'Then we sail without him and you will have nothing to worry about again.'

'I should not have climbed the mast, should I?'

'No you should not!' He cocked his head inquisitively. 'Though I would have liked to have witnessed it. I have to say it was a brave thing to do – albeit foolhardy.'

'It was a wonderful view.'

'I don't doubt it.'

Emma smiled and looked at the line of small boxes on the cabin table. 'Some things you collected?' she asked.

He nodded.

'Perhaps you would show me.'

Charles looked at each box in turn, examining the name he had scribbled on the label. 'You will like this one,' he said eagerly. As he lifted the lid, the closed wings of a butterfly fluttered as if a breath of breeze had blown on them.

'Is it dead?' Emma asked.

'Almost.'

She regarded it sadly.

'They have an extremely short lifespan,' he said. 'And I am sure it has served its purpose on this earth. Now it will serve my purpose and be immortalized.'

Emma laughed. 'Immortalized?'

'It is true. By drawing its likeness I will record the life which is gone. It is important to remember that.'

Emma turned her face towards his but the scientist was engrossed with the new additions to his collection.

'Will you go ashore tomorrow?'

'No!' he said. 'I have more than enough samples to keep me busy. Tomorrow I will pack most of them away and would be most grateful if you could assist me.'

Emma nodded. 'Certainly.'

'The captain tells me that we will be heading south to catch the westerly wind which will carry us to our destination. He also says the southern latitudes can have a tendency to be "a little lumpy" at times.' He smiled. 'Believe me, Emma, when he says that, he means we could be heading into some fairly heavy seas.'

'Hard to port!'

The helmsman spun the wheel pulling the rudder hard across.

'What is the matter with him? Damn Yankee fool must be blind! Hard to port I say!'

'Port on, Captain!'

With a laboured crack and squeal of timber on timber, the *Morning Star*'s bowsprit slid on to the deck of the larger ship. It settled for a moment resting like a sperm whale being dragged on to a whaling vessel, then slowly, as if the chains had broken, it started to slide back on to the water. The American clipper shuddered and slowed as the pair still tangled together turned in an arc of ninety degrees. Shouts rang out from both decks but the voices were drowned by the sound of three-dozen luffing sails, flapping violently like angry geese.

'Starboard rudder, Mr Wortley! We must get off her back before she breaks us in half. Get the jibs down before they are shredded!'

With each passing swell the *Morning Star* rose up and crashed its bow back on to the deck of the American vessel. The sails were flapping uselessly.

'Braces, Mr Thackray! Get the yards around!' The calls were echoed along the deck. Seamen ran to their stations.

The ships were stuck together like two flies. And they were drifting with the current towards the rocky coast. As the men hauled the yards around, the wind began to fill in the square sails and with help from the waves the *Morning Star* separated herself from the unwelcome union.

'Watch the forestay!' the Captain yelled. Too late. It caught the clipper's forecourse yardarm. The *Morning Star*'s bowsprit, with a girth of two feet, heaved and creaked. Drawn tight as the string on a bow, the forestay snapped and catapulted loose. The topmast cracked and fell, rattling to the deck in a rumble of crackling canvas, yards and falling rigging.

The two ships floated free.

'If I had a thirty-six pounder, it would give me the greatest pleasure to put a hole right through her! Damn that ship! And damn the master! He must have been drunk to sail across us like that! Or blind! Did you get her name, Mr Wortley?'

The second mate did not answer. 'Up there, Capt'n.' He pointed to the broken rigging. 'Man down and another caught in the lines!'

Shouts were coming from the deck.

'Mr Thackray, get someone up there, quick as you can. I don't want to lose another sailor!'

Another cry rang out. 'Man overboard!'

The captain, unable to see what was happening from the helm ran along the deck gazing up at the tangle of wreckage suspended above. As four sailors climbed the rigging, two others scrambled down. On the deck a seaman nursed his head in his arms, another held out his hands, the brand of the running rope burned into his palms. A third was helped aboard, wet, but otherwise unharmed.

'Get some help up there!' the captain shouted. 'Mr Thackray, can you see what is holding that man?'

'There's two of 'em, up there. Young Sam's got his leg hooked between the sheet and the clew line. Looks like he is trying to cut himself free.' He shook his head. 'If he falls from there he will hit the deck.'

'Tell the men to climb warily. She's not holding by many threads.' The seamen already aloft were securing the broken mast which was swinging perilously above the deck.

The sound of the collision had brought Emma hurrying on deck but she had stopped clear of the damage. She was unable to see what was happening around the foremast. She could see François leaning against the rigging, his head resting against it. His foot on the bottom rung. What was wrong?

'Get up there Frenchy, what are you waiting for?' the mate ordered.

François climbed slowly and Emma lost sight of him behind the canvas.

With a resounding thud a body fell on to the deck. Almost instantly a pool of dark blood flowed from the man's head. There was no movement. Hal Dodd would climb no more.

'Below!' the cry came down. 'We need more hands! We've got Samuel but he's a dead weight.'

Half an hour later, with a rope tied around his chest, the unconscious boy was lowered slowly down the rigging, passed gently from the arms of one man to another, down to the deck.

'Mr Witton, would you take a look?'

Charles watched as the young seaman was laid on the deck. His eyes were open. Not far from him his dead mate was ignored. The pool of blood had already congealed. It was almost black, like spilled pitch and had set hard on the teak deck.

The rope was eased from Samuel's shoulders. He would recover.

'Mr Kaye, get up and see what the damage is!'

The carpenter touched his knuckle to his head and scrambled up the rigging against the straggle of men still climbing down.

The captain sighed. 'Let's get that mess cut down, Mr Thackray.'

'Aye, sir.'

Charles watched as the men set about the laborious task of removing the damaged timbers. The work went on throughout the afternoon. As it proceeded, little was said. Hal Dodd's body was neither moved nor covered. The men merely worked around it as though it was another piece of fallen debris.

Charles posed the question cautiously to the captain. 'Will you take the *Morning Star* back to Cape Town?'

'And chance being buried in that salty graveyard? No, thank you! I will find a sheltered cove and providing there is no major damage to the hull, we will repair at sea. Mr Kaye assures me we have enough timber onboard for a new topmast. The carpenter is a good man. I trust him. He has checked the two yards which came down and they are not cracked. The sails have only suffered minor damage and can be patched. And we have lockers full of shrouds and rope. They may be old but at least they will not stretch. Once the mast is up we can head for the forties.' He looked at Charles's concerned expression. 'It will not delay us long.'

'And the man who fell?'

'We will bury him in the morning.'

'What of the other ship?' said Charles. 'Shouldn't the accident be reported to the authorities?'

'That was hardly an accident, the fool sailed across my bow!' He calmed himself. 'But in answer to your question, officially, yes. But I doubt it will serve much purpose as I do not have the ship's name and I'm damned if I am going into that port again, even in a small boat. If I am not wrong, she is a tea clipper making for the Indies. Did you see how she headed out with all haste not even stopping to offer us assistance? She suffered less damage than us, and time for her is money.' He sighed. 'If I complained about her it would amount only to one captain's word against another. And by the time that ship sails this way again it is unlikely this incident will be remembered.

'This is a cursed place. I have a broken mast and have lost another good man. The sooner we are away from here the better.' He smiled wryly. 'Let's hope the American's next encounter is with *The Flying Dutchman*. That ship will give her a run for her money.'

Charles laughed. 'You believe in such legends?'

Captain Preston took a deep breath before answering. 'I have seen some strange things at sea which beggar explanation.' He paused. 'You may well smile at me for saying so. You are a man of science and you know many things. But ask any man who sails the sea, officers or able seamen alike, they will all answer the same way. They will tell you there are things at sea which are never spoken of in jest. I have witnessed strange happenings, inexplicable sights, sounds which would make your blood curdle, and, I might add, not alone, but with good men alongside me. As to *The Flying Dutchman* and believing in phantom ships, I prefer to keep an open mind.' He turned. 'But if you will excuse me,' he said. 'I have a ship to sail and I do not have the time for idle talk.'

Despite the lack of canvas, the *Morning Star* made four knots as it sailed south. The wind was favourable and the sea current assisted their passage. They passed the Cape of Good Hope and headed south by east until they rounded the southernmost tip of the African continent. Late the following afternoon, they found a cove with a clear deep water channel leading into it. Sheltered by a peninsular of land on the eastern side and a narrow reef to the south, the water in the bay was flat as a mill pond and blue as any Pacific lagoon. Around its edges the sand was white. The crystal water abounded with fish. It was an ideal location to refit.

As night fell, small fires flickered on the surrounding hills. Natives perhaps? In the morning naked men carrying spears were seen running along the beach. With no knowledge of the area Captain Preston ordered the crew to stay on board. There was a job to be done and he did not intend risking the loss of any more of his crew. The combined watches were already short of five seamen. The order to stay on board was extended to include Charles Witton. The entomologist was both disappointed and disgruntled but after presenting his arguments, realized it was pointless trying to sway the captain. His decision was final.

Mr Kaye and his mate worked amidships. The timber yards resting on the gunnels protruded from both sides of the ship. It took four men to haul the topgallant sail along the deck, and finding enough space to accommodate the folded canvas was not easy. Jack Burns, the sailmaker crawled over it, scouring every inch, checking his old patches, cutting and stitching new pieces to it. Curling smoke from the brazier ran up the rigging carrying with it the reek of tar. Ropes were cut, spliced, tarred, stretched and oiled. The clang from the blacksmith's anvil rang out across the peaceful bay. At midday the sun burned overhead. There was little breeze. The men's eyes squinted against the reflected glare on the water.

The seamen not engaged in the repairs, wallowed on the deck. There was no space to swab or holystone the teak. Woodwork was varnished, brasses polished and polished again and yards of old rope converted into oakum. Were it not for a large shark, which constantly circled the ship, the men would have been occupied caulking the hull or scraping the barnacles from below the water-line.

Although a couple of the men were prepared to chance their luck for the sake of a swim, the threat of punishment deterred them. As it was, the cook caught a small shark on a baited line. Not all the men would eat the flesh, claiming they were eating fellow sailors, but for those who did, it provided three good meals and soup for several days. Needless to say, the buckets of water hoisted from the bay served to cool the men, though the carpenter was not amused when a gallon of salt water hit him full in the face.

To escape the sun, Emma stayed below occupying herself with her drawings. She had only seen François from a distance since they left Cape Town. There was much she wanted to speak to him about but he had ignored her and appeared preoccupied. She wanted to tell him how relieved she was, knowing that Thomas Barstow was not on board. She had worried at first that he may have sneaked on to the ship and be hiding somewhere. But as the days had gone by she had worried less, realizing the sounds of scratching she heard at night, and the squeaking of timber outside her cabin door were the sounds made by the ship itself.

She wanted to talk to François the way they had talked on the deck. She had told him of her past life but she wanted to hear more about his life and the places he had visited. She wondered if she had upset him. She knew he was jealous of the time she spent in Charles's day cabin. Then she remembered what he had said about being in harbour. How he hated it. How it made him feel confined. She told herself he would be different when they were sailing again. Once the ship was underway there would be ample time to talk to him at length.

On the afternoon of the fifth day, the jury rig was swayed up and bolted into place. The yards were raised and lowered several times to test the running gear.

'I will speak to Mr Kaye,' the captain said. 'He did a first class job. This afternoon we will see if the sailmaker's work is equally sound. Prepare the ship, Mr Thackray! We sail out with the tide!'

# Chapter 23

'Mama! Mama! Open the door. It's me, Josh! Please open the door.'
Emma put down her pen.

'Hush, Josh, don't make so much noise. What's wrong?'

'François is sick!'

'Sick? Where is he?'

'Come with me, Mama, I will take you to him.'

The air which greeted them as they climbed down the steep ladder smelled foul. The bottom of the ship was dank and dark. Light spilling from a single lamp was unable to penetrate far into the bowels of the ship, unable to penetrate the black crevices which separated the piles of stores, cases, bails and barrels crammed into the hold. In a space barely wide enough to fit a man's shoulders, François was curled against the ship's hull, cradling his arms around his chest. He was wet and shivering like a cornered rat.

'Gracious! What has happened?'

'I don't know. I heard Samuel calling for Mr Witton not more than a few minutes ago. He said he had found Frenchy and he thought he was dying.'

'Don't say that, Josh. Please don't say that.'

François opened his eyes but did not move. 'I am fine,' he said, looking no further than the barrels against his head.

'What is wrong, François? What are you doing down here?'

'I heard a rumour the captain had purchased some casks of Verdelho in Madeira. It is a mighty fine wine they make on the slopes of that island and I thought I might sample some.'

'François, how could you? You're drunk. Josh said you were sick. Get up! You are wet and dirty. You can't stay here.'

'Leave me!' He demanded. His eyelids drooped, then closed.

177

'I'll get him up.' Josh leaned forward and grabbed François' arm. The seaman's body arched. He groaned. He tried to rise but he flopped back banging his head on the side of the ship.

Joshua leaned forward to try a second time. He grabbed the Frenchman's arm and pulled. 'Mama, look!' he cried.

The sight made Emma clasp her hand to her mouth. A brackish yellow stain had soaked the front of François' blouse. Dirt had encrusted the blood-streaked matter across his chest. His shirt was stuck to it. The smell was putrid. It sickened her. 'Oh, God! Hurry, Josh, get Mr Witton.'

'I'm here,' Charles was standing behind her along with several other men all crowded into the small area. 'We must get him out of here and quickly!' he said. 'The air is foul. You boy! Samuel! Can you get your legs behind him and lift him a little so we can get him out of there.'

'Where are you taking him?' Sam asked. 'You can't put him in his hammock! He made me promise I'd not let anyone put him in his hammock. I think he's afraid he might get sewn in it before he's dead.'

'Please help him,' Emma begged. 'You must do something.'

'To begin with, we must get him out of here. The galley will not do. We must get him up on deck if he can he lifted up the ladders.' Charles looked around for the strongest men to lift him. 'Look lively, but gentle as you can.'

From the hatchway a crowd of faces peered down into the semi darkness.

'I want warm water from the galley,' shouted Charles. 'Take it amidships on the weather deck. And I want it in a basin and not a bucket, mind. And the apothecary's chest from the captain's cabin. And some clean rags.' He touched Emma on the sleeve. 'It is best you go up top and wait there. I will look after François from here.'

Emma hesitated then nodded. The men stood aside for her to pass.

François' head rolled on to his chest as Samuel eased him up from the side of the ship.

'Gently, men!' Charles called.

Heavy as a sack of sodden wool François was carried up to the fresh air. On deck the afternoon sun still burned bright but had lost its heat. With no wind, the *Morning Star* was as still as a ship in dry dock.

'Lay him down there. Something for his head. Those sacks will do. Help me to sit him up. Stand back! Let him get some air. You there! Get some drinking water!'

Emma helped lower François' head on to the cushion of sacking. 'What happened?' she whispered.

He opened his eyes.

'Did you fall? How did you get hurt?'

Charles interrupted, 'Emma, please. No questions. First I must see what I can do for him.' He looked up at the group of men. 'Does anyone know how long has he been down there?'

There was no response. No one had seen him go into the hold. No one had missed him.

'Who is on his watch? Surely one of you must have known he was not on duty?'

A seaman volunteered the answer. 'Been no call for sail these past two days.' He looked up to the dead canvas. 'A man's left much to his own devices when conditions are like this.'

'Emma, when did you speak with him last?'

'I cannot think. Was it yesterday or the day before?' Her eyes were filled with tears. 'I have been busying myself below deck,' she said. 'I have seen little of him since we left Cape Town. I thought he was avoiding me. Angry with me. I never once considered he could be ill.'

'Emma!' Charles's tone was quietly stern. 'I suggest you go to your cabin while I look at this wound. It may not be pleasant.'

'I will stay.'

Perspiration filled the furrows on François' brow. He ground his teeth and groaned as the piece of folded rag was peeled from his chest. A soft cheesy substance oozed out of an open wound.

François cursed.

'This is a mess,' Charles said quietly. The measure of his fears showed unmistakably on his face. 'How on earth did you do this, Frenchy?'

François closed his eyes and turned his head away. It was indeed an ugly wound. Not a long slice, but deep and damaging. The skin around was mottled, red and blue and too dead to be stitched together.

After cleaning the wound the best he could, Charles bound François' chest with lengths of linen sheet. A cut he had noticed on the seaman's arm he left uncovered. It was dry and crusted.

As he wiped his hands, Emma sat down on the deck beside him.

By this time, the sun had dipped behind the gunnels and was about to sink. The interest the crew had shown at first had dissipated. Most had gone below or moved to another section of the deck.

Despite Emma's efforts, François refused to eat, taking only a few sips

of warm rum with sugar and a little water. The sweat from his forehead
dripped on to the deck. She wiped his face and neck.

The captain remained on the quarterdeck throughout the proceedings.
He was advised of the progress by Len Thackray. As the day ended, he
wandered along the deck. 'It's time we spoke,' he said, addressing his
brother-in-law. 'Join me in my cabin when you can.'

Charles looked down at Emma. 'Will you stay with him?'

'Yes.'

'Then I will come back later.'

'What are you looking for?' François asked quietly.

Emma turned back from the rail, surprised he was awake. The moon
was shining in his dark eyes.

'I am looking for the tiny stars which sparkle in the sea. But tonight
they are not here.'

'They will come back,' he said. 'I promise you.' He tried to sit up but
he could not hide the pain burning in his chest.

'Let me help you.'

'Promise me one thing,' he said, as she leaned towards him. 'Whenever
you see the stars in the sea you will think of me?'

'Why do you say that, François?' A deep sadness welled in her eyes.
'You will get well . . .'

'Promise me!' he said.

'I promise.'

'My knife,' he said, feeling for it on his hip. She touched his hand to the
scabbard. 'Take the belt. Slide it from me. Give it to your son. A seaman
needs a good knife. This is the best. I bought it in Toledo.'

'I cannot; you will need it.'

'I have another,' he said wearily. 'It is in my sea chest. Do as I say. Give
this to your boy.'

Emma slid the belt from around his waist. 'But François, I am afraid.'

'Of what? You have nothing to fear.'

'The things you are saying make me afraid.'

'That is no cause for fear.'

'But this thing which has happened to you makes me afraid. Who has
done this to you? Was it Thomas Barstow?' she asked anxiously. 'Is he on
board the ship? Is he hiding somewhere? In one of the lockers where you
hid me? Tell me he is not here. I am afraid of him. Afraid of the darkness.'

François reached up and touched her face, brushing the tears from her cheeks.

'My dear Emma, I swear the man you fear is not on this ship. Believe me, Tom Barstow will never bother you again.' He tried to lift himself. 'Help me,' he begged. 'I want to smell the sea. I want to look at it with you. Perhaps together we can conjure up those diamonds you like to see.'

With one hand resting on Emma's shoulder, his other pressed across his chest, François struggled to the rail. Each breath he took pained him. He coughed, leaned on the gunnels and rested his head on the rigging. Across the glassy surface, the moon splayed a broad path of silver. It stretched from the ship to the distant horizon.

'How beautiful she is,' he said gazing at the sea. '*La mer*. So like a woman.' His body tensed. 'Look,' he said. 'How soft and flat she lies in the night. Smooth, like silk. Black. Beguiling.' His tongue touched his lips, 'I can taste her salt,' he said, his voice barely a whisper. 'Listen. Hear her breathe. Softly. Slowly. She sleeps.' His fingers gripped the rail as his body rocked back. 'It is time to go,' he whispered, placing a gentle kiss on Emma's mouth.

'No, François!'

'Remember me.'

She could not hold him. His skin, wet as an eel's, slid through her hands. There was hardly a splash as he slipped into the water.

Emma's cry reverberated across the ship. 'François. . . !'

But the Frenchman did not hear her and the sea was quick to swallow him up.

# Chapter 24

As the sea battered the ship's bow, the luminescent particles flickered then faded. Hundreds of them. Thousands of them. Hour upon hour. Shining and dying throughout the night.

'You must go to bed! Get some sleep! This is doing you no good!'

Emma ignored Charles' advice and remained on deck all night gazing into the water or staring down at the strips of bleached teak between her feet.

'Penny for them?' the sailmaker said when he came up on deck.

She looked up. 'It's nothing.'

'You might call it nothing,' he said, shrugging his shoulders. 'But if you'll pardon me for saying, miss, I see a spare anchor hanging round your neck and if you're not careful it will carry you to the bottom of the sea.'

He leaned against the rail beside her, puffing smoke as he sucked on his pipe.

'See out there! See that splash of white water.'

Emma looked in the direction he was pointing.

'Whales!' he said. 'Killer whales. Pod of them, if I'm not wrong.'

'Killer whales?'

'Don't fret about the name. Docile they are. I seen a man swim beside them and not get hurt.' As he spoke, in the distance, a giant black head, streaked with white, broke the surface, raised itself to an enormous height then flopped heavily on to its side. A gush of spray shot high in the air.

'They be swimming from the Southern Ocean. Heading for the Arctic.'

'That is a long way.'

'Aye. But they're always on the move. If they stay in one place too long the whalers get them. But I reckon you would know that coming from Whitby. Now seals,' he said, 'they're different. They just stay in one place.

182

Seems they are waiting to be killed. If the sealers don't get 'em, the great white bears do.' He prodded his finger into the smouldering leaf and gazed out to sea. They watched the whales in silence until the last one dived.

'If you'll take my advice, missy, you'll not let your heart stay in one place too long. Pull anchor and sail even though the sky looks black. Believe me, lassie, there'll be fair winds waiting for you beyond the horizon.'

Emma smiled. 'Thank you,' she said.

He touched his cap. 'My pleasure, miss.'

Standing beside her at the rail, Charles looked into her eyes. 'You are thinking about François, are you not?'

Emma nodded.

'You have not spoken of him since his death. I do not mind if you want to talk to me about him.'

She turned her face to the wind and let it blow the hair from her eyes.

'He would have died, Emma. You realize that, don't you?'

She nodded.

'And François knew it. That is why he did what he did.'

'But what had happened to him? What had caused that horrible injury? He must have fallen, yet I saw him two days before he died and he was well.'

'He may have appeared well,' Charles said, 'but I think François had been carrying that wound for several days before the infection got the better of him.'

'But why didn't he say something to one of the men? Why did he go away and hide like a cat waiting to die?'

'From what I have learned of seamen, they are insular men. They are tough also. They have to be. And if you begin to understand them you will know they think they are invincible.'

'But François was hurt. Badly hurt.'

'Indeed. It was a deep wound and hard to say what caused it. When I saw it, I was afraid for him. I could see that the poison from it was spreading through his body.'

'Couldn't you have done anything to help?'

Charles clenched his fingers. 'How many times in my life have I asked myself that question? If only I had learned more when I was a young man. If only I had become a doctor, maybe I could have helped him.

Maybe I could have helped my wife. My daughter. Maybe I could have helped the man who fell and many similar poor souls. Look at me now,' he said. 'I rather spend my time looking through the eyepiece of a microscope than looking at my sick neighbour. I know more about the house fly than I know about the human body. That is no boast to be proud of. Yet here on the ship, irony has it that I am regarded as some sort of man of science, a medical man who can perform surgery, a man who has the knowledge to administer to all manner of ailments.' He sighed. 'But that is not so. I am none of those things and, at times, it depresses me. I did all I could for François. I am sorry, Emma, there was nothing more I could do.'

She wanted to reassure him. To tell him he should not feel the way he did. She wanted to tell him she admired him for what he had done and for how kind he had been. But, though her mind fought to find the right words, they would not come, and the silence which existed between them carried with it an air of uneasiness.

Charles continued, 'Like many young men of my time, I was a fool. The idea of being famous, of making great discoveries, appealed to me. I wanted to be like John Henslow, the botanist,' he laughed. 'Yet I had neither the tenacity nor the brain.'

'But you studied. You are a scientist and are well respected. How else would you be invited to join a scientific expedition?'

'I have a wild iris named after me,' he said, with some degree of pride. 'A distant relative of the saffron crocus. But one cannot measure the name of a plant against the value of a man's life.'

'You must not denigrate yourself. You did all you could for François and I doubt a medical doctor could have saved him. Even I could smell the badness which was eating him. I saw it oozing from his chest.' Her brow furrowed. 'And I know he would not have wished to die in a hospital bed.'

'Strange as it may seem,' Charles said, looking up as the yards were braced and the ship slowly began its turn towards the east. 'It was those things which you talk about which took me away from medicine.'

Emma listened. It was good for him to talk.

'I had planned to be a doctor, like my father. I moved to Leeds to study. There is a fine infirmary there. But I found the work depressing. So much infection and death. I was a young man and I could not bear to see it. The prospect of the profession disillusioned me, yet I became intrigued with the bacteria which live inside our bodies, those tiny organisms only the microscope can see. Because I was tired of seeing people die, I chose to escape. I went overseas in search of the exotic things I had only read about. I suppose I was a selfish young man.'

Emma passed no comment and listened.

'When I returned to England three years later, I went back to the university, but it was not medicine I studied, it was insects – entomology. So now,' he sighed, 'I can tell you what insect a man crushes beneath his feet – but not what disease he is dying of.'

They stepped aside as the cooper rolled a heavy barrel along the deck towards the galley hatch.

'Now, if you will excuse me,' he said. 'I am a little tired. I was awake early and I think I will retire early.'

'Of course,' she said quietly.

He inclined his head. 'Good night, Emma.'

'Good night.'

Emma woke late feeling stiff and sore. The air in her cabin was stuffy. She wanted to get out.

'May I get something from the chest?' she asked, from the doorway of Charles's day cabin.

He looked up from his journal. 'Please help yourself,' he said, and continued writing.

With a selection of clothes draped over her arm, Emma thanked him and reached for the doorknob.

Turning in his chair, Charles said softly, 'I am pleased to see you, Emma. I have missed you these past few days.'

She stopped as if wanting to say something.

'I have been watching you on deck, gazing out to the horizon. What was it you were searching for?'

She shrugged.

'You must excuse me for saying, but at times you seem lost. And very alone. Yet you have acquaintances on the ship. Many of the seamen enjoy having you on board and they respect you. And you have your son,' Charles said. 'And, for what it is worth, you have me. It saddens me to see you like this.'

Emma thought about his words and sighed. 'I sometimes think I am like the tiny diamonds in the sea. While the ship sails they live, they shine. But when the ship stops, their light is extinguished. I feel my life is the same. While we are sailing I am safe, alive, content. But when the ship docks in Sydney, what then? What will become of me? Where will I go? I do not like to think of that time. It frightens me.'

'You must not be afraid.'

'But I have never been alone before. Not completely alone. For thirteen years my son has been with me. But when we reach Sydney that will change. I know of no one there. Joshua has said he will care for me, but I know his heart is set on staying with the ship. It is his wish and I would not press him to leave.'

'Then I should stay in Sydney and not join up with the rest of the party. Then, at least, you will know me.'

'How can you even consider that, Charles? The expedition is the purpose of your voyage. That is your wish, your dream. And besides, you do not know me.'

He turned and looked away.

'No,' she said. 'I must consider my future. I will have to find a job. I can offer my services as a governess. A lady's companion perhaps. Even a housekeeper. I have never been in service but I am sure I know what is required.'

Mr Witton looked troubled. 'Please, Emma, before you say more, listen to what I have to say. I have friends in Sydney. Influential friends. When the ship docks I will make enquiries with them. At least allow me to do that.' He shuffled in his seat. 'What you have just said makes it easier for me to speak. Emma, I have a proposition, but I find it somewhat embarrassing to put to you.' He turned his chair towards her and sat down. 'You are a good artist. Very skilful. And I have watched you drawing. I know how much pleasure it gives you. Would you consider following in your father's footsteps and earning money from your talent?'

'Do you want me to paint your portrait?'

He laughed. 'No. Forgive me, I am talking in riddles. As I explained earlier, I am an entomologist. I study insects, all manner of small creatures – crawling, flying, swimming. I have hundreds of specimens which I have collected in England and overseas. Amongst them I am hoping to discover some exotic species which has never been recorded before. But that involves a lot of work, examining each one, weighing, measuring, dissecting, cataloguing the details. And when I make my notes I draw a likeness of the specimen.'

'To immortalize it,' Emma said, grinning.

His face was serious. 'My artwork is poor. Like a child's compared with yours.' He leaned forward. 'Emma, while we are on the ship, would you do some work for me? I have a chest bursting with specimens which require attention. I have the new microscope which I collected in Madeira. And,' he added with some embarrassment, 'I will pay you for your effort.'

'But I have never drawn an insect before!'

He waited as the idea flitted through her head.

She smiled. 'But tomorrow I will try.'

Above the deck of the *Morning Star* the seamen released the replacement sail. Standing along the yardarms they looked like wooden pegs on a giant washing-line. Emma recognized some of the sailors. They belonged to François' watch. He should have been up there with them.

The square of canvas crackled and slapped as it dropped and filled. On the deck the sheets were trimmed. The *Morning Star* was making six knots, sailing tight on the strengthening wind.

Overhead, a huge flock of migrating birds clouded the rising sun. They flew in formation, the shape twisting and turning like the changing pattern in a kaleidoscope.

The smell of cooking drifted up through the galley hatch. Mr Sung's head popped up from below. 'You want breakfast?'

Emma nodded gratefully.

'You stay. I bring breakfast.'

The sailmaker bade her good morning. Another sailor nodded to her.

Emma smiled. She was feeling better.

'Please come in, Emma. I have everything ready.'

The day cabin was cluttered. A second, slightly smaller, wooden trunk had been hauled into the room. It was pressed against the chest containing clothes which already occupied much of the floor space. The trunk was open and almost empty, its contents having been placed on the oak table.

Stacked one on top of each other, were numerous small boxes, each bearing a neatly written label. In front of those was a pile of books and journals and beside them a flat leather case. A pair of tweezers, a small sharp-bladed knife, scissors and pins lay in its blue velvet lining. A light wooden box, divided into compartments, held a quantity of circular dishes and several small bottles. The coloured fluids swilled from side to side though there was little movement of the ship. With the microscope taking pride of place in the centre of the table, there appeared little space for Emma to work.

He anticipated her concern. 'Let me clear some of this away. Draw up a chair and sit down.'

Emma watched him as he contemplated where he could store his possessions. After realizing that his desk was also littered, he returned the piles to the chest.

'Paper,' he said, 'water-paint, ink, quill, penknife, pencil, charcoal, blotting paper, water, rag. There,' he said, pleased with the provisions. 'I think you have everything.'

Emma dusted the table top and placed the sheet of paper in the centre. After sharpening the quill she waited, poised like a scholar, for her instructions to commence.

'What do you want me to draw?' she asked.

He examined the labels on several of the boxes, reading some, opening others and examining the contents. He talked to himself in what sounded like Latin though Emma did not recognize any of the words. After sorting through the pile, he reached for a glass dish. It was covered in a white cloth.

'This,' he announced, 'is fresh! A beautiful specimen!' He picked up the insect with a pair of tweezers and placed it on the paper. The smell of ether hung in the air.

Emma recoiled.

He regarded it carefully through a magnifying glass. 'Now that is nice,' he said. 'Very nice indeed. *Periplaneta orientalis.* A common cockroach.' Enthralled with his specimen, he failed to notice the expression on Emma's face. 'Take a closer look. The glass enlarges it. It truly is a lovely specimen. Excellent for dissection.'

As if expecting it to crawl across the paper, Emma touched it gently with the tip of the quill feather. It did not move.

With Charles standing beside her, she pushed the lace cuffs back into her sleeve, draped the rag across her knees, dipped the pen, shook off the excess ink and drew the first lines on the paper.

Charles Witton smiled contentedly.

'Excellent. Excellent,' he said, as the insect developed. 'Female!' he announced. 'If you look carefully you can see the joints in the antennae,' he added pointing with the tip of a pin. 'Yes,' he said excitedly, as Emma transcribed the details, the armoury of the femur's minute spines, the fine hairs covering the *cerci anales.*

Suddenly she felt flushed. She blotted her forehead. Beads of sweat were starting to trickle towards her eyes. The air felt heavy. Perhaps it was her nervousness at being observed so closely.

'Charles!' The captain's cry sounded urgent. He stopped at the door when he realized his brother-in-law was not alone.

'Do come in, Nathan. There is something I would like to show you.'

'Later, Charles,' he said. 'I fear we may be sailing into some rough weather. The barometer has dropped too quickly for my liking and I fear this is an ominous calm we are suffering. I would like you to join me on deck. But,' he said, pondering the multitude of objects scattered around, 'I would suggest that everything which is not bolted to the floor is housed securely.' He turned to Emma. 'If we strike a storm, I suggest you remain here or in your own cabin. The sea could get quite rough.'

# Chapter 25

The air in the stateroom was stagnant. On returning from the deck, Charles had lit the lamp and though eager to continue with his specimens had heeded the captain's advice, stowing everything back in the trunk. Though not wishing to, he had to satisfy himself with his reference books. Emma tried to read, but the shadows see-sawing across the page made it difficult.

The storm hit with almighty force laying the ship almost on its beam. Men were thrown to the gunnels as the sea foamed across the deck. Barrels torn from their lashings spun like tops. The pitch kettle steamed.

The helmsman lay sprawled unconscious against a locker. The helm was spinning free. Cries could be heard from all directions. The ship vibrated with each wave. The sailors, soaked to the skin, scrambled to gain a footing, to bring the ship around and haul in the remaining sails. Water flooded the deck cascading through the hatches to the decks below.

Charles had been standing by the bookcase when the force of the storm hit.

Emma's breath was punched from her chest as she was thrown forward from the chair into the edge of the table. Above her head, the lamp shattered, showering her in glass. Burning wick and oil floated down like tiny incendiaries. Smelling her hair singeing, she brushed the particles from her head instinctively. Falling into her open book, the pages ignited. The flames lit the room. Emma grabbed the book and dashed out the fire, the tips of her fingers caught by the flames. She fell forward. The ship had righted itself. They were still afloat.

The ship shuddered ominously. From the weather deck came the sound of muffled cries. Their frantic tones were unmistakable.

'Charles!' she called in the darkness. There was no answer. She reached out along the floor. 'Charles! Where are you?'

The floor was strewn with books, the fiddle on the bookshelf had broken showering the books and journals across the floor. A strange rose-coloured light was filtering through the window. It was the colour of the storm.

Charles was on the floor. The initial impact had thrown him across the cabin. He was motionless, his face pressed between deck and cupboard.

'Help! Someone please help!' Emma cried.

But the thunder of the sea and roar of the wind swallowed her voice.

Afraid to stand, she slid down to where Charles had fallen. As the ship listed again she rolled him on to his back.

'Charles,' she called softly, stroking her hand across his face. His brow was wet and sticky. Blood. But he was breathing. 'Please wake up,' she begged. There was no response. She must go for help.

It was even darker outside the cabin. The companionway hatch had been fastened down. The boards under Emma's feet were wet.

The door to the captain's cabin was swinging. She shouted again. No answer. Every able-bodied man was on deck. She must go through the companionway in the mess. She hoped it would still be open. She knew of no other way.

Emma was no longer afraid of the darkness. She had survived days of blackness in the sail locker. All the men were on deck. And Thomas Barstow was no longer a threat. Providing the ship stayed upright, she had nothing to fear.

She climbed down to the mess deck and let her hands guide her along the low passageway. A glow from the mess encouraged her. It was the galley stove. And the smell. Burned broth. Memories of Seal Street.

The tables suspended from ropes were swinging in unison. She grabbed the ropes to support herself to the far end of the long room. As she got closer she could see the hatch above the ladder was closed. A noise, like a rat scratching in the corner, attracted her. Then a groan.

'Who's there?'

'It's me, ma'am. Samuel.' The boy pulled himself up into a sitting position. She could see his face in the pale light.

'Are you all right?'

'Not really.' he said. 'I fell through the hatch when she went over. Twisted me leg. I'm afraid I've broken it good and proper this time. Can you get Mr Witton to take a look, do you think?'

Even in the shadows Emma could see the boy's leg was folded at a strange angle.

'Mr Witton is hurt too,' she said. 'Are all the men on deck?'

'Aye, ma'am, all hands.'

There was no one to help Charles or Sam. She must do the best she could.

'I will be back,' she said. 'Wait a while.'

It was a foolish statement. The boy was going nowhere.

Charles Witton opened his eyes.

'Please do not move,' Emma said, as she wiped the blood from around his nose. A lump had already risen on his forehead. Emma pulled a thick woollen cloak from the chest of clothing. It made a good pillow.

'Now please stay where you are,' she said. 'You will be all right, won't you?'

She got no reply. His eyes had closed again.

Amongst the books scattered on the floor were the pieces of the wooden fiddle broken from the bookcase. They would make a good splint. Strips of cotton from her petticoat would serve for the binding.

Emma returned to the boy as quickly as she could and with his help applied the splint to his leg.

'I'm sure Mr Witton will fix it properly and the carpenter will make you a crutch.'

'I reckon you did a good job. See, I can move my toes.' The pain showed on his face. 'I just hope me leg'll fix quick. I don't want to be put ashore.' He sighed. 'I ain't been too lucky lately, 'ave I? What with the mast breaking and now this!'

'I think you are probably very lucky!' Emma said, as she looked down on the boy who was Joshua's best friend. Samuel was the same age but six inches shorter than her son. He was a mere slip of a boy and the soft blond curls which bubbled from his head were a refreshing change from the untended greasy mops which most seamen hid under their moth-eaten hats.

'I suggest you don't try to climb,' Emma said.

'I ain't going nowhere while she's blowing like this!'

As she left him, Emma felt inclined to touch his hair or plant a maternal kiss on his forehead. He had not complained once about the pain. He would make a good seaman!

Emma returned through the darkness to the stateroom and her other charge. As she kneeled down beside Charles, she could feel his eyes examining her face. The pale light from the window was reflecting in his eyes.

Outside, the storm clouds were finally breaking up.

'I think the worst is over,' she said.

'I hope you are right.'

Despite opening the cabin door slowly, the hinges creaked. Charles ducked his head as he stepped into his day cabin. The lump on his forehead had gone leaving only a yellowed bruise.

'Shall I leave?' Emma said, the quill poised in one hand, a piece of rag in the other.

'No! Stay. I just want to sit and rest my legs for a while. I find it tiring standing for long periods on the deck. Please,' he said, 'do not let me disturb you.'

Charles flopped back into his wingback chair. It was the only comfortable chair on the ship, even the captain did not have such a luxury. As he closed his eyes, Emma wondered if he would fall asleep.

As she worked, her hand hardly moved. The tip of the feather waved very slightly. On a tin plate in front of her, its wings fanned flat, was a dead moth.

Charles was watching, not sleeping. At first, his eyes followed the movement of the quill, a soft heron feather which turned in a curl at the tip. The hand holding it was equally soft. Fine and delicately boned. Fine like the French lace around her wrist. He followed the line of her arm resting gracefully on the table. Her back so straight. He studied her neck, slender with soft wisps of hair falling on to it from her bun. The same curling wisps framed her face.

As Emma's eyes bounced back and forth from paper to specimen she sensed she was being watched. She turned. 'What is it?' she asked.

'Nothing,' he said. 'I was just watching you and thinking.'

'I must finish the fringes on the wings,' she said, as she continued drawing.

'Young Samuel is doing well,' he said. 'You did a splendid job on his leg. Tell me, where did you learn to fix a fracture?'

'The doctor mended my sister's leg when I was a child. It is something I will never forget. I remember the sound of the bones grating together and her screams when the doctor straightened it.' She shook her head. 'But Samuel never murmured. He was very brave.'

'Very brave!' he echoed.

'It is finished, I think,' she said, as she smoothed the blotting paper over her work. 'I will add the colour later.'

Charles stood beside her chair.

'Lovely,' he said.

'I hope it is correct.' Emma waited for his comment but he made none. Wondering if she had omitted something or not copied the specimen correctly, she looked again at the markings on the moth's wings and compared them with the zigzag lines she had etched on her paper. She studied the wings' circular spots which stared back at her like a pair of large round eyes.

But Charles's eyes were set on neither insect nor picture. He was gazing at Emma with a warmth she had not seen before.

'Lovely,' he repeated, as he lifted her chin and placed a kiss on her forehead.

Emma closed her eyes.

'Please forgive me,' he said 'It is a long time since I have felt this way. I did not think it was possible. Thank you.'

'It is I who should say, thank you,' Emma said. 'You have given me so much.'

'I have done nothing,' he said.

On the desk, the quill rolled round in the inkwell as the ship slid gracefully down the side of the swell. In a few more days they would be disembarking in Sydney and their journey would be over.

# Chapter 26

'Mama, I want stay with the ship.'

'Yes,' Emma said.

'Mr Thackray said I have done well, and for him that is indeed a compliment. And the captain told me because I learned geometry and algebra at school, he would teach me to use the sextant on the next voyage. The captain was in the Royal Navy when he was young,' he added.

Emma was not surprised.

'He said if I was serious about a life at sea I should think seriously about joining the service. He said if I worked hard I could become an officer.'

'Really! And when did he say this?'

'Some weeks ago.'

'But you did not tell me.'

'I thought you would not approve.' He paused as he looked at his mother. 'I thought you disliked seamen.'

'I think perhaps I have learned to know better. My only wish is that you will be happy with the choice you make.'

'But I have never been so happy.'

'So I see.'

Joshua laughed. 'I can also say I have never been so cold, so afraid and so tired all in the same day.' He looked out to sea. 'When I climb the mast, Mama, and sit up top and the horizon is one big circle around me, I can tell you, there is no feeling to equal it. Imagine, Mama, if one day I was master of my own ship. The captain says it is not impossible.'

Emma smiled anxiously. The memories of the voyage had left her with mixed feelings. 'But the types of men on board,' she said. 'The dangers, the hard work and the weather. Don't they bother you?'

'Of course not. Those are the things I enjoy.'

Emma touched his hand. 'We have come a long way, you and I, and I am not speaking of miles from England. You have grown to a man, and I . . . well, I am not sure, but I feel my life has changed.' She sighed. 'I have thought for some time that you would choose to stay with the ship, so what you say is no surprise. I love you, Joshua,' she said, 'and I wish you well. But promise me this: promise you will write and tell me about the places you visit and the things you do. And whenever you dock in Sydney, you must find me if that is possible.'

'But, Mama, what will you do? Where will you go?'

'I will work. Perhaps draw as I have been doing these past weeks. And Charles has friends. Do not worry about me, Joshua. Just promise me you will write.'

'I promise, Mama, I will.'


Nathaniel Preston looked uncomfortable as he ushered Emma into his cabin.

'Please, take a seat.'

He waited until Emma was seated. He chose to stand. His face wore a concerned expression as he picked up a roll of patterned cloth from his desk.

'There are two things I must speak with you about before you leave the ship.'

Emma watched as he turned the bundle over in his hands.

'Firstly,' he said gravely, 'I will give you this. In doing so, I must add that I have considered my actions carefully, and in this instance have again taken the liberty of asking the advice of Mr Witton. This,' he said, looking down at the item on his palm, 'was amongst the personal possessions of the seaman, François le Fevre, the man we knew as Frenchy.'

Emma cast her eyes down.

'I understand it was his last wish that your son, Joshua be given his knife.'

'Joshua already has François' knife.'

'So be it,' the captain said. 'However, this knife,' he said, offering the package to her, 'was found in his sea chest. Perhaps your son should have this also. But I think you should see it first before you decide. The rest of Frenchy's property, his clothes and sea chest, will be auctioned amongst the men as I understand there is no family to claim them. As for the pay which is owing to him, that will be given to the seaman's fund for the widows and orphans.'

Emma took the bundle and could feel the metal folded inside it.

'Be careful when you open it. It is very sharp.'

Emma nodded.

'Now I come to the second matter,' he said, as he cleared his throat. 'It would appear I owe you an apology.'

Emma was puzzled.

'I am referring to the money which you had with you when you . . . how shall I put it . . . embarked on this voyage.' He leaned back against his desk, his hands behind his back. 'I am afraid I accused you of various offences, not least of being a thief. For that I offer you my apology.'

'Thank you,' she said. 'I can understand you would question a person in possession of such a large sum.'

'I am afraid your appearance made me assume you were a vagrant. And the fact you were in the company of a sailor, made me think your morals were those of a woman of the taverns. For that I am sorry.' He inclined his head to one side. 'You must agree, the circumstances relating to our first introduction were somewhat unusual. However,' he said, 'before I go further, let me say my opinion was influenced by Mr Witton who, I might add, has nothing but praise for the assistance you have given him with his work these last two weeks.'

He continued, 'Knowing everything is not always what it appears on the surface, I must admit I find myself intrigued with the circumstances which led to you stowing away on my ship and the fact you were carrying a bundle of gold coins. Of course, I cannot press you for an explanation if you do not wish to speak of it, but,' he said, 'it would be interesting to hear. Material for my memoirs, perhaps, or a story to tell to my grand-children.'

Emma smiled as she imagined Nathaniel Preston surrounded by an audience of boys and girls. 'A story for your grandchildren then,' she said.

Leaning back in the chair she began. 'I told you my father was a portrait artist. His work was perfect in technique, proportion and perspective. It was what the art world wanted at that time. He not only reproduced an almost identical likeness of his subject on canvas, but was able to tran-scribe their thoughts and feelings with his brush. As if he could capture their very souls. Because of his special gift he was in great demand and he worked very hard.'

The captain nodded.

'And I regard myself as fortunate; not only was I his daughter, but I was also one of his pupils. He taught me from a young age.'

Emma paused. 'But I digress. You asked me about the gold coins. As I told you, my father sold one of his paintings and, I might add, was paid handsomely for it. He gave me the coins on the day I left home to be married. I remember his words well: "Take this", he said as he pressed them into my hand. "It is a gift, but mind it carefully". He made me promise I would tell no one about it, not my husband-to-be, my sister, or Joshua, who was a baby at the time.

'I did not want to take it but he insisted. "This is not for you to waste on frivolities", he said. "It is for that time in your life when you have need for it". I asked him when that time would be. "You will know when that time comes", he said. I remember his words clearly. "Trust me", he said. "You will know".

'Papa and I were very close and I could see he was troubled. He was not a well man.' There was a sadness in Emma's tone. 'His sight was leaving him.' Emma sighed. 'How tragic that is for anyone, but for an artist . . .' She shook her head.

'When I came on board the ship, I had few possessions. But I carried the gift my father had given me. During the dark hours I spent in the sail locker, I thought about him a lot. I decided he would have wished I used the money to pay for my passage. He would have been happy that his gift would give me the opportunity to find a new life.'

'I think I would have liked to meet your father,' the captain said.

'It would have been his pleasure, sir.'

'Then you accept my apology.'

'Yes, Captain, I do and I thank you for not putting me ashore in Portsmouth.'

Nathaniel Preston smiled. 'It is the Almighty you must thank for that, not me.'

'I do,' said Emma. 'Every night in my prayers.'

Emma returned to her cabin, warmed by her conversation with the captain, but saddened by the reminder of François which she carried in her hands. He had told her he had another knife, but she had forgotten. It was rolled in a sleeve torn from a woman's blouse. She laid it on her bunk and unwrapped it carefully.

The knife was old and unpretentious, but its blade had been honed so many times it was worn thin, its tip sharpened to a point like a stiletto. A rust-coloured stain ran down the length of the blade and, despite the wooden hilt being ingrained with grease and sweat, the brown stain had seeped into it. A length of plaited twine was bound tightly around the cracked wood preventing it from splitting further.

Turning the knife over, Emma noted several notches and scratches pecked into the hilt. They appeared to be deliberate marks. Apart from the row of single lines, two figures had been carved into the wood. They had worn smooth over the years and were difficult to read. At first glance Emma interpreted the scratchings as the numbers, '8' and '1' but as she turned the knife around she realized what they were. The letters carved into the wood were the initials 'T B'. The knife was not François'. It had belonged to Thomas Barstow.

His knock was soft yet it startled her. Charles closed the door quietly as if entering a room where someone was sleeping.

As Emma looked back towards the door, the fine brush trickled a line of water droplets across the table top. Quickly dabbing the pearl beads, she laid a sheet of blotting paper across her work. She stood in front of the table, shielding the drawing. 'This is your room,' she said. 'You should not knock.'

'I'm sorry to interrupt you,' Charles said, conscious of an expression on Emma's face he had not seen before.

'I was just finishing. I will put this away.'

'Will you show me what it is you are working on?'

Emma looked guilty.

'It is nothing in particular,' she said. The brush in her hand was dripping spots on to her apron.

Charles looked down. Her eyes followed.

'How careless of me.'

He lifted the chair from in front of her, took the rag from her hand, kneeled and carefully dabbed away the marks. 'There,' he said. 'It is gone.' As he returned the cloth to the table, his hand reached out towards the picture hidden behind her on the desk. 'May I?' he asked.

Emma nodded and sat down.

The picture showed a man and woman. Neither was young nor well dressed. The man was slender of build and appeared rather frail. He was seated in an old armchair. Beside him was a walking stick with a metal handle moulded to form a duck's bill. Standing beside him was a lady of similar age. She was more robust than the man, of proud stature and with a kindly expression, though her face was touched with an air of sadness. One of her hands rested on the man's arm. The other held a full blown rose. A dog rose. A petal had shed from it and was falling to the floor. The rose was tinted with a touch of paint – the softest pink. It was the only dab of colour on the pen and ink work. It was still wet.

Charles sighed heavily. 'Your parents?'

'Yes,' she said, as she looked down at her work.

'There is something about this drawing which is remarkable. Your father, I think. Yes,' he said. 'His eyes! They are so striking, so intense, so alive. I feel they are looking out at me from the page.'

Emma smiled.

'Did you copy this from a photograph?' he said, looking around the desk expecting to find one.

'It is a picture I carry with me all the time,' she said. 'In my heart.'

He looked from her to the drawing and back again. His hand enclosed hers.

She was still holding the sable brush.

'Is there space for another in your heart?' he enquired, drawing her towards him.

Her throat was full. Her eyes welled with salty tears. 'You are so kind,' she said. 'You remind me of my father.'

He tensed.

She sensed his disappointment. He had misunderstood.

'I loved him very much,' she said.


The evening was cool.

From her favourite place in the bow Emma listened to the group of seamen huddled around the blacksmith's fire. Joshua was amongst them. She heard his voice. Heard him laughing with the others.

When a piece of wood was thrown into the embers, sparks danced into the air and she thought about François. She thought about the tiny stars which shone in the sea and wondered if she would forget him when she left the ship. Leaning over the rail she looked down at the water curling from the bow.

In her hand was the roll of cloth. She opened it. The blade glinted in the moonlight.

Emma gazed at the sea as she let it fall. She knew that soon she would never see the tiny stars again.

The knife sliced silently into the water and disappeared.

# Chapter 27

## Sydney, New South Wales,
## 3 July 1856

A s the rain stopped and the sun, rising from the Pacific, breathed gold on her tired canvas, the *Morning Star* eased through the mile-wide Sydney Heads. Emma stood in the bow as the barquentine sailed slowly towards the quay. By the time it tied up against the wharf the sky was clear and the chill had gone from the air.

It was a grand harbour, broad and deep and well sheltered from the open sea. So different from the sandy flats of the tidal estuary of the River Esk. Some of the vessels moored around the semicircular quay were grand also. Tall masted clippers and schooners, far bigger than the ships which moored in the Yorkshire port. But, Emma considered, the Whitby wharfs were always congested. Here there was more space and fewer ships.

Like Whitby, the shops and houses around the wharf area reached almost to the waterfront and the sounds of machinery and the clatter of wheels and hoofs was the same. But unlike the North Coast fishing village, the boats in this harbour lacked the bright colours of the herring fleet.

It was not what Emma had expected. On the dock there was a lot of noise with raised voices and everyone appeared to be in a hurry. Waifs wearing little more than rags were the only ones loitering about. They looked like beggars. Emma asked herself, wasn't Australia a rich country like America? Wasn't Sydney like Boston with fine houses and elegant families?

Having dressed in pink satin she felt uncomfortable. She did not belong in this foreign port. Where would she go? What would she do when the *Morning Star* sailed and she was alone? How many times had she asked herself these questions and still she had no answer.

From the aft companionway Charles appeared followed by another gentleman whom she had not noticed come aboard. As they approached, she heard Charles say, 'I would like to introduce my widowed cousin, Mrs Emma Quinlan.' They all smiled as the introductions were made.

'Emma, this is the friend I spoke of, Sir Percival Seaton.'

The older man bowed. 'I am pleased to make your acquaintance, Mrs Quinlan.'

A tentative smile hid Emma's surprise.

'I have received good news of my expedition,' Charles announced. 'The main party were delayed on their voyage. After more than three weeks of idling in the Doldrums, they had to sail almost to South America to catch the westerlies. The group is no more than a week ahead of me.'

'That is good news indeed.'

Charles turned to his friend. 'I must admit, I had not relished the idea of travelling the countryside alone. Now I shall be able to catch up with them before they get too far ahead.'

'And what of your young cousin?' Sir Percival said, as he glanced at Emma. 'Where will you be staying, Mrs Quinlan?'

Before Emma had the opportunity to say anything, Charles interrupted.

'Would you permit me to answer for you, Emma?'

She nodded, relieved.

'As you know I had originally intended to arrive in Sydney some months ago which would have allowed time to organize accommodation for me and my daughter. But under the circumstances . . .'

'Yes, I understand.'

'My predicament now,' said Charles, 'is that I am undecided about my future. The expedition will take me into the hinterland for six or maybe nine months. When I return there will be considerable work to be completed, namely cataloguing the specimens which I collect.' He turned to Sir Percival. 'Emma is assisting me. She is an invaluable help. I do not know what I would do without her.'

'You are very lucky, Charles, to have such a talented cousin.'

'I am indeed,' Charles said. 'And Emma has graciously offered to put my work in order while I am away, a chore, I must admit, which has been eluding me for some time. But she will need somewhere to work.' He took a deep breath. 'The problem I have at the moment is that I am undecided if I am going to make Sydney my permanent home. I may seek to gain an appointment with the university, but if nothing is forthcoming, I will consider leaving the city and buying a parcel of land in the country. At present,' he said, 'I feel it is unlikely I will return to England. There is nothing there for me now, but it is a decision I must give some thought to.'

'And your position, Mrs Quinlan,' the gentleman asked. 'Will you be staying in Sydney? I do hope that the answer is yes.' He continued without giving Emma the opportunity to answer, 'If you will excuse me for saying so there is a considerable shortfall in the number of educated and well-bred young ladies in this town.'

'I have no plans at the moment,' Emma said, 'But as Charles says, I will require somewhere to live and a place where I can continue with the work I have been doing for him.'

'Emma is a talented artist,' Charles said.

'Indeed? That is very interesting,' he said. 'Tell me, Mrs Quinlan, would you consider accepting my hospitality for a short time? I know my wife would be delighted to have an English lady for company. We have a large residence and we can make ample space available for you to pursue your work. If it is suitable, you could stay with us at least until your cousin returns and you are both able to come to a decision about your future.'

'That is very generous of you, Percy. Is it not, Emma?'

'Extremely,' said Emma cautiously.

'Excellent! My wife will be thrilled.'

Despite the freshness of the winter air, Emma's hands were clammy. She watched as the two gentlemen left the ship and talked together on the wharf. Emma looked across to the buildings behind them. They were grey and daunting.

'And welcome to New South Wales, Mrs Quinlan,' Sir Percival called as he climbed into his carriage. A boy dressed in tatters hurtled past Charles, almost knocking him over. Further along the wharf a policeman blew several sharp blasts on his whistle.

'I hope you will forgive me for taking certain liberties,' Charles said, when he stepped back on board. 'And I apologize, I did not give you the opportunity to answer for yourself.'

'I did not have an answer,' Emma said.

He paused. 'What I said is the truth. When I return from the expedi-

tion I must make a decision about my future and it will not be easy.' He
took Emma's hand. 'There is another question I wish to ask you and I find
it difficult.' He led her to the boatswain's deck locker and invited her to sit
with him.

'I think fate had a hand in throwing us together on the *Morning Star* and
for that I will be eternally grateful.' He spoke softly. 'Sadly, when we
embarked, we were both burdened with grief and for you in particular the
voyage has not all been smooth.' His eyes settled on the ships bobbing on
the harbour. 'I believe a ship is an artificial environment. Like a cocoon.
And like a cocoon, sometimes strange and unexpected things emerge
from it. On the ship there were dangers for you, and the life for both of
us was foreign to any life we would have encountered had we been thrown
together on the land. But I believe we have both emerged from the voyage
somewhat stronger and wiser for the experience.'

He continued, 'Sydney also is a strange place. It is a city filled with
English folk but far different to any English town you or I have ever
known. It is a town you will either love or hate. Whichever the case, you
must live here for sometime before you can make a decision.

'If you will take my advice, Emma, you will accept Sir Percival's generous offer of hospitality. You will be living with genteel people in most
respectable surroundings. I could think of nothing better. And when I
return then you will be able to decide what the future holds for you.

'I want to help you, Emma, and I would like to be part of your future.
With your artistic talent you are invaluable to me, but what I am thinking
of is far greater than that. In the meantime if you are in agreement, I will
leave you with sufficient work to keep you occupied, and, if possible, I
will arrange to have items sent back to you while I am away. As I said on
the ship, I do not expect you to do this work for nothing. I will arrange
for an amount of money to be paid into an account for you. It will not be
a great deal but it will be sufficient to provide you with some indepen-
dence. And if I could be so bold as to state, your talent as a portrait
painter would be well sought after, were it made known. A reputable lady
artist would be very well received in this new country.

'Now,' he declared. 'I have spoken too long and probably said too
much. But before I finish there are two more things I must beg of you.'

Emma inclined her head.

'Firstly, I ask that you remain in Sydney until I return. And secondly,
that while I am away you will allow me to write to you. May I do that?'

'Yes, of course,' she said. 'My dear Charles, it seems to me from the time of my accident on the ship, I have been in your debt, and I have done little to show my gratitude. Without you I would not be here and none of this would be happening.' She rested her hand on his. 'I promise I will be here when you return, and I will look forward to receiving your letters and news of how the expedition is progressing. As to my decision whether I leave this town or stay, that is something I will save for your return. I am sure that with your help I will not make the wrong decision. And,' she said, 'as for the drawings, it will be a pleasure for me to continue. I will try not to disappoint you with their quality.'

'Excellent. Then that is settled. I am relieved.' He stood up and filled his lungs with air. 'Mrs Quinlan, if you would care to take my arm, I will take you for your first stroll on Australian soil.'

With one hand grasping Charles's and the other on her skirt, Emma stepped from the gangplank on to the quay. The smells reminded her of Whitby; seaweed, fish, and meat roasting.

'If you bought a farm in the country,' said Emma, 'would you have a house cow?'

'No!' he said grinning. 'I would have a herd of cows. And all the milk you could drink.'

'Then I will think about what you have said.'

'Now it is my turn to say, thank you.'

The ship had been Emma's home for almost four months. Leaving was not easy.

It was midday when the carriage stopped on the wharf opposite the gangplank. It was followed by a dray wagon. The ship was quiet. Most of the men had gone ashore. Others were resting below decks.

Though Emma had boarded the *Morning Star* with nothing she was leaving with two large trunks: one full of clothes, the other packed with Charles's exotic specimens, equipment and journals.

Beside his own trunk, Charles had an extraordinary number of boxes and cases. Joshua and two of the seamen hauled them up from the hold and loaded them on to the wagon. Charles made sure everything was secured firmly.

For Emma, saying goodbye to Joshua was the hardest. She tried to joke with him and make light of the fact he would soon be sailing away, but when he hugged her for the final time the tears flowed fast and free.

'Your boy will be fine,' said Charles. 'He is in good hands.'

Joshua rubbed his face with the back of his sleeve. 'Goodbye, Mama,

I will write, and I will visit when I can. I have not forgotten what you asked.'

Two seamen appeared from the companionway. 'Begging your pardon, ma'am, we got something for you.'

Jack Burns had a sheepish expression on his face. Standing beside him was Mr Kaye, the ship's carpenter, the quiet man whose skill had repaired the ship several times during the voyage. 'The *Morning Star*,' Burns said, as he handed Emma a model ship rigged in fine twine and boasting a full complement of square sails.

'Replica she is,' he said. 'A bit smaller than the real one. Kaye whittled it. I just did the sails. And she's rigged right. Just like the *Star*!'

'Thank you, gentlemen. This is remarkable.'

'Might do to give the wood a bit of an oiling occasionally,' the carpenter said.

'I will, and I will treasure this along with my memories of my time on board.'

'Aye, well, best be off.' Jack Burns lifted his cap.

Mr Kaye touched his knuckles to his forehead. 'Good luck,' he said.

'Aye, and to you too, governor.'

'Thank you, Mr Kaye,' Charles replied. 'And I wish you both a safe voyage home.'

Emma stood by the gangway cradling the model in her arms as the two men climbed back down the hatch.

'I believe you have won a few hearts,' Charles whispered to her. 'Let me help you. We must get started. We have a long drive ahead of us and our hosts will be expecting us before dark. It will feel strange to sleep on beds which are not rolling but I think by tonight we will both be ready for sleep.'

'Goodbye, miss! Good luck!' a voice shouted, as the carriage started to roll. Young Samuel was balancing on the rail, waving his crutch in the air.

Joshua ran up the gangplank and on to the quay. ' 'Bye, Mama!' he yelled.

Emma waved her handkerchief until the carriage turned away from the water and the two boys were lost from sight.

It was early the following Monday morning when Charles slid the canvas bag hard against the saddle on the back of the same flat wagon. This time his luggage consisted of few items and he insisted that he load them himself.

'You are taking so little with you,' Emma said.

'Too much, I think. I have to be prepared to carry everything by horse or mule as the wagon will probably be unsuitable for the route we are taking. Dear Emma, I wish you were coming with me, but such a journey is no place to take a lady. But,' he said, 'it worries me to leave you.'

'I will be fine. I could not have imagined a situation more generous and Lady Seaton is a dear kind lady. And this lovely house . . . and the people I have been introduced to over this last two days, I could not have wished for anything better.'

'Then I am pleased. While I am away I will write, but despatching mail may not be easy.'

'I understand.'

'If all goes well I may be back by Christmas. Are you sure you will be all right alone, Emma?'

'I will not be alone.'

His face was serious. 'You will stay here until I come back, won't you?' 'Yes.'

'Good. Then I must say goodbye.' He held Emma's hands in his. As she leaned her body towards him he reached his arms around her.

'I did not think it would be so difficult to leave.'

'God speed and bring you back safely,' she said.

Charles climbed on to the seat next to the driver and with a flick of the whip the pair of horses snorted and carried the wagon slowly down the dusty driveway. Emma watched it disappearing into the distance.

Lady Seaton was standing at the doorway. 'He will be back in quick sticks, my dear, you mark my words. Come along, we have work to do. You must help me with my preparations for next week's reception. We will be entertaining over a hundred guests. Everyone who is anyone will be here. It will be a wonderful opportunity for you to be presented and make some new acquaintances.'

Emma looked down the track, but all she could see was a cloud of settling dust.

'Come inside, dear, Mr Witton will be back before you know it.'

# Chapter 28

Though it was still early, the large reception room was filling quickly. Lady Seaton descended on each group of newcomers as they arrived, flitting between guests like a nervous butterfly. Emma had feared awkward questions, but against the background of voices, the clink of crystal and the rustle of silk on silk, conversation began to flow freely. Most of the Sydney residents wanted snippets of information about England. Anything, from the amount of snow which had fallen the previous winter, to the state of the railways, to Palmerston's power as Prime Minister and the growing legend of Miss Florence Nightingale. Emma answered as best she could and listened to various opinions. At times she would have preferred to listen to the string quartet which was playing in the ballroom.

'Mrs Quinlan. I hardly recognized you.'

Emma spun around to the familiar voice. 'Captain Preston,' she said, holding out her hand. 'I am so pleased to see you. Lady Seaton said you might be attending. I was surprised to hear you had not sailed.'

'Unfortunately we are waiting on a consignment of wool. As soon as it arrives and is loaded we sail for London.'

A servant approached with a platter. The captain waved him away.

'Perhaps we could get away from the noise for a moment,' he said. 'There is a small matter I must speak with you about.'

Somewhat surprised by his request, Emma accompanied him through the French doors. The courtyard, bordered by a garden, overlooked an apron of neatly trimmed grass which sloped to the banks of the Parramatta River. Across the water a herd of long-horned cattle were grazing in the marshes.

'Is it something about my son, Joshua?' she asked anxiously. 'He has signed on for the return voyage.'

'No, it is another matter,' the captain said. 'I have something for you.'

Reaching in his pocket he took out a black satin purse and placed it on Emma's palm. 'A gift from your father, if I am not mistaken.'

Emma closed her fingers around it. She could feel the coins inside. 'Thank you,' she said quietly. 'You are a kind man.'

'I am not sure everyone would agree with you on that matter!' Captain Preston allowed himself to smile as he offered Emma his arm and escorted her back into the main reception area. 'Now, if you will excuse me, I will leave you to enjoy your evening. I plan to return to the quay early.'

'Would you tell my son you have seen me?'

Nathaniel Preston bowed. 'I will. Goodbye, Mrs Quinlan.'

As Emma watched him walk away, she thought of the ship which had carried her halfway across the world, of its captain, and of her father whose gift to her was far greater than mere pieces of gold. As she clutched the purse to her chest, her eyes filled with tears.

'Now my dear,' said Lady Seaton, as she swept across the floor. 'I do not want to see you on your own. There are so many people to whom you must be introduced. Come with me. You must meet the Governor and Lady Denison. They arrived a few moments ago and I have just told them what a talented young lady you are.'

Emma followed as the hostess skirted the ballroom, nodding pleasantries to everyone she passed.

Though the governor was surrounded by a group of people, Lady Seaton bustled her way through. 'Sir William, may I introduce Mrs Emma Quinlan?'

Emma curtsied.

'Mrs Quinlan,' the governor said. 'I am pleased to make your acquaintance. I trust you like our town.'

'Indeed. It has a beautiful harbour and the countryside around is very pleasant. I hope to see much more of Sydney in the near future.'

'And I hope we will see a lot more of you in the future.'

'That is very kind of you.'

'Tell me, how was your passage? A good one I hope?'

'It was a good journey.'

'I am pleased to hear it,' he said glancing at his wife. 'We found the passage most tedious, didn't we, my dear? The accommodation was terribly uncomfortable and the service quite abominable. However,' he sighed, 'we have to make these sacrifices at times, do we not?'

Emma was obliged to agree.

When Lady Seaton appeared with another group of guests, Emma was relieved. It gave her the opportunity to escape from the noise and chatter to the peace of the small garden. Outside the sun was bright but the day cold. There was no breath of wind. How different she thought from her special place on the ship's weather deck. How she longed, at times, to again hear the sound of the sea, to feel the salt on her face, and to gaze out at the changing hues of the evening sky colouring the horizon.

The room provided for Emma to work in was delightful. It was a long, narrow room, on the ground floor, with French windows which overlooked the river. Facing north, it allowed the winter sun to stream across its polished floor.

It took Emma quite some time before she could commence the work Charles had left with her. Lady Seaton left her little time to herself, interrupting continually, enquiring if she needed anything, offering assistance, requesting her company on a visit into Sydney or to stroll with her in the gardens. She even insisted Emma take time to read the British newspapers, despite the fact on arrival they were four months out of date and any significant news had already been printed in the *Sydney Morning Herald*. It was only when the novelty of Emma's presence had worn off, Lady Seaton allowed her time to herself.

Apart from work, Emma wanted to write to Charles and Joshua but she had no way of contacting either. Her correspondence would have to wait until she received a letter from them.

It was with some difficulty she wrote to her sister telling her briefly about the voyage and what had happened since she left Whitby. About Lord and Lady Seaton and the fine house she was living in. And about Charles Witton, saying how kind he had been and the opportunities he had provided for her. Emma concluded by mentioning Joshua, saying he was well but not telling Anna he had sailed away with the ship.

When the letter was sealed she handed it to Sir Percival. He assured her it would despatched on the next mail packet sailing to England.

September brought spring to New South Wales and it was beautiful. Though the eucalyptus trees showed little evidence of the changing season, the wild flowers bloomed in a rainbow of colours – red spider flowers, blue leschenaultia, golden wattles, and wild orchids. At night the fragrances of the garden drifted in through the open windows, the scent of daphne and boronia, and native frangipani. Emma listened to the clicking of cicadas and the hum of the beetles' wings as they buzzed frantically around the room. But as she lay on her bed and looked at the white ceiling, her mind always wandered back to her bunk on the *Morning Star* and the man who had nursed her when she was sick.

With every passing day, the midday sun rose higher and the temperature grew warmer. The freezing mornings, when she had to scrape ice from the bird bath outside the French windows, were soon gone. By seven o'clock the days were hotter than she had ever known in Whitby, by midday the heat almost unbearable.

Emma's work with the specimens kept her busy. She began early in the morning when it was cool, but by noon found it impossible to draw as the sweat from her hands dripped on to the paper. During the afternoons she would spend her time reading, referring to Charles's journals. The study absorbed her.

Occasionally when she wandered in the garden she would catch an insect and take it indoors and attempt to identify it and draw a likeness of it, carefully recording each specimen in the hope she might discover something new before Charles returned. It was three months since he left and Christmas was still two months away. She tried not to think too hard about him.

But Emma's progress with the backlog of work was halted when Sir Percival requested a portrait of his wife. He described it as a commission though Emma refused to accept payment saying it was the least she could do to repay their kindness.

Lady Seaton was not the easiest of subjects. Unable to sit still, or sit quietly, she was constantly talking and shuffling, adjusting the folds in her skirt or tilting the angle of her head. But three sittings were all Emma needed. She could have managed with less but Lady Seaton insisted.

The long room had become both laboratory and studio for Emma. She was mostly left alone and particularly enjoyed working after supper when the household had retired and everything was quiet.

When the portrait was completed, Lady Seaton was ecstatic and immediately requested Emma paint Sir Percival, insisting she start right away. With her ladyship's wide circle of friends, word of Emma's talent quickly passed around and soon she was receiving requests for her services. She refused them all, but one gentleman was not easy to deter. He visited the house on three occasions expressing interest in her talent. Emma accepted his compliments politely though she felt unsure of his intentions.

As the weeks passed Emma thought more and more about Charles and when Lady Seaton asked for help in making plans for the forthcoming Christmas festivities, Emma accepted, pleased at the distraction.

Lady Seaton mopped her brow as she wandered over to the easel by the window. A white tablecloth was draped over it. 'May I see what it is that you have been working on, my dear? I do so like looking at your pictures.'

Emma lifted the cotton from the canvas.

'My, my! Mr Witton. And such a perfect likeness.' Clapping her hands, she stepped back. 'How did you manage to capture his face without even a single sitting? You must carry his image in your head.'

'In my head – and here,' Emma said, resting the flat of her hand across her chest. 'I did not realize it myself until I started painting.'

'Oh, I must show Percy, he will be so impressed. And when Charles returns, I am sure he will be delighted. That won't be long now. Didn't he say he would back for Christmas?'

'If all went well.'

'Have you received word from him?'

Emma shook her head.

'Don't worry, dear. He'll be all right. You wait and see.'

Christmas came and went with all its celebrations, as did New Year. The house had a constant stream of guests passing through, even the governor and his wife called in one afternoon to take tea. Much to Emma's embarrassment Lady Seaton made sure Sir Percival's portrait was displayed to advantage.

But despite the hubbub of activity, Emma could not stop thinking about Charles. Even when entertaining visitors, she found herself not listening and having to ask them to repeat their questions before she could reply.

Where was Charles? What had delayed his return? Was anything amiss?

As the weeks passed with still no news, Emma grew more anxious. She did not discuss her concerns with Sir Percival, but she knew from the whispered words spoken with his wife, he too was worried about Charles's welfare.

It was an oppresive afternoon in late March. The intense heat of the previous few days was suddenly dowsed by a wild thunderstorm which unleashed its full force directly over the house. Emma was standing beside the window watching the courtyard as it turned white under the barrage of hailstones. She didn't hear the knock or see the door open. When she turned, Sir Percival and Lady Seaton were in the room standing beside each other. Something about their stance was unusual, almost childlike. Sir Percival had a piece of paper in his hand. Lady Seaton a handkerchief.

'Sorry to interrupt you, dear,' Lady Seaton said.

'Please come in.' Emma had to raise her voice to be heard above the thunder. 'You are not interrupting me. I was just watching the weather. The contrasts here are so stark.'

There was silence.

'You tell her, dear,' Lady Seaton said nudging her husband.

Sir Percival spoke as he stepped forward. 'I am sorry, Emma, but we have received some bad news and felt that you would want to be informed.'

Emma's fingers covered her lips. She sat down. 'It's news of Charles, isn't it?'

Lady Seaton walked over to her and took her hand. 'No, dear, it's not that. It's the ship you sailed on, the *Morning Star*. She has sunk!'

'No!' Emma cried. 'Where! When!'

'Bass Strait, off the Furneaux Islands. She was due to dock in Sydney two weeks ago.' Sir Percival shook his head as he handed a sheet of paper to Emma. 'Here are the names of the survivors.'

She took it and ran her eyes down the list. She read it again. Joshua Quinlan's name did not appear on it.

'We are so sorry, dear,' Lady Seaton said.

Emma face was pale. 'But what happened?'

'I am told there was a fire as the ship was sailing through the strait. It started in the stern section below deck. The men managed to put it out, but not before it had disabled the rudder. Without steerage the ship drifted. The master thought they would clear the islands as they were well to the north but a gale blew them on to an uncharted reef.' Sir Percival shook his head. 'Treacherous currents and winds in those waters! I understand the captain stayed on board with a handful of crew while two boats were lowered. But one was swamped and several of the men drowned. The other boat picked up the survivors and managed to make the shore. But it seems that when the men returned the following day they found the ship had broken in two and there was no sign of anyone on deck.

'But how do you know this?'

'Word came from the men who survived. They were lucky. They had landed on one of the larger islands and were able to make their way to the lighthouse. They stayed with the lighthouse keeper until they were picked up by sealers and eventually landed in Melbourne.'

'But what of the captain and men who stayed on board? Could they have got away on another boat perhaps? Drifted to the mainland or another island?'

Sir Percival looked grave. 'It is unlikely. We would have heard by now. Unless they landed on an uninhabited island. Even then their chances of survival would not be good.'

Emma spoke calmly. 'Do they have the names of the men who drowned?'

'No, only this list of the men who survived.'

She read through it again slowly.

*Leonard Thackray – First Mate*
*William Wortley – Second Mate*
*Alfred Burns*
*Neville Gill*
*Kenneth Kaye*
*Jack Mahoney*
*Mikael Mikelsonn*
*Leslie Mundy*
*Harold Pickersgill*
*Walter Womersley*

'I remember them all,' she said softly. 'Mr Burns and Mr Kaye were good men. I am pleased they survived.' She turned the page to see if any names were entered on the other side.

'Is there anything we can do?'

'No, thank you. It was my son's choice to sail and he was aware of the perils. I am sure Captain Preston did all he possibly could to safeguard his men and ship.'

Sir Percival held out his hand towards his wife. 'Come along, my dear. I think Emma would like some time to herself.'

As they left, Emma walked over to the window. She gazed at the rain streaming down the pane until her eyes filled with tears and she could see no more.

# Chapter 29

A hot wind was blowing from the interior when the rider arrived with the mail. After handing the leather pouch to Sir Percival, the man was conveyed to the kitchen for some refreshments. After briefly perusing the contents of the pouch, Sir Percival walked into the conservatory.

Lady Seaton was sitting with her eyes closed, her embroidery resting on her lap. It was too humid to sew, her hands had been clammy and as a result she had used barely six inches of silk the whole afternoon. Emma was reading.

Saying nothing, Lord Percival handed an envelope to Emma, turned and walked out studying the other letter in his hand.

Lady Seaton opened her eyes and frowned. 'Who is it from, Percy?'

He did not answer.

Emma examined her envelope. It had taken over four months to arrive.

'Is it from Mr Witton?' Lady Seaton enquired.

'No,' said Emma, recognizing the writing. 'It is from my sister, Anna in England.'

She wandered over to the window to read it.

*Dearest Emma*

*How good it is to hear you are safe and well. I was delighted to receive your letter telling of your voyage to Australia and your new life in the colony. How exciting that must be. How brave you are to travel to the other side of the globe. I do envy you.*

*I hope Joshua is well. Daniel and the boys are well and wish to be remembered to you.*

*I needed to contact you several weeks ago but having no forwarding address it was not possible. Are you aware that George is dead? He was found in the house in Seal Street. The doctor said he had died from the drink.*

*I was contacted because my name and address was found amongst your letters in the house. It appears George had no relatives.*

*In your absence and with no other monies available, Daniel decided it was best to act on your behalf and advise the authorities to sell the house in order that George's outstanding debts (and they were quite considerable) were paid.*

*I know this news will come as a shock to you and I am sorry that this is the main thrust of this my letter.*

*My dear Emma, I know you have suffered in the past but now you have a new life and all that is far behind you. You mentioned a gentleman you met on the ship. I hope you will find happiness in that direction if that is your wish.*

*I think of you often and miss you.*

*Your loving sister,*

*Anna*

Emma folded the letter and placed it back into the envelope.

'Good news, dear?' Lady Seaton said inquisitively.

Not knowing what to say, Emma didn't answer. How could she say George's death was good news? That would be terrible. But she remembered how many times in her heart of hearts she had wished that to be the case. Now he was dead she found herself devoid of feeling. She felt neither elation nor bitterness, guilt nor sorrow for the man to whom she had been married for twelve years. As she stared at the envelope, all she could feel was emptiness.

The arrival of the maid with the afternoon tea trolley came as a relief.

'Splendid,' Lady Seaton said. 'This heat makes one so dreadfully thirsty. Don't you agree, dear?'

'It does indeed.'

After setting out the crockery, the maid disappeared and returned with a plate of cheese and fruitcake. 'Will there be anything else, ma'am?'

'No thank you.'

Emma was pouring tea when Sir Percival appeared at the door. As he wandered over to his leather chair his wife observed him quizzically. He appeared preoccupied with the letter he was holding in his hand.

'What is it dear?' Lady Seaton said, pushing her needlework to one side.

'It's Charles's party,' he sighed. 'It appears things are not well.'

Emma's heart sank as she waited for him to continue.

'It is written by a man I do not know. He was with Charles on the scientific expedition. Let me read an excerpt:

*We were beset by problems from the very start. After only a week the shaft on the wagon broke. A week later, one of the horses went lame and had to be shot. The following week two of the horses wandered off one night which meant discarding some of the equipment. After that we were almost consumed in a scrub fire and then some of the men became sick. When Henry Machin fell and broke his leg a decision was made to abort the expedition. Charles Witton volunteered to remain with Mr Machin while we returned for help. We left the pair in a small clearing beside a river, with two tents and sufficient rations. They were aware it would be at least six weeks before we would get back to them.*

'But surely they should have been back by now!'

Sir Percival shook his head. His expression was grave. 'It says here the rescue party returned as quickly as they could but it took them seven weeks.' He referred to the letter:

*When we located the place we had left them, we found the river had risen and the campsite was under water. With the volume of water and speed of the current we were unable to cross. There was no sign of the men on the other bank and after an unsuccessful search, the rescue was called off.*

'What is he saying, Sir Percival? What does he mean?'

'He is saying, though he does not write it, that the conditions in the area are extremely difficult. The terrain is near impossible to penetrate, the country is inhospitable, the heat unbearable. There are natives about and animals. Snakes. Deadly spiders. God only knows what lurks in the bushland.' He sighed loudly. 'I do not want to say this, but in all truth, if we do not receive word within another week or two, we can only presume that Charles and Henry Machin are dead.'

Emma collapsed into the chair. 'No,' she murmured. 'No.'

Emma could not work. Nor could she sleep.

Whenever a rider appeared on the drive she would rush to the door to find if there was any news.

Lady Seaton tried to be of comfort, but nothing worked, until one afternoon when a letter arrived. She bustled into Emma's studio waving an envelope.

'Emma. A letter from England. This will cheer you up. Maybe it's from your sister.'

Emma smiled faded when she recognized the handwriting. It bore none of the delicate style of her sister's hand. The strokes were thick and uneven. It had been written by her son and posted in London in October 1856. As she opened it she felt the tears running down her cheeks. She knew he had sent it sometime before the *Morning Star* had embarked on its fateful voyage.

'Perhaps it is better if I leave you alone,' Lady Seaton said.

Emma didn't reply. She was reading.

*Dearest Mama*

*I hope you are well and send you my love.*

*My friend Samuel also sends his good wishes. I am sure you will remember him. His leg is healed, the only sign of the break is a little thickening where the bones fitted together. He walks and runs with no limp and can climb the rigging as swiftly as any man.*

*The return voyage from Sydney was good. We made good way up the coast of Africa and apart from a few sails blown out and the smell of sulphur (used to get rid of the lice) there were no problems. We docked in London on 10 November.*

*The Morning Star was due to sail again for Sydney last week, but when Samuel and I heard that Captain Preston was leaving the ship and that it was to get a new Master, we decided instead to go to Portsmouth.*

*Two days ago Sam and I joined the Royal Navy. I hope you will be happy for me. It is what I want to do. I do not know when, if ever, I will sail to the Southern Ocean but hopefully, one day I will visit you in Sydney.*

*Give my regards to Mr Witton.*

*I have not forgotten my promise and I will write to you again.*

*Your loving son,*

                                                         *Joshua*

From the doorway Lady Seaton could see Emma bent over, her face buried in her hands. 'What is it dear?' she said, putting her arm around her shoulders. 'Not more bad news?'

'No,' Emma sobbed. 'Wonderful news! Joshua didn't sail with the *Morning Star*. He wasn't on the ship when it sank. Nor was Captain Preston. They are both alive.'

'Praise be!' Lady Seaton shouted. 'Praise the Lord!'

It was the first week in April. The ground was cracked and corrugated. On the driveway the horses' hoofs churned up a cloud of dust which floated on the warm air and seemed unwilling to settle. Watching from her window, Emma recognized Sir Percival's carriage and returned to her work. Ten minutes later there was a knock on her door.

'Emma, there is someone here to see you,' Lady Seaton called.

'If it is that fellow Winterbourne who has been begging me to paint his portrait, please tell him I am not available.'

'It is not Winterbourne.' The voice was gentle; she recognized it instantly.

'Charles!'

As she rose, he held out his arms.

'Oh, Charles, dear Charles,' she said, as she felt his arms close around her. 'We thought you were dead. I thought I would never see you again.'

'My dear Emma, how much I have wished for this moment. Sometimes I thought it would never come.'

Lifting her head, she looked into his face. 'But you are so thin! Come. Sit down.' She led him to the armchair which faced the river and sat beside him on the foot stool. After a few moments silence, Emma asked, 'How did you manage to survive? Sir Percival told me what happened, that you stayed behind and the river flooded.'

Charles gazed through the window to the river lazing between the fields like a silver snake. 'It is a long story.'

Emma smiled kindly at him. 'Please tell me.'

His eyes looked tired as he spoke quietly. 'We had been waiting for the party to return, when a summer storm struck. The rain was torrential, I have never witnessed anything like it, and the river broke its banks. We woke in the night to find water lapping at our feet. The current was strong. It carried everything in its path. We could see the level rising by the minute.

'Our only escape was to scramble up the side of the valley. It wasn't easy for Henry. At times I dragged him, at others he crawled on his belly. There was no path through the bush, only tracks made by kangaroos and wild pigs. Apart from a bag of biscuits everything in the camp was washed away. Including my microscope.'

'Then how did you manage?'

'We were found by a group of natives. Women and children gathering berries. They were very wary of us at first but offered us food. After two nights they helped carry my friend to their small camp. It was not much more than a clearing in the bush with a few shelters made from woven reeds, but they shared their meat with us and in their own gruff manner, were kind.'

He paused and inclined his head. 'If only I could sketch the way you do. You would have loved their faces. Their expressions. The stories hidden deep within the blackness of their skin.' He sighed. 'I am sure it spoke of their hardship and told of their history reaching back for many generations.

'All that changed when the menfolk returned. There was a commotion in the camp and for a time Henry and I feared for our lives. The next morning the natives moved off without saying a word. But they left us food, and the women had shown me which berries I could pick, which grubs and insects we could eat.'

Emma's nose curled as she smiled.

'A strange diet,' he laughed. 'But we survived and stayed in that camp for almost four weeks until Henry's leg had healed sufficiently for him to walk on it. Then we travelled along the ridge keeping the river in sight hoping it would eventually lead us to the coast. When we stumbled across a wagon track we rejoiced. It was on that track we were found ... and now we are back. Oh, Emma, how I missed you.'

'And I missed you more than you would know. Let me show you something,' she said, as she offered him her hands and led him to the portrait on the easel. She regarded the man standing beside her, his face burnt brown, his cheeks hollow from hunger. Apart from the hues, it was the same face she had painted. The likeness was remarkable.

'You made room in your heart for me?' he said.

'Yes. More room than you can imagine.'

'Emma, there is so much I want to say, I do not know where to start. Would you walk with me for a while?'

'Yes,' she whispered.

Taking her hand he led her through the French doors.

On the grassy slope a flock of pink cockatoos screeched and chattered. As the couple approached, they lifted in the air and, like a rose-coloured cloud, floated across the river to the line of gum trees at the other side. The cattle wading amongst the reeds ignored them.

'You once said you might become a farmer,' Emma said.

'Yes,' he replied.

'And I asked if you would buy a house cow.'

'And I replied that I would buy a whole herd of cows.'

Emma slid her arm through his. 'I hear there is good land south of

Sydney. Where the rolling hills are as green as England's and the fields slope gently to the sea; where you can watch the sun as it rises from the ocean and the horizon stretches forever.'

'A perfect place for a farm, you think?'

Emma smiled. 'Perfect,' she said.

.